A FAERY ON MY SHOULDER

a metaphysical comedy
by Lisa Bonnice

also by Lisa Bonnice

Shape Shifting – the Body/Mind/Spirit Weight Solution

The Shape Shifter's Daily Diary

Fear of Our Father
(co-authored with Stacey M. Kananen)

Castle Gate
(Book 1 in *The Maxwell Curse Trilogy*)

The Faery Falls
(sequel to *A Faery on My Shoulder*)

in the works …

Books 2 & 3 of
The Maxwell Curse Trilogy:

A Curse by Fire
&
Kind Miss

Why has this book had so many doggone names?

Lo these many moons ago (2009 to be precise) the first edition of this book was published under the title *Be Careful What You Witch For!* It rested quietly on the "shelves" of online booksellers until 2017 when Lisa met Marc Allen, the publisher at New World Library. Marc read the book and loved it but suggested that Lisa add a new ending and change the title. Since 2009, much to Lisa's chagrin, a slew of other authors had published books using that same title.

After implementing Marc's suggestions, in 2019 the newly reworked book was published as *The Poppet Master*. Not a great title, but Lisa was coming up empty and she had to call it something.

Meantime Lisa was working on the sequel, *The Faery Falls*. In 2024, the sequel was finally complete and ready for publication. This seemed like a great time to revisit Book 1 in the Lola and Twink saga and freshen it up a bit. So what you hold here in your hands is the same basic story as *The Poppet Master* with a little dusting off and the language updated (it's amazing how quickly our technological changes have been occurring to make some of the references in *The Poppet Master* downright archaic).

The newest (and final) title, *A Faery on My Shoulder*, is the title that was floating around in Lisa's head when she first got the idea for the book during the hurricane-filled summer of 2004 on the west coast of Florida. As she walked barefoot down a sandy road past a massive thatch of bamboo in the oppressively humid after-storm, she felt a tap on her shoulder and the story began pouring in, along with that title. Perhaps if she had paid attention to what she was told in the first place, this book wouldn't have had to go through so many iterations.

Sensitivity note: This book contains a characterization of a person in transition. She is based on a combination of real-life experience, interviews with friends and experts, and a tremendous amount of love for her. Her experience is her own and no disrespect to the trans community is intended.

Cover by Jessica Bell Design
Character illustrations by Justin Spyres

ISBN 10: 0-9799999-7-9
ISBN 13: 978-0-9799999-7-0

A note from Marc Allen:

Once upon a time (because, what better way to begin an introduction to a modern-day faery tale?), I founded New World Library with my dear friend, Shakti Gawain, who wrote our first bestseller, *Creative Visualization.* At that same time, the author of the book you're holding, Lisa Bonnice, was living a dull Midwestern life, much like this book's heroine, Lola Garnett.

By the time Lisa discovered Shakti's book a few years later, she was beginning to gradually experience the kinds of bizarre psychic awakenings that Lola gets blasted with all at once. And, similarly, Lisa thought she was losing her marbles. No one she knew was meeting future selves, for example, so she kept these experiences between herself and her journal–just like Lola.

While there are plenty of differences between Lisa and Lola (this is, after all, a fictional book) many of the strange things that happen to Lola are based on true events (except, to Lisa's chagrin, Lisa has no faery 'helping' her–at least, not like Lola has Twink–Lisa's faery friends are not quite so visible ... or obnoxious).

Fast forward too many years to count, I met Lisa and Lola. I fell in love with Lola and Twink and wanted to publish this funny and intriguing book. Unfortunately, however, New World Library doesn't publish enough fiction to make this viable. We're best known for non-fiction books by authors like Eckhart Tolle, Deepak Chopra and Joseph Campbell.

In lieu of publishing this delightful story, I'm offering this introduction and endorsement. I want this book to be read far and wide, opening the doors for its delicious sequels. Read it, love it, tell your friends about Lola Garnett and her reluctant faery sidekick, Twink. Your life will never be the same.

And, you might just live happily ever after.

Marc Allen
Publisher
New World Library

A few words from energy healer Desda Zuckerman

To read is to learn and laugh and fall in love with the magic on the page. Lisa Bonnice is a magic maker. Her characters leap into your heart with lighthearted inspiration. She tells the story of a woman discovering her hidden gifts with humor and love. Her process of realizing who she is and what she intuitively knows is filled with authentic understanding and real knowledge of the subject. Lisa knows what she is talking about and her heroine is filled with the insights of a deep inquiry of life. I recommend this book to those on the path of awakening their sensitivities and empathic gifts.

Desda Zuckerman
Author- Your Sacred Anatomy
Founder- Sacred Anatomy Academy and Sacred Anatomy Work
www.yoursacredanatomy.com

TABLE OF CONTENTS

Journal Entry 1

I haven't kept a diary for over twenty years, since I was a teenager, but I think it might be a good idea to start typing a journal before I lose track of everything that has happened. The story is getting too complicated to keep up with. I type about a hundred words a minute (one of the few advantages of working as a secretary—excuse me—executive assistant), so it'll be a lot faster than scrawling this out by hand in a notebook. Besides, I can't read my own writing half the time because my hand can't keep up with my thoughts.

I haven't kept a diary for over twenty years, since I was a teenager, but I think it might be a good idea to start typing a journal before I lose track of everything that has happened. The story is getting too complicated to keep up with. I type about a hundred words a minute (one of the few advantages of working as a secretary—excuse me—executive assistant), so it'll be a lot faster than scrawling this out by hand in a notebook. Besides, I can't read my own writing half the time because my hand can't keep up with my thoughts.

And, even though my memory can be very sharp (I can summon up the most picayune details of events I'll never need to recall), I can also forget the important details quickly. So, it would be wise for me to log this stuff as it's happening.

For example, I can vividly remember an incident that happened when I was six years old, suffering from an ear infection and a high fever that left me bed-ridden for several days. There was even talk of surgery to remove my adenoids, I was so sick. One morning, during that illness, my mom cooked breakfast (bacon, eggs, toast, etc.) while I entertained myself with my toy makeup kit, which included a bottle of toy perfume. It was sweet and cloying and would be disgusting to an adult's olfactory sensibilities. While the house still smelled of frying bacon, and with the scent of this awful perfume still lingering in my nose, my sinuses slammed shut and stayed that way for a week. I was stuck with that god-awful mixture of odors in my head the whole time I was sick so I was nauseated the entire time as well.

I can vividly remember useless information like the stench of that perfume and bacon combo. Just writing about it here brings it intensely to mind. I can smell it now and it makes me queasy. But if I'm under pressure you can ask me the name of an important client, or my family's birthdays, and I'll stare at you like Michigan J. Frog and only croak out a single, "Ribbit."

So, that's why I've created you, a Microsoft Word document, to be my virtual BFF and confidant, to listen as I ramble and rant, and to help me keep track of this strange tale.

Therefore, here I sit at my keyboard in my second-floor home office with a bird's eye view of Melinda's house. My "office" is just an unused third bedroom where we stuff all the things we can't put elsewhere. In addition to a desk for my laptop, it holds my grandmother's antique rocking chair, some bookshelves, a small filing cabinet filled with old tax returns and an ancient wrought iron stand that holds an obsolete TV that I never use and my husband refuses to get rid of.

With apologies to Mr. Rusk, my favorite high school English teacher, I'm not going to worry about perfect punctuation and syntax. Please pardon any grammar gaffes because I'm going to type this as it flows. Otherwise, I'll waste too much time repairing typos.

These psychic events—the reasons I'm even sitting here writing—have been going on for a couple weeks. I had hoped they would stop, but they're just getting stranger and scarier. It occurs to me that it might also be a good idea to keep a journal so they have something to read when they lock me up. They'll be able to track the downward spiral of one Lola Garnett.

That's me, Lola, short for Dolores. Why my parents chose to hang a handle like that on me I don't understand. I always hated the name Dolores because it makes me sound like an old lady. Plus, if you look it up, you'll see that it means "suffering" and "sorrow." Why would anyone wish that on a kid?

"Lola" at least sounds like the person I'd like to be: fun, festive and flirty. The reality of me isn't quite so exciting, but at least a sexy name like Lola beats the snot out of Dolores and lets me occasionally pretend I could be a showgirl at the Copacabana if I wanted to.

Instead, I live a dull life in Chagrin Falls, Ohio. I work as a secretary (*pardonez moi,* executive assistant) at a welding supplies company in Cleveland Heights. This is not what I longed to be when I grew up—I never actually had any big dreams beyond marrying my teen idol Cameron Carter, whose posters wallpapered my bedroom during my adolescence—so this is what I ended up with. It's dull but it pays the bills. I dress like a grownup every day in boring business-casual clothes but can't wait to get home so I can tear off the elastic and underwires and put on something comfy, like my sweats and bunny slippers.

I'm married to my high school sweetheart, Chuck. We didn't get married straight out of high school. We both dated around some, before we decided that we got it right the first time and made it permanent in our early-twenties. Chuck is a contractor. He owns his own tile installation business in Mayfield Heights.

That's not what he intended to be when he grew up, either. It sort of happened by accident. When we moved into our first home together, we kept getting phone calls from strangers asking about having tile work done. After weeks of telling these people they had the wrong number, that we had just moved here and this was a new phone number for us, Chuck finally asked one of them where they were getting the phone number from. It wasn't listed under "Tile Installation" in the Yellow Pages—which was the only resource, back in the old days pre-Google. The caller told Chuck that there was a sign on a pole at the corner of North and High streets.

Chuck drove to that intersection to check it out and found a sign—handwritten with a Sharpie on 12x16-inch piece of heavy cardboard—nailed to the pole. I would certainly never employ anyone who only bothered to scrawl out a sign similar to "Will work for food" to perform fairly involved work in my home and sanctuary but, apparently, all of these other people would, because our phone was ringing off the hook!

Inspiration struck my industrious man. Chuck was working as a shipping and receiving clerk and hated it so he took this, literally, as a sign from God. He took an hour-long class at one of the big hardware store chains and learned the basics of how-to install tile. For the first year or so he cut his teeth on small tile jobs, like bathroom floors and tubs, until he found some training and learned how to do bigger jobs.

Before long, he got his license and now has a dozen or so employees. Now that he's reached this point, I think it's a funny story that shows a lot of initiative on his part but at the time I was terrified that someone would bust him for being unlicensed. Nowadays, there's no way anyone could pull this off, but back then he muscled through and grew into a legitimate business owner—one who works too many hours.

This leaves me to deal, most of the time, with our teenage daughter, Amanda. She's at that borderline age (fifteen) where she's ashamed to be seen with her parents most of the time, but not so proud that she won't be seen with us at the mall buying clothes for her.

She's too skinny, in my opinion, but at least she eats (boy, does she eat!). She's fortunate enough to be genetically blessed, unlike me, with my chunky butt and thighs. Oh sure, to look at me you'd think I'm thin enough but, without clothes, I'm a mess. I hate my body and wish that plastic surgery wasn't such a vain and risky proposition.

Thank God Amanda doesn't have an eating disorder. I know she doesn't, because I've paid attention. I've tried to teach her to have good self-esteem about her body, and it hasn't been easy, considering how lousy I feel about my own. It makes me mad that we parents even have to be concerned about this type of thing, with all the pressure girls feel to look the way Amanda looks, naturally. I wouldn't be a teenage girl these days for all the money in the world.

Of course, raising a teenage girl these days isn't very easy, either. I adore Amanda but, at this age, she's barely bearable. I miss my little girl, my baby. I miss the old days when she still looked up to me and wanted to spend time with me, when she still wanted me to help pick out her clothes and do her hair. But now, I have to admit that I cannot wait until she turns eighteen. Chuck and I are both counting the days.

Sorry—went off on a tangent. Anyway, looking back, I think I can pinpoint when the weird stuff started happening. I'm pretty sure it was that weekend that Amanda tried to get me to do her homework for her. She was supposed to watch the movie *Gandhi* for her history class and then write a report.

Must be nice, right? When I was in school, back in the Stone Age, we had to open a book once in a while! Why her teacher isn't making them read Gandhi's biography I'll never know. Plus, what if the movie uses poetic license with the details and facts, as so many do?

On the other hand, at least this way they have some idea of who he is and what he did. I guess maybe teachers find it hard enough to make a class full of fifteen-year-olds stop texting each other long enough to pay attention for an hour, much less read an entire book about some "… old, dead guy," as Amanda called him.

But that's not what she told me. Instead, Amanda brought home a *Gandhi* DVD from the school library, saying she thinks I'll "really enjoy it." She said, "Here, Mom, watch this and let me know what you think."

The deception begins.

I'll admit that I've always wanted to watch the movie. It's one of those old, "must see" classics that I've felt a little guilty about never sitting through, like *Lawrence of Arabia* and *Out of Africa*. So, I suggested to Amanda that we watch it together. I told her I'd make some popcorn and we could make an afternoon of it.

No, she reminded me, she had plans all weekend. This was the weekend she and her girlfriends were planning to spend at Kirsten's dad's cabin. "I guess I'm watching it alone," I told her.

Well, it's not like I had anything else planned over the weekend, other than the never-ending housework that awaits me after a week of nine-to-five idiocy. It's not like Chuck would care that we have the whole place to ourselves for the first time in months. The idea of doing it in every room in the house, any time we're alone, flew out of his head right around the time he watched a football-sized baby squeeze its way out of my formerly unspoiled girly bits.

I shouldn't say that. Our sex life isn't bad—in fact, when it's good it's very good. It's just been a while and I guess I'm feeling neglected. Chuck is a great guy and I'm happy we got married. He's a better dad than most and he makes a decent living. Unfortunately, he's also a major slob and I hate cleaning, which is a recipe for a cluttered and messy house. I neither have the time nor the interest in picking up after a perfectly capable grown man, who should be picking up after himself.

And maybe, if I'm being honest, that's why I stopped caring about doing it in every room every chance we got. Once I became a housewife and office drone, I lost my will to get up in the morning, much less to play the sexual temptress. No, I'm not suicidal; perhaps I'm being a tad dramatic. I get that way sometimes.

But seriously, I just hate cleaning the house and doing the laundry and cooking the dinner and doing the dishes and on and on, ad nauseum, especially since it just has to be done again tomorrow and the next day and the next—kinda takes the edge off of one's libido, scrubbing lover boy's shit off the toilet again and picking up his crunchy socks for the umpteenth time because he sure as heck isn't going to do it.

I tested once to see how long he would go before picking them up himself. He literally ran out of clean socks in his drawer before he noticed them scattered all over the house.

On the other hand, he does have to carry the load of fixing stuff around the house as it breaks, mowing the lawn and taking the trash out. I do appreciate having a man around the house. It would be nice, though, if he didn't spend so much time undoing my hard work.

Amanda has chores but sometimes it's easier to do them myself because at least they get done right and when I want it done. Plus, I get tired of hearing myself nagging her to help me. It always leads to the same argument: "Geez, Mom, why do you have to scream at me?" followed by my usual response, delivered through clenched teeth, "Because you don't listen to me until I do!"

God, I should stop bitching. I'm very happy. I love my husband, I love my daughter, and we have a nice, middle class life—not wealthy enough to live in Pepper Pike or Gates Mills, but that's fine with me. I wouldn't feel comfortable in that kind of ritzy environment—my sensibilities are borderline blue collar, the way I grew up, and I have to deliberately remind myself to not swear like a trucker. Being around the ultra-rich makes me so nervous that filthy, obscene things pop out of my mouth before I realize that words are coming out.

So, I'm grateful that I have my pleasant little life, the life many people aspire to attain. We have the house, the cars, the occasionally snarling teenager with no drug habits or pregnancies, and we do have sex often enough. It's just not the way it used to be before we became grownups and both developed trouble 'getting it up', so to speak.

See why I'm journaling? I get distracted from keeping track, far too easily.

Back to the Ghandi evening: while Amanda was coercing me to watch her DVD, Chuck yelled from the kitchen as he came in from the garage with dinner, "Amanda, come get your homework off the table or it'll get all greasy from the pizza box, which I am about to put down right on top of it!"

Homework? The child had said nothing about homework on cabin-getaway weekend.

Go figure.

She hurried to the kitchen to snatch it before I could. Too bad for Amanda that her dad beat both of us to it. He started reading as we raced into the room, "Watch the movie *Gandhi* and answer the following questions. One, how would you feel if you were subjected to the unfair treatment ..."

Amanda managed to grab it out of his hand before I could but not before I got the gist, most important of which was she had homework. This changed her plans for the weekend, at least as far as I was concerned.

Chuck asked, incredulous, "Your assignment is to watch a movie? What happened to reading a book?" but I waved him off. I gave Amanda the stink-eye and grabbed the paper, giving it a quick glance.

Due date: this coming Monday. Assignment date: two weeks ago!

Know this—I'm not one of those hard asses who would make a normally good kid miss a weekend of fun with her friends because of homework, especially since I don't believe kids should be assigned homework over the weekend. I would usually try to find a way to help her do both. But the little brat lied to me and tried to trick me into doing her homework for her. Homework that had been assigned *TWO WEEKS AGO!*

So, the next day, she and I sat ourselves down on the couch to watch *Gandhi*. Together. She wasn't getting out of this one and I was going to see to it, even if I had to sit through a three-hour movie about the history of some old dead guy in India instead of Chuck and I having the house to ourselves for the weekend.

Now that I'm typing this out and putting it all together (See? This idea of a journal is already paying off!), I can say that it was definitely the *Gandhi* weekend that things started getting weird, because I know for a fact that I had never seen Melinda before that day, and I would have remembered her wild, red hair. This is especially strange, because Chuck tells me she's lived across the street from us for almost half a year. I remember waking up from a strange dream (I'll tell you about that in a minute) and watching her chasing a terrified young woman out of her house.

I remember noticing the dichotomy between this movie I was watching, about someone who was practically a saint, and the seemingly crazy-violent redhead who I never knew lived right across the street from me.

I'm getting ahead of myself...

I fell asleep watching *Gandhi*. Sue me. It's long, I was tired, and how often do I get to lie down on the couch, on purpose, for three hours?

I stayed awake until about a half hour in before I drifted, and I really did enjoy what I saw. What an amazing man he must have been! To stand up to the kind of oppression that Indians faced in South Africa and take deliberate beatings just to prove a point. Wow! I wished I could be more like that—not to get beat up because of the color of my skin, but I wished I could make a difference in the world, instead of filing and typing correspondence for my illiterate creep of a boss.

My boss really is a creep, too. Ron Montgomery is his name. He's one of those smarmy jerks who wears too much cologne, expensive golf shirts and tailored khakis to work. He smugly looks down his nose at the women in the office, as if they were all members of his private harem, scraping and bowing, hoping to be the one chosen to pleasure him. Problem is, three of them play that game with him, making it harder for those of us who don't—especially those of us (me) who have to report directly to him and who have to share office space with him.

My desk is right outside his door, in sort of an anteroom office, between his office door and his private executive restroom (la di da!) so I can see when these simpering pinheads go into his office, all flirty, and close the door. Fifteen minutes later, they come out with their hair all messed up and God only knows what kind of DNA stains on their persons. It's simply revolting. Personally, I'd rather have sex with a pig.

He better watch his step, too, because—with only fifty-four employees—this pond isn't big enough for word to not eventually get out that there's a fisherman on the pier with three hooks on his line. It baffles me how they don't know about each other, because everyone else sure does.

So, yeah, working for Ron gives me nowhere near any kind of feeling that I'm contributing to the betterment of mankind or fighting for equality like Gandhi. Watching the movie only made me feel worse about myself, so I guess I had yet another excuse to fall asleep only thirty minutes into the movie.

I last remember a scene where Gandhi was telling his wife that he gladly took his turn cleaning the latrine because they were all equal on the ashram. I recall thinking that Chuck would let the latrines in our house look like we live in a service station before he'd ever lift a toilet brush and, even then, only to use as a retrieval tool if he dropped his watch or phone in there.

I was sincerely wishing to God, as I drifted off, that there was more meaning to life than being so deeply grateful for a quick, precious nap on a Saturday afternoon.

What I remember first about the dream, itself, was the singing. Not singing, actually, more like a long, melodious "Ahhhhhh." I wouldn't quite describe it as an angelic chorus, because that's not exactly what it was. It was an exquisite tone that I slowly became aware of, and it did make me think of angels singing, even though I never actually saw any angels. I don't know how else to describe it, though. It literally gave me goose bumps.

It was so beautiful! I'd never heard anything like it before, but I also recognized it. Does that make sense? I still haven't puzzled that one out, but it is what it is—this serene, alien-yet-familiar, singing tone.

And then I saw this sort of cloud-like thing (how do you describe the indescribable?). It wasn't really a cloud. It was more of a vaporous form that kept changing shapes, with the most incredible colors! You know how sometimes when you blow bubbles one of them catches the light and you get a mini laser show in its iridescence? It was kind of like that, shimmery and colorful, and … happy.

Yes, it was a happy cloud and, yes, I know how crazy that sounds. I told you I was questioning my sanity, didn't I?

The shimmering not-a-cloud pulsed and throbbed along with the angel tone. It was the greatest dream I'd ever had and I hoped that I wouldn't wake up just yet. I wanted more of this. It was the closest thing to great sex that I'd experienced in a long time, but it wasn't like dirty sex: it was like those fleeting moments that happen once in a blue moon, the kind of sex that feels like you've touched God.

I know that sounds wrong—God and sex do not go together. I know that. But, since it's just me and my diary here, I have to admit that once in a while I do feel like I'm communicating with God during sex. And then I remember that sex is supposed to be sinful and all that, and He immediately leaves.

Anyway, enough blasphemy. The cloud seemed like it was getting closer to me, reaching for me as I reached back. It wanted me as much as I wanted it. We touched … hands? Does a cloud have hands? This one seemed to, because it reached out and when it touched my hands I was instantly filled with a brilliance that took my breath away. I gasped and sat, bolt upright, on the couch and saw Amanda, startled, asking me, "Mom, are you okay?"

And that's when I turned my head and saw—out the living room window—my across-the-street neighbor Melinda chasing that skinny hippie chick out her front door and down the street.

Journal Entry 2

Okay, I'm back. I swear, I never have any time to myself. Today, though, Chuck went downtown to the hardware store where he always spends hours talking to the old timers about the good old days before the big chain stores came along and closed down the Mom and Pop shops (Chagrin Hardware is more than that—it's a pretty historical place—it's been around since the 1850's). Amanda is at Kirsten's house, as usual.

Hopefully, now that everyone is out of the house I can finish the story. Or, at least, continue it because I don't know if it will ever be really finished. Sure feels like it won't.

Okay, I'm back. I swear, I never have any time to myself. Today, though, Chuck went downtown to the hardware store where he always spends hours talking to the old timers about the good old days before the big chain stores came along and closed down the Mom and Pop shops (Chagrin Hardware is more than that—it's a pretty historical place—it's been around since the 1850's). Amanda is at Kirsten's house, as usual.

Hopefully, now that everyone is out of the house I can finish the story. Or, at least, continue it because I don't know if it will ever be really finished. Sure feels like it won't.

I was talking about watching my neighbor Melinda running crazily after a young woman, chasing her down the street. That was a strange enough sight on its own, but witnessing it while still feeling the glow of that amazing dream gave it an entirely surreal edge. One minute I was blissfully asleep—a state I never manage to attain—and, the next minute, my senses were assaulted by the sight of Melinda's front door flying open and a slightly built, twenty-something hippie girl with long dishwater blond hair tied back in a braid, bursting through the doorway and running as fast as her twig-like legs could carry her.

For a moment, I thought she was my daughter, they look so much alike. If Amanda hadn't been on the couch with me I might have sworn it was her that Melinda was chasing, even though Amanda is younger.

The young woman's eyes were wide with terror and, once I saw

Melinda following close behind—waving some kind of stick around, looking like she was going to kill this girl—I didn't blame her for running. Melinda is a tall, hardy woman and, with that crazy hair, she looks like she wouldn't think twice before wiping the floor with you.

Let me clarify. Her hair style isn't crazy—just short and spiky—but it's an extreme red, dyed an unnatural color. It's almost as red as her beat-up Camaro, which is always parked in front of her house. Like me, she doesn't use her garage. I don't use ours because Chuck has it so packed full of his stuff that there isn't room for both my car and his truck. God only knows what she has stuffed into hers.

I think that was the first time I felt one of the twinges in my head that I've been getting more and more frequently. They're hard to explain, like a teeny-weeny bolt of lightning in my brain. I checked with my doctor to make sure I wasn't having seizures or a stroke, but everything checked out fine. I didn't tell him the whole story, about all the weird stuff, just the lightning bolts. I was afraid he'd commit me.

After one of these lightning bolts, I just … *know* … something I have no way of knowing. Just like I knew, in a flash, that Melinda was so angry at Tammy—I somehow knew the girl's name, too—because she had done something to Melinda's doorway. It makes no sense, I know. I'm just telling you what flashed into my head after I woke up.

For the rest of that day I felt out of sorts. Angry. I really didn't want to wake up from that glorious nap and now my day-to-day life looked even more mundane than before, which I didn't think was possible. Amanda was whinier than usual and Chuck was kind of a jerk that night about dinner not being cooked the way he liked it.

They were both ticked off that I put the kibosh on Amanda's cabin weekend. Chuck thought she should have watched the movie on Friday night, so we could have the house to ourselves over the weekend. I knew there was no way she would stay awake that late to watch the whole three hours and write a report.

I hated them both and just wanted to be left alone. Apparently, they think that I have nothing I'd rather be doing, either. I don't enjoy being the only responsible one, the buzzkiller. What I wanted was to go back to sleep forever and find my way back into that dream.

Unfortunately, that night, the dream didn't come back. Instead, I felt like there was a convention in my head. Talking, talking, talking. Snippets of conversations that made no sense.

Hang on—it's coming back to me—I knew typing it out like this would help me see the bigger picture! I'm beginning to remember, I had a dream about Melinda that night. How did it go? Let me think ...

She had a vengeance list, and Tammy was now on it. She was furious about the broken doorway. I could see it now, and it wasn't a doorway like the kind you have between rooms with a wooden frame, hinges and a door with a knob. It was ... hmmmm ... a better word would be a portal. It was a translucent membrane between—something—I don't know. That part is fuzzy. But it didn't look broken to me. I felt like I could step through it easily, although I didn't try because it was way too alien for me. It made me queasy to think about it.

And then the dream went to another scene. Hold on—now that I think about it, this part was so vivid and real that I wrote it down the next morning so I would remember. I'm going to go find the paper I wrote it on. I think it's on the nightstand, still buried under all the other Notes-to-Self that I've left there.

###

Okay, found it. My note says that, in the dream, there was a cute little shop, the kind I try to find when (if!) I ever go to a new city, the kind of place that sells things made by local artists—not quite a tourist trap, but the kind of place that all the locals know about, off the beaten path. Chagrin Falls is full of those kinds of shops, but they're mostly down Main Street, in the center of town.

This shop was a yellow-painted brick building with the large plate glass window, painted with suns, moons and fairies, and an "olde" looking sign hanging over the arched, wooden door saying "Karma Korner." I noticed the odd spelling because I've always had an aggravated, knee jerk reaction against cutesy kitschy spelling like that. I don't know why … it just brings out the grammar nazi in me.

For example, food processing companies are legally allowed to call their artificial crab meat product "krab" meat, as long as it's spelled with a K. Or a company can say that their product is "chocolaty," meaning that it's not real chocolate, it's chocolate flavored. It's how they trick consumers into thinking they're getting the real deal. God only knows what "cheeze" really is.

I wondered, in the dream (yes, I'm even a cynic in my sleep), if spelling Korner with a "K" meant that it's not really a corner, and if not, what was it? A Karma Kul-de-sac?

As I was nitpicking to myself about the spelling of the sign, I saw a couple of dark, menacing figures approach the storefront and throw something through the quaintly-painted plate glass window. Next thing I knew, the place went up in flames and I felt such a sense of loss, like I had been stabbed in the heart. I knew that something very, very wrong had just happened. Something precious had just been destroyed.

I'd forgotten until now that I dreamed about Karma Korner that very first night! The puzzle pieces are beginning to fall into place. Good. That's what I was trying to accomplish with this journaling exercise.

The timing of the dream makes a little more sense now because a couple days later, in real life and on my way home from work, road construction forced me to take a detour through a somewhat bohemian section of town (if you can call it that—Chagrin Falls doesn't have many bohemians unless you count Dave's Cosmic Sub shop, which has kind of a 60's, hippie theme, or the psychic astrologer down the street from the Popcorn Shop).

As a result of the detour, I ended up on a side street that I would never otherwise take. Right there, as big as life, was a shop just like the one in my dream, complete with the painted plate glass window, and the "olde"-looking sign saying "Karma Korner."

And, even though I was dumbfounded by the coincidence, I still took the time to be mildly annoyed by the stupid spelling of the name. Plus, the shop was in the center of the block, so it wasn't even a corner. What's up with that? Is that why it's spelled with a K? Grrr...

The plate glass window was intact and painted exactly like it was in my dream, and there was no sign of there ever having been a fire, so I didn't know what the dream was about. Was it one of those dreams you hear about people having that predict a plane crash or something? Was it just a fluke? What?

I was half tempted to park the car and go inside, but I was running late because of the detour and had to get home. I figured I'd go back another time. And honestly, I wasn't all that concerned. It was an interesting coincidence, that's all. Very interesting, in fact, but not worth messing around with finding a parking spot and all that.

Besides what if, while I was in the store, two dark figures came up and threw a Molotov cocktail through the window? What if I was the something precious that had been destroyed in my dream? Thank you, no.

I'm getting waaaaay ahead of myself again. I guess that's the problem with trying to tell so much story at once.

Anyway, when I woke up from the Gandhi dream, I saw Melinda chasing Tammy down the street looking like she wanted to ring her neck, or worse.

I never saw the end of what happened between them because they disappeared down the block and Melinda didn't come back before I gave up gawking out my window in morbid curiosity.

That was my first impression of Melinda and, it turns out, it was a pretty accurate one. Since that time I've learned more—thanks to those little lightning bolts chock full o' psychic info—than I ever wanted to know about my neighbor Melinda Underwood.

For example, I've learned that she carries a major grudge against the owner of Karma Korner, a woman by the name of Raven Starcloak.

Yes, the shop is owned by a woman who actually calls herself Raven Starcloak. How do these people take themselves seriously? We live in Ohio, for crying out loud, not Oz. When Raven first introduced herself to me (obviously, my curiosity eventually got the better of me and I did stop in, but I'll tell that story later) my eyeball tendons practically froze up in my head from being so suddenly shifted in reverse. Otherwise I never would have been able to stop rolling my eyes. Why not just name yourself Sunbeam Moonchild, or Moron Deluxe? Honestly, I just don't get it.

The thing is, she's a very nice woman. I have grown to like her and wish that she didn't have such a stupid name because I feel stupid saying it! "Pardon me, Ms. Starcloak, would you please pass the batwing dip?"

Getting back to Melinda's grudge against Raven, "How do I know about it?" you ask. Good question because I still don't understand how it works. I just know and I wish I didn't. What I can tell you is that she hates Raven with a passion that burns to the depths of her dark and tortured soul.

This knowledge, of course, came to me riding on the back of one of those little twinges of lightning I was telling you about earlier, the ones I thought were me having a stroke. I was suddenly blasted with a vision, for lack of a better word, of Melinda pacing around her house, concentrating very hard on coming up with some way to get revenge on Raven for humiliating her. Just as quickly, the vision was gone and I was left to wonder what Raven did to her.

Ya know, come to think of it, I didn't get this information until after I met Raven. Interesting—another puzzle piece. It's like I'm only shown a scenario when I know who all the players are.

Yikes! I wonder if that means I know who the two dark figures are, the ones who are going to throw a Molotov Cocktail through Raven's shop window. If that dream comes true, that is. And if it works the same way with dreams. It might just be the case with lightning bolts.

That's kind of a scary thought. What if those figures are Melinda and Tammy? Think about it. Up until I met Raven, I was only getting flashes of information about Melinda and a little bit about Tammy.

For example, and this is sad information about her, Tammy is a bit of a masochist. She can only feel seen if she's being emotionally stomped on. Her friendship, if you can call it that, with Melinda carries that dynamic. It feels like Tammy is Melinda's toady, yapping around her heels asking "Did I do good? Huh? Did I?"

It was almost as if I could taste it about her, like it was part of her flavoring—the damaged/yet-sweet essence of Tammy-ness. I don't mean I could taste it with my tongue, but it's the only way to describe the way this knowing feels. Just like I can taste the bitter sadist in Melinda. The two of them get off, emotionally and psychologically, pairing up in this type of symbiotic interaction. It's what holds them together.

Tammy has some role to play in Melinda's plan to mess with Raven, but that's the extent of my awareness. I wish I could pick and choose what I suddenly know. Apparently, this ability – for lack of a better word – doesn't come with an on/off switch. It seems to work when it wants to, not when I want it to.

It's puzzling, too, this intense hatred Melinda has for Raven. I've been to Raven's shop a couple of times and I can't imagine her doing anything to make anyone that angry, although Melinda is a generally enraged person. It doesn't seem to take too much to piss her off. Still. To throw a flaming bottle into Raven's shop goes beyond reason.

I'll write more later. Amanda's home. I can hear her coming up the stairs looking for me.

Journal Entry 3

Now that I have a little more time to write, let me tell you about the first time I met Raven.
I did finally drop in at Karma Korner owned by Raven Starcloak on Fairy Moon Day (also known as Friday-hey, I can play crazy-name-game, too) because the road I usually take home from work was still closed and I was still detoured. I had to drive by every day. I figured I might as well go inside, especially since I feel this strange pull to do so every time I drive by.

Now that I have a little more time to write, let me tell you about the first time I met Raven.

I did finally drop in at Karma Korner owned by Raven Starcloak on Fairy Moon Day (also known as Friday—hey, I can play crazy-name-game, too) because the road I usually take home from work was still closed and I was still detoured. I had to drive by every day. I figured I might as well go inside, especially since I feel this strange pull to do so every time I drive by.

The day I finally did stop, it was almost as if the car steered itself into the parking spot that seemed to magically appear out of nowhere right in front of the store as I was stuck in traffic. Call it Karma. (Ha! Sometimes I crack myself up.)

First thing I noticed was that I loved the way the place smelled—it took me back to the time I snuck into a head shop when I was a kid, with its incenses all intermingling into one big aroma that smells like a mixture of orange baby aspirin and Catholic mass. Wind chimes tinkled when I opened the door and I could hear fountains bubbling from every direction. I swear, the woman had at least six fountains running. Her electric bill must be through the roof.

The place was filled with books, gorgeous figurines and knick knacks, and lots of little bins filled with different kinds of crystals. I spent some time gazing around at all the pretties, hungry to take them all home with me. At first I thought someone was playing a flute in the back room, but it turned out to be a Native American flute music CD (I ended up buying a copy). Overall, I found the place to be very peaceful and relaxing.

And then Raven came flowing into the room, and I do mean she flowed into the room. She wore a long, elegant silky sweater atop a gorgeous multi-colored full-length skirt, and lots of sparkly crystal jewelry. Her waist-length, black hair glistened like that of a model on a shampoo commercial. She entered from behind a beaded curtain that separated the shop itself from, as I later learned, the Reading Room. She saw me looking at the crystals and asked, "Can I help you find something?"

I stammered, "I don't have a clue what I'm looking for.

She approached and said, "Let me help you find the perfect crystal, the one that's meant for you. Hold your hand over the bins and allow it to be guided to the place that feels right." She held her hand out, palm downward, a few inches above the bins to demonstrate. "Sweep your hand slowly back and forth until you feel a bit of a downward tug. Some people have a hard time doing this the first time, because they expect it to be stronger than it usually is. It's sometimes more of a notion that 'this would be a good place to stop' than it is an actual physical feeling. Just trust that you can't do it wrong. You'll end up with the right crystal for you, whether you feel it or not."

I did as she suggested and, surprisingly, felt my hand being guided toward the bin of quartz points.

When she saw my hand stop over the quartz crystals, she said, "Now, reach in and take the stone that feels like it belongs with you."

I held my hand still, "listening" for that stone. I felt a mild, magnetic tug downward and to the right side of the bin, where one of the stones felt like it was practically leaping into my hand. I picked up the crystal and was rather disappointed that it wasn't very pretty. It wasn't as clear and sparkly as some of the others—it was sort of foggy, and had a chip in it. If she hadn't been standing right there, watching me, I would have been tempted to put that one back and find one that I liked better. Even so, I was impressed by this trick.

"That's amazing," I said. "How does that work?"

She chuckled and replied, "I don't think anyone knows for sure, but one theory is that each crystal has sort of a sentience—their own personality—and they know better than we do if they can help us or not. Another theory is that our spirit guides, who always help when we ask them to, direct our hands to the crystal that is most in tune with our needs. Crystals are sort of like tuning forks. They each have their own vibration—some match ours, and some don't."

Although there was plenty to ask about there, I focused on only one of her statements and asked, "Spirit guides? What are they?"

"Oh, there are all sorts of spirit guides surrounding each of us," she said. "Some are angels, some are relatives and ancestors who have passed on and are hanging around to help us when needed, and some are spirits who have never incarnated whose purpose is to watch our backs and give us an assist when we ask. And, all you have to do is ask."

I mentally filed this information away under "Good to Know" and then noticed the time. I had to get going. I put the crystal and the flute CD on the counter to pay for them and asked what was behind the beaded curtain. That's when she told me it was the Reading Room. Raven offers Tarot readings. I haven't gone quite that far, yet, because I'm not sure how safe that is, with the occult and the Devil and all. I'm surprised that this kind of shop exists here in town and that I've never heard of it.

I know we don't live in the Dark Ages but I've heard that you shouldn't mess with that kind of thing. It sounds silly to say it, but what if there really are evil spirits attached to psychics and stuff? Is it worth taking a chance, just because I'm curious?

Now that I bring it up, that's another thing that concerns me. What if I'm possessed? I don't mean like the *Exorcist*, where I'll be wetting the rug and puking pea soup, but seriously. What if all this stuff that's going on with me and Melinda is something evil trying to take over my body? They say the Devil takes many forms and will trick you into following him by pretending to be something he's not, something perfectly lovely.

But then I remember how amazing that first dream felt, how it felt like touching God. How can that possibly be evil?

"Ah," the doubt in my head responds, "that's exactly how the Devil tricks you! He makes you believe you're doing God's work, and then pulls the rug out from under you in the end!"

Something tells me, though—a second voice in my head—that as long as my intention is good, as long as I know that I'm doing what I think is truly right, then I can't do any harm.

Yet a third voice piped up with, "Sounds like Fundamentalist rationalization to me!"

And then another voice in my head cries out, "*You've got voices in your head! Get thee to a nunnery!*"

I'm tired of even thinking about all this. I know I didn't write much today, but I'm not in the mood. I'm going to have a cup of tea and chill out for a while. More later.

Journal Entry 4

I haven't been able to journal for several days because life got too busy. I know I'm not quite finished laying out the background but let me tell you the new stuff first and then I'll get back to telling the story.
A few days ago I was on my way to the grocery store to do the week's shopping and, as I was stopped at a stop sign in a residential neighborhood, I noticed a dog lying in the grass inside a fenced-in yard. It was a typical dog, perhaps a Lab mix, just like any other … nothing remarkable about it. Yet somehow I

I haven't been able to journal for several days because life got too busy. I know I'm not quite finished laying out the background but let me tell you the new stuff first and then I'll get back to telling the story.

A few days ago I was on my way to the grocery store to do the week's shopping and, as I was stopped at a stop sign in a residential neighborhood, I noticed a dog lying in the grass inside a fenced-in yard. It was a typical dog, perhaps a Lab mix, just like any other … nothing remarkable about it. Yet somehow I knew that it had just had puppies. I knew how she felt inside, raw and scooped out like I felt after Amanda was born.

As I was puzzling this out (How do I know this? Am I right or am I delusional? How weird is it to be able to feel what that dog feels, physically?), the dog's owner opened the back door and she got up to go inside. I could see physical evidence, the new mom boobs (Is that what you call a dog's mammary glands? Do they have a name?) that come with a fresh litter of puppies.

I would be willing to chalk that up to daydreaming, coincidence, or even hallucination if something similar didn't happen the next time I went to Karma Korner.

I've begun sort of hanging out there because I'm learning so much. I'm getting to know Raven a little better and plan to take a class or two soon. She teaches Tarot, Psychic Development and something called Reiki. I've heard of the first two, because they teach them at the Y, but

Reiki I've never heard of. However, it's the book selection that really caught my attention.

The day after I had the puppy mama experience, I was at the shop browsing through the books when the hippie girl that Melinda chased out of her house came in. And, like the first time I saw her, at first glance, I thought it was Amanda. I wondered what on earth Amanda was doing there until I finally realized it was Tammy.

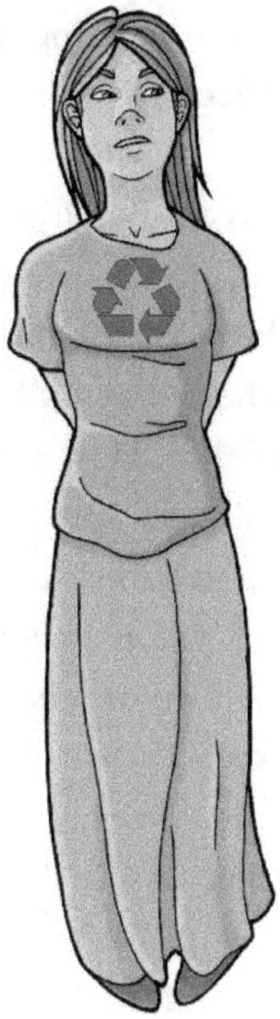

Tammy, if you recall, is the one in whom I sensed masochistic tendencies which play into her friendship with Melinda. That time, when I received that information, it was one of those lightning bolts I've told you about. I just knew. But, this time, what I felt was more like my experience with the dog.

Suddenly I was inside Tammy's body.

Keep in mind that I still, up to this point, had no confirmation that her name really was Tammy or any of the other things I knew about her. But now I was walking around in her skin, feeling what she was feeling, hearing her thoughts. And what she was thinking and feeling felt horrible. She was thinking about hurting Raven.

The feeling was so intense and alien that I felt waves of nausea overtake me and I hopped out of her body from revulsion. She was feeling a desperate desire to cause pain to someone else (not necessarily Raven, but she would do), mixed with a fear that it would never alleviate the extreme pain that she, herself, felt.

She felt pressured to do something she didn't want to do. That pressure was coming from Melinda. I wondered if this is what the guards at Nazi concentration camps felt like, knowing they had to overcome their basic humane instincts to follow orders. But was that my question? Or Tammy's?

Raven said hello to her, and Tammy smiled back, shyly. I could feel her fondness for Raven so she was especially torn inside. If I hadn't just been inside her skin, there would have been no way of knowing her inner turmoil. She appeared, for all intents and purposes, to be a sweet, shy young woman who hugged trees and ate granola while writing songs on her acoustic guitar about saving baby seals.

Tammy told Raven, “I’m just here to check the bulletin board to see if anything new is going on.” Raven directed her to a new flyer, offering the Tarot classes, and Tammy thanked her. I didn’t need the intuition that told me that what she was really doing was checking the date for the next coven meeting, because she went directly for a flyer advertising the local Wicca group’s schedule.

Wicca, by the way, is something I still don’t quite understand. Raven says it’s a religion, but they practice witchcraft. That, to me, is an oxymoron, much like the concept of Vacation Bible School. They just don’t go together. But she says Wicca is an Earth-based, pagan religion, where they call upon the gods and goddesses of nature. She says it’s one of the oldest practices in history, and that many of the major Christian holidays were created to overlay pagan holidays because the Church wanted to ease its way into people’s lives.

I don’t know about all that. I don’t think I’m quite ready to entertain the idea of witchcraft and I’m surprised that there’s an actual witch coven here in town, but Raven is a Wiccan and I’m not getting any lightning bolts of doom coming from her, just from Melinda and Tammy. In fact, if I get any feelings at all from Raven, they’re very calm, nurturing and loving. We’ll see.

After Tammy hurriedly scribbled something on a notepad she’d pulled out of her voluminous bag and rushed out the door, I asked Raven who she was. Maybe I could finally get some confirmation that these lightning bolts were accurate. I told Raven that I thought the girl looked familiar but couldn’t place her name.

“That’s Tammy Webster,” Raven said. “She was in our coven for a while but she dropped out recently. She works over at the library. Is that where you know her from?”

I pretended it was. Actually, I was surprised that I had never seen her at the library because I go there with Amanda from time to time and thought I knew all the librarians. Apparently not.

But I was right about her first name, wasn’t I? Does that mean I’m right about all the other stuff and about her planning to hurt Raven?

I had to stop thinking my own thoughts for a minute because Raven was still talking.

"Tammy's a nice girl," she was saying, "but she fell in with someone we don't associate with anymore, someone who was banished from the coven who doesn't understand the Wiccan Rede, which is 'An it harm none, do as thou wilt.' Basically, that means that as long as your intention is good, as long as you know that you're doing what you think is truly right with loving intent for all involved—for the highest good of all—then you can't do any harm. If so, you may do whatever you wish."

I was momentarily stunned because that's exactly what I was saying just the other day when trying to figure out if what's going on with me is the Devil's work—the difference was the addition of the concept of "for the highest good of all." That helped to alleviate the fundamentalist rationalization I wondered about. After all, plenty of people justify brutal actions when trying to control the lives of others because they honestly believe that what they're doing is right. But if you add "with loving intent for all involved—for the highest good of all," then that removes a lot of possible actions from the list of things that it's okay to do.

Raven continued, "It's our version of the Golden Rule—you know, do unto others and all that. Anyway, I'm afraid this woman is up to no good and has Tammy mildly brainwashed. The last time I saw her she was very angry with me ..."

That explained Tammy's thoughts about hurting Raven.

"... and she has apparently coerced Tammy to stop coming to coven meetings."

I blew off the fact that I saw Tammy writing down the next meeting date because it seemed more important to ask Raven why "the woman" was angry with her. She seemed in a gossipy mood, so I poked my nose in a little.

"I probably shouldn't be telling tales out of school," she replied, "but she was campaigning during coven meetings that she wanted us to cast a group spell to get revenge on her ex-boyfriend for some wrong he had committed against her. I think he was cheating on her but I don't know for sure. I didn't ask because it's irrelevant. We don't do revenge.

She wouldn't take no for an answer, no matter how often I reminded her that responsible use of power is the Wiccan way and if she can't be responsible, she needs to at least heed the law of karma, which states what she does will come back to her threefold. I wanted no part of it. Since then I've been receiving anonymous threatening emails, but I can't prove it's her so I depend on binding and protection spells."

Unfortunately, her business phone rang and the conversation was over. I wasn't able to ask all the questions I had, like "Binding and protection spells?" and "Law of karma? Huh?"

All the talk about Wicca made me curious to learn more so I grabbed the first book I saw on the subject. I haven't started reading it yet, but I'm looking forward to getting more information that might help me understand what's happening to me. If Melinda's involved and she's into this witchcraft stuff, then it wouldn't surprise me if I found some answers there.

Journal Entry 5

I haven't been able to write much lately because I've been busy at home. For a while, I got so interested in the Melinda/Raven/Tammy triangle that I completely neglected my family and the housework. Or so Chuck says, anyway.

As much as I hate to confess that he might be right, I must admit that I got a little obsessed for a while with these new powers I have. Once I learned that I could see inside other people, it's been pretty much how I spent most of my time.

First, I wanted to learn how to do it on purpose, because when it initially began happening, I had no control over it. I was at its mercy and, once in a while, I'd become overwhelmed when I

I haven't been able to write much lately because I've been busy at home. For a while, I got so interested in the Melinda/Raven/Tammy triangle that I completely neglected my family and the housework. Or so Chuck says, anyway.

As much as I hate to confess that he might be right, I must admit that I got a little obsessed for a while with these new powers I have. Once I learned that I could see inside other people, it's been pretty much how I spent most of my time.

First, I wanted to learn how to do it on purpose, because when it initially began happening, I had no control over it. I was at its mercy and, once in a while, I'd become overwhelmed when I was in the grocery store or mall. I found myself slipping in and out of random people so rapidly that I couldn't keep track of who was them and who was me. I considered taking Raven's class in Psychic Development, but it doesn't start for a few weeks and I need help now!

It makes life at work hell because these weren't strangers I was dipping into, these were people I work with and I was getting information I really didn't want to know. For example, I now know that one of the other secretaries, Caroline, is a kleptomaniac who loads her purse down with office supplies daily. I'm sort of duty-bound to report her but I like her and don't want to get her in trouble.

Less harmful, I know that Tony from Accounting spends most of his lunch hours writing desperate love poems that he'll never have the courage to give to Alexis, the receptionist.

Not surprisingly, I've learned that my boss, Ron, is a far bigger jerk than I ever imagined (and I have a healthy imagination), but let's not even go there right now.

Those juicy tidbits weren't the worst of it, though. The hardest thing to deal with was feeling their pain. Oh my God, the things that some people are carrying around inside their skins is enough to make me never stop crying, and that's what finally made me realize that I have to find some way to access the Off switch for this power.

What I've discovered is that I can control this if I pay attention and focus. The reason I'm able to easily slip into most people is because they're daydreaming and have let their guard down, so to speak. In fact, that's how I was so out of control in crowds, at first, because I was daydreaming—inattentive and unfocused.

It feels like we're all blobs of goo, like uncooked eggs without a shell—the yolk is our solid self and the egg white is our psychic edges, which are so undefined that we melt into each other when we're near, like cracked eggs in a bowl. I believe that, if they tried, other people would probably be able to feel into me, but they don't know they can. That's how natural this has begun to feel, a real no-brainer.

This was sort of a creepy feeling when it first occurred to me, knowing that anyone could poke into my private thoughts if they knew they could—just like I had been doing, and if I can do it, then anyone can! I instinctively reacted by creating a psychic 'thought-wall' to keep them out.

That was interesting! Didn't even know I could do that! I'm not sure how to explain what a thought-wall is or how I did it because I don't really understand it myself. It was sort of like a reflex action, like you would do if someone was taking a swing at you. Your first instinct would probably be to throw your arms up to protect your head. As soon as I realized that someone else might be able to see into my noggin as clearly as I can see into theirs, a part of me instinctively erected—for lack of a better word—a wall of "Oh no, you don't!" thoughts to protect my privacy, by thinking it into place.

Fortunately, I know from experience—from being inside them—that it never occurs to the vast majority of people to deliberately try. Many are mindlessly surfing one another, but are unaware that the thoughts and feelings they're experiencing are not their own. They have no intentionally-defined boundaries, so they go about their lives all sort of mushed together in a confused stew, just like I used to.

Not that this is bad, necessarily. I spent most of my life that way and didn't mind. It was just the way life was, and it came with a mildly comfortable feeling of "We're all in this together." On the flip side, this default sleepwalking mode is also how people become mindless sheep, blindly following government or religious leaders, some of whom aren't worthy of being followed. For the most part, however, it is kind of nice to feel like we're all connected and part of something bigger than ourselves.

I miss that because, now that things have changed so much, I feel very alone. I have no one I can talk to about what's happening to me. I certainly can't tell Chuck! I've tried to bring it up, but I have a hard enough time getting him to talk about our budget or other day-to-day household conversations. I have to get his attention right away or he tunes me out and, because I don't know what to say, he loses patience with my hemming and hawing.

Even if I did find a way to tell him, he wouldn't take me seriously. It's all too weird and he'd send me to a shrink. He's very down to earth and skeptical, and he'd never believe me. Or maybe he would. I don't know. I'm afraid to take the chance and find out.

Even Raven, who I think would understand, isn't someone I can talk to about it because I don't know her that well and, also, I'm not sure I want to encourage this being real enough to talk about. Ya know? Telling someone else about what's going on within me makes it real. Meantime, I can pretend like it's a fun game I'm playing. It's interesting trying to figure out the rules by myself, but I could sure use some help. These abilities didn't come with an instruction manual.

I'm pretty sure I'm on the right track with all this because I've been experimenting on Amanda and Chuck. I've noticed that there are times when I can easily know what they're thinking and feeling and times when they are completely closed off and I can't get in, especially when I'm trying to prove that I can. The easy times are usually when they're not doing anything very important, like mindless chores. It's harder when they don't want anyone in there, when they're thinking private thoughts or they're mad at me. That's when they tend to censor out any intrusion.

There was a hilarious instance with Amanda, after I yelled at her for missing the school bus. She felt perfectly justified in being late because she couldn't find her shoes and they were in my closet for some reason (I didn't put them there!!!). She was using that as her rationale for this being someone else's fault. The poor, innocent thing was being persecuted!

Anyway, she was giving me the cold shoulder/silent treatment—on the outside. On the inside, she was boiling with rage and couldn't decide whether she wished I could hear how much she hated me as she shrieked in her head, or whether she knew that she better not cuss at me, even in the privacy of her own noggin.

It sounded, to me, like this:

"Oh my God, I ***HATE*** you, you [silence for enough seconds for her to call me a couple of filthy names]! I should steal your [silence] shoes and see how you like it!"

It felt, to me, like a blast of fire as if a furnace door had just been opened, followed by what it must be like in the calm eye of a hurricane, then the open furnace door, then the calm, then the blast of heat again.

It was a real eye-opening experience. And I loved that it came right after I began questioning how this thing works. Almost as if it was delivered to me, on purpose, as a demonstration.

Chuck is another story. We already had a rapport like this intuitive thing I have going on, but to a lesser degree, in a way that he can comprehend and be comfortable with. I mean, we do the typical couple things like finishing each others' sentences and the psychic things you hear about people doing all the time, but he can accept that because it's easy to understand how that can happen after two people have lived together for many years and have grown comfortable with each other. After all, he is my best friend and I spend most of my time (outside of work, that is) with him. But what I have learned about him since the Gandhi dream is both delightful and disturbing.

For example, I learned that most of the time when I used to think he was deep in thought and pondering important things like philosophy and the human condition, one of the things that always made me swoon over him—he seemed so deep—instead, he was actually thinking of something mundane like drilling holes in wood, or car races, or bunnies, or whatever.

I never caught him thinking about other women. I think it's mostly because he respects our relationship and that's one of those things he naturally shields from me. I'm not naïve enough to think he never thinks about having sex with someone else, he just doesn't do it when I'm around. But I was stunned and hurt when I became aware of the involuntary erection he experienced as we strolled past a pretty, much younger woman in Riverside Park, when we went uptown recently for an ice cream at the Popcorn Shop.

He hasn't popped instant wood for me in many years. That stung. It made me feel old, fat and ugly, and I hid any of my own nudity from him for the next few days. I mean, I used to just dry off from a shower or get dressed in front of him, because that's part of being so comfortable with my best friend, but I was very self-conscious after that incident. It also made me very critical of his body, in self-defense, "Mr. High-School-Football-Star has grown a little soft and round himself!"

On the other hand, I never realized before how deeply he loves me. Now I know what that expression on his face means, when he looks at me "that way." It brings tears to my eyes, just thinking about it.

This, by the way, led to the most amazing sex you can even imagine. Talk about connecting at a soul level! I know what he's thinking about while we're in bed, what he secretly wishes I would do (and is too shy to tell me), what he wants to do to me, and I respond accordingly. I can tell what he's fantasizing about and I play the role exactly how he wants it (fortunately, so far, he's not fantasizing about anything I would object to—most of it's quite fun!).

I never realized that sex, for men—or, at least, Chuck—is about conquest, urgency and explosions, both his and mine. I could see/feel from inside his body as he was inside mine, and I found that it's a totally different experience for men than it is for women. I'm seeing him through completely new eyes.

Which leads to my frustration about him saying that I'm neglecting the family! Here I am, feeling so much closer to him, and he's accusing me of spending all my time at the Karma Korner or reading my "woo-woo" books, as he calls them. He bitches that the laundry isn't done and that the house is messy, but I don't see him lifting his delicate little fingers to do anything about it, or riding Amanda's ass to pick up after herself and help out a little. Speaking of which, there goes the dryer buzzer.

I can see how this may become a real challenge.

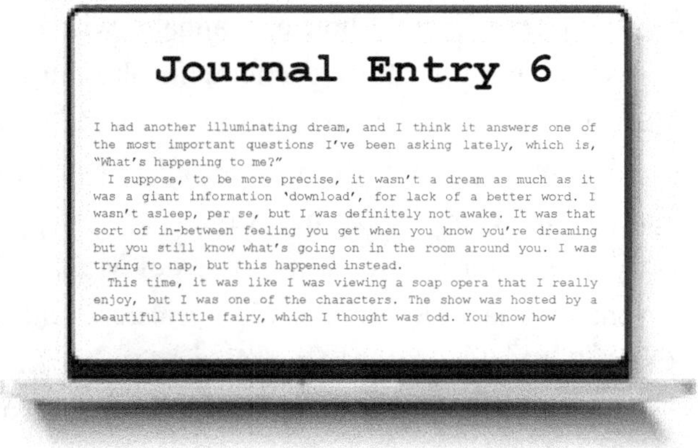

Journal Entry 6

I had another illuminating dream, and I think it answers one of the most important questions I've been asking lately, which is, "What's happening to me?"
I suppose, to be more precise, it wasn't a dream as much as it was a giant information 'download', for lack of a better word. I wasn't asleep, per se, but I was definitely not awake. It was that sort of in-between feeling you get when you know you're dreaming but you still know what's going on in the room around you. I was trying to nap, but this happened instead.
This time, it was like I was viewing a soap opera that I really enjoy, but I was one of the characters. The show was hosted by a beautiful little fairy, which I thought was odd. You know how

I had another illuminating dream, and I think it answers one of the questions I've been asking lately, which is, "What's happening to me?"

I suppose, to be more precise, it wasn't a dream as much as it was a giant information download, for lack of a better word. I wasn't asleep, per se, but I was definitely not awake. It was that sort of in-between feeling you get when you know you're dreaming but you still know what's going on in the room around you. I was trying to nap, but this happened instead.

This time it was like I was viewing a soap opera, but I was one of the characters. The show was hosted by a beautiful little fairy, which I thought was odd. You know how Tinker Bell always opened the show for *The Wonderful World of Disney*? It was sort of like that.

Plus, I—the watcher—wasn't even me, I was a nameless/faceless being watching a show about a woman named Melinda and her neighbor, Lola. It was almost like I was sitting in front of a TV, being shown—by this fairy—a dramatic reenactment of what happened that day I had the Gandhi-induced dream. It will probably be better to tell the story that way, as if I'm telling you about a TV show I saw. I think it'll be easier to convey:

###

Across the street from Lola's house, wannabe-witch Melinda Underwood was cooking up a little excitement. She felt as if she wanted to break out of her skin, to smash some heads. She wanted revenge on a cheating man and the woman he left her for. She wanted things to be different—to be her way.

Unfortunately, this bitter lust for vengeance got Melinda kicked out of her coven. Just days before, her high priestess had tried to tell her that she didn't fit in, that she didn't quite get it. "Harm none." Raven had warned her, "It's against the Rede to cast spells at someone. Remember the laws of karma ..."

"Screw that," Melinda thought. "What is the point of having power if you can't use it to get what you want? And sometimes 'other beings' stood in the way!"

After the third time that Raven had to counsel Melinda on the gentle ways of the Wiccan, the coven had taken a secret vote and ousted her.

Melinda's face still burned with red-hot anger at the memory of the scene where she was given the news—Raven's condescending, yet placid tone droning on and on after taking her aside from the rest of the coven, "Melinda, dear, until you can live up to the high standards decreed by the Goddess, until you can learn that we work with Nature, not against Her, then I'm afraid you will be banished from working with our group."

In the background, Melinda could see the coven sitting in circle, chatting and laughing—at her, no doubt—their camaraderie like a nail through her breaking heart. Only one member of the circle paid any attention to Melinda and Raven. Little Tammy Webster was watching the whole thing.

Tammy was new to the coven and had been instantly drawn to Melinda. They had just started to become good friends, if friends you can call it, when this disaster struck. Their relationship was one of "big dog, little dog," with Melinda—of course—as the big dog. Tammy played the role of the subordinate, looking up with wide-eyed admiration at someone she perceived to be powerful and wise. Melinda enjoyed the vision Tammy held of her and encouraged it to grow. She liked the idea of having a minion.

Seeing Tammy's horrified face as she watched her mentor's humiliation was Melinda's undoing. She grabbed her things and stormed through doorway, the beaded door-curtain flying in her wake, shouting, "You'll pay for this! You all think you're so much better than me. We'll see who's more powerful!"

She rather hoped that Tammy would follow her and was disappointed when there were no breathless, rapid footsteps behind her as she stomped through the parking lot to her car—the red Camaro with the "My other car is a broomstick" bumper sticker.

Once behind the wheel, doors-shut-windows-closed, she allowed herself a full vent. Howling with rage, she pounded on the steering wheel, pretending it was Raven's stupid face. Eventually she realized that she was hurting her hand, so she finally turned the key in the ignition and drove home, cursing all the other drivers on the road for their incompetence and for being in her way.

She'd make them pay. They'd see. She knew a lot more about this magic stuff than they gave her credit for.

The moon wasn't exactly in the right phase for the kind of magic Melinda planned to work that following Friday night in her home, with Tammy drafted as her reluctant accomplice, but she was too impatient to wait another week. She wanted to get the ball rolling on the giant whammy she was planning for Raven. She intended to open a gateway through the veil that cloaks the physical world from the etheric realm. Once through the veil, she would have access to all the power she needed to blast that simpering priestess senseless.

Tammy stood by, watching Melinda prepare to cast her spell. She was still too new at this magic stuff to know exactly what Melinda was doing, but she knew enough to be afraid. Melinda was furious, and Tammy had learned from Raven that only bad things could come from manipulating power from this state of mind. The only reason she was still there was because she was more afraid of what Melinda would do to her if she dared to leave.

"Okay, here's what I need you to do," Melinda barked, "I want you to keep a chant going after I begin. I want you to chant, 'Powers that be, Come through me.'"

"But," Tammy shyly interjected, "Don't you want the power to come through you?" She was terrified to invoke any sort of power through her uninitiated self. She had no idea how to handle that sort of thing.

"No, dummy! Let me finish!" Melinda snorted, and continued, "You'll be wearing one of my cloaks and pendants." She tossed a bundled cloak and necklace at Tammy. "Pretend you're me, and you'll be an extra conduit for power to flow for me!"

"Oh," Tammy replied, densely. "Will that work?"

"It will, if you do it right. Now don't screw it up." Melinda continued laying out her altar tools, mumbling to herself.

Tammy didn't like this idea, not one little bit. Desperately, her thoughts darted around in her brain, as she dressed in Melinda's giant things, casting about for a way out of this. Suddenly, a fresh thought took hold: while chanting, she could volunteer her services to the Goddess to help to keep Melinda in check, by acting as her second, never leaving her side. This was the only way she could see around playing a part in something she knew could cause so much harm.

"Okay, let's do this," Melinda finally said, her tools in place, incense and black candles burning. "You stand right here." Melinda moved Tammy toward the center of the room and picked up her ritual knife to begin psychically tracing the circle around where they stood. "Keep your focus on being an extension of me."

Tammy tried to recall instructions that Raven had once given her about harming none, but they were a jumble in her frantic mind. She would just have to do the best she could.

Melinda completed the circle and stepped into the center. She knelt in front of her altar and began. Tammy stood nearby, dressed in the oversized cloak and pendant made of pitch-black jet. "Stand behind me and put your hands on my shoulders," Melinda said. "I'll tell you when to start chanting."

Tammy did as she was told, as Melinda began reciting her spell.

Gods and Goddesses of war and destruction,
I invoke thee.
Form for me a gateway through the veil
Through which I may access your power.
Work through me to defeat my foes,
And let all tremble in my wake.
So mote it be.

"Okay," Melinda instructed, "start chanting now."

Together, Tammy and Melinda chanted, "Powers that be, Come through me. Powers that be, Come through me." The chant continued as Tammy felt the room getting dark, far away and out of focus. Not really expecting the spell to work, she was terrified at this apparent result.

Quickly, she added her own twist to the mix. Silently, she added to the chant. "Great Mother, protect us and keep us from harm. Let me act as a guardian to my sister and keep her from doing too much damage."

Unseen by them both, an upward-pointing cone of swirling, misty light formed around them as they chanted. The combination of Melinda's dark thoughts and Tammy's hope-filled counteraction caused a beautiful mix of colors, both deep and light. Tremendous, yet neutral now due to Tammy's innocent plea, it grew upward, spinning and expanding, stretching into the ethers. The passion with which Melinda cast her spell energized and strengthened the cone as it reached ever higher into the non-physical realm of infinite power. The tip of the cone bit into the veil that divides the realms and broke through just as…

…a loud shattering of glass shook Melinda into startled consciousness, breaking her connection to the cone.

"God damn it!" she shrieked. "What the hell was that!?"

As Melinda raged at the interruption, which turned out to be her black cat, Onyx, knocking over a vase, the cone of light broke away from the circle and left the room, drifting up and away, like a helium balloon escaping the grip of a careless child. Tammy, although she didn't know why, felt a tremendous physical relief as it let go of her and Melinda.

Melinda, on the other hand, took out her fury on poor Onyx. "Stupid animal! I thought I locked the cat door after I put you outside!" Onyx blinked at her and ran under the altar to hide. While the cat may have been clumsy, he was not brainless. He knew when to dart into an out of the way place to escape his mistress.

The angry witch dove under the altar with a ferocity that knocked her tools to the floor. All her work had now been undone. Onyx was going to suffer. Tammy was only mildly relieved that it wouldn't be her.

After chasing the cat around the house in a way that Tammy would have found comical if she weren't so nervous, Melinda finally gave up. Onyx was under the couch and wasn't coming out, even with Melinda swiping at him with a broom handle.

"Well, that was a big waste of time!" she announced. "Let's try again tomorrow, after I have a chance to calm down and start over. Come over at one o'clock and we'll do it again."

Tammy already had plans for the next day, but knew that Melinda wasn't going to take the news well, so she agreed to come back. In the meantime, she prayed, maybe a good excuse would come to her. She removed Melinda's cloak and pendant, throwing them over the back of the couch, and gathered her things to leave.

"One o'clock!" Melinda shouted as Tammy made a hasty departure. "Don't be late!"

Above Melinda's house, a cloud of swirling lights—invisible to the average naked eye—bored its way into the veil between the worlds like a termite munching happily on a support beam.

"Form a doorway, form a doorway, form a doorway …" its intent was clear. It didn't know why: it didn't care why. It just knew that was its purpose "… form a doorway, form a doorway, form a doorway …"

The next afternoon, Tammy picked up the phone to call Melinda. She had practiced the speech in her head before dialing, "I can't make it today. My car won't start. I don't know what's wrong with it, but my brother is coming over to take a look at it."

Once she felt she could be convincing, she punched the numbers in and waited—butterflies in her stomach—for Melinda to answer.

Caller ID alerted Melinda to Tammy's identity. "You better not say you're not coming over," she answered, without saying hello first.

"Uh," Tammy stammered, "My car …"

"What about your car?"

"It … uh … doesn't work." Tammy silently cursed herself for sounding so lame and unconvincing.

"I'll be there to pick you up in ten minutes. Be ready when I get there." Melinda hung up as Tammy resigned herself to her fate. She made the call to cancel her original plans and prepared for Melinda's arrival.

Melinda hurried Tammy into her house, "Come on, come on! Don't let the cat in!" she hollered as Onyx tried to dart inside through the open door. Tammy managed to slip inside quickly and keep the cat out. She couldn't understand why he would even want to come in, but thus is the nature of cats. They have their own logic.

"I've got everything all set up, already, so all you have to do is get dressed." Melinda gestured toward the cloak and pendant that Tammy had left on the couch the day before. "I'll get the candles and incense going."

Tammy reluctantly pulled the garments over her head. Having all night to think about the events of the previous evening, however, gave her more time to think about how to handle her uncomfortable situation. While she looked up to Melinda and desperately wanted her respect in return, she knew that she had an important role to play in this work. The Goddess had delivered her to Melinda's side as a helpmate, to keep a watchful eye on her. This knowledge gave her more confidence in her ability to perhaps sidetrack, or at least help to control, what Melinda was about to do.

Overhead, unbeknownst to Melinda, the doorway she requested had already been formed. The swirling, munching cloud had succeeded in breaking through the veil between the physical world and the astral world, and it floated blissfully in the opening, having accomplished its work. It knew not what to do next. No further instructions had been given. So, it was content, in its mindlessness, to sit and enjoy the completion.

Meantime, across the street, the edge of slumber was a delicious thing as Lola contentedly drifted along sleep's periphery, half wishfully fantasizing about how nice a meaningful life would be, and half simply enjoying the serene atmosphere in the living room, the hum of the TV fading in and out. Amanda had been sucked into the movie and Gandhi's message of peace, so there was no tension in the air. Lola felt absolutely yummy.

The good feeling was accompanied by lilting, Indian-accented voices, voices from the TV that filtered into her resting mind, speaking of nonviolence and passive resistance. She liked that and wanted more of it. It felt so much better than the boredom and aggravation that she had become used to in her daily life.

As she slipped toward dreamland, new images began filtering into her head—images of anger and naughty witchery. She lightly dreamed of a scene with two women, one fierce and one submissive, building a cone of some sort. It made no sense, and didn't feel very good, so she absently drifted back into the yummy feeling that she preferred.

"Yes," her dream-self stated, "That's what I want my life to feel like. Yummy."

Meantime, the joyful little cloud felt a downward tugging and chose to ignore it—the tugging didn't feel nice. The cloud was perfectly content to stay right where it was, in the exquisite doorway of its making. But the tugging became more insistent, more aggressive. The cloud felt itself being pulled downward by some unknown force, which was stretching it into the shape of a cone. It felt another cone's point reaching upward, striving to meet and conjoin.

The cone felt vaguely familiar and if the cloud had more capacity for memory it might have more easily recognized its own energetic roots, the mixture of passionate rage and pleading resistance from which it had been formed.

But, wait! Another cone, a smaller and less powerful one, was being formed nearby. This cone felt different. It felt warm and happy—what was the right word to describe it? Yummy? Yes, yummy.

Lola dreamed on, the movie and her teenage daughter no longer a part of her consciousness. In her dream, she was dressed all in white and was gazing up at a sky of swirling colors. She watched, fascinated, as the swirl pulsated and formed itself into a cone. It seemed to be making a decision. "Pick me," she thought at the cone, not having a clue what she was being picked for. She just knew that it felt good and she wanted more of it.

"Powers that be, Come through me. Powers that be, Come through me ..." Melinda and Tammy chanted in unison, raising the cone of power. Tammy's heart wasn't in it today, however. She allowed her mind to wander here and there, wondering where the cat was and if he would interrupt again, thinking about the dishes she had left in the sink at home, and occasionally back to the task at hand—undermining Melinda's efforts.

The cloud/cone played joyfully with its two points of attraction, bouncing back and forth between them. They both called out for it to join them, and the cloud enjoyed the Is-ness of the moment, the wanting-ness of it. Such happy happy! Such deciding-ness! This or that? That or this? Both and none, none and both.

All at once, the power of one cone faded, allowing the other to become stronger. But before the fading cone disappeared entirely, it managed to snag a large portion of the cloud's mojo into its own beingness.

"Damn you, Tammy, you're not concentrating!" Melinda scolded.

"Pick me!" Lola's dream-self cried out, "Let's play!"

What was left of the cloud/cone made its easy choice. Happy, happy! Happy felt better. Happy felt complete. The connection was made and the cones touched points, united in an instant of cosmic ecstasy. They formed a swirling vortex of bliss that rocketed Lola's dream-self through the doorway to the other side of the veil.

Images of stunning shards of light blasted into her vision as she gasped with elation. "Welcome," she heard a genderless voice say, "Glad you could join us! You asked for some excitement, right?"

"Mom? Are you okay?" Amanda was asking, as Lola sat bolt upright on the couch. Lola ignored the question and looked out the window to see Melinda chasing Tammy, like a crazy person, waving her wand around as if it were a club.

###

That's when I woke up. And that's how I finally know what happened to me, and what started this whole mess.

Speaking of mess, I'm going to have to chew out either Amanda or Chuck, because there are a bunch of pens on the floor near my desk. It would certainly be nice if they'd stay out of my office or, bare minimum, pick up after themselves when they knock things over.

Anyway, I wish that fairy in my dream was real so I could ask it to explain the movie. Maybe it would be able to help explain a lot of things.

Journal Entry 7

I can't keep pretending this isn't real. A part of me stays skeptical, telling myself this is all my overactive imagination, or that I'm crazy, or a dozen other ways of convincing myself that what's going on isn't reality.

But, Melinda intends to hurt Raven, and she's serious about it. And I'm the only one who can do anything about it because, other than Tammy, I'm the only one who knows about it.

Shit.

Why did this have to happen to me? I was just idly wishing for life to be more interesting! Don't we all do that??? I didn't mean by being given psychic powers, with no instruction manual, and being asked to take on an evil witch!

I can't keep pretending this isn't real. A part of me stays skeptical, telling myself this is all my overactive imagination, or that I'm crazy, or a dozen other ways of convincing myself that what's going on isn't reality.

But Melinda intends to hurt Raven, and she's serious about it. And I'm the only one who can do anything about it because, other than Tammy, I'm the only one who knows about it.

Why did this have to happen to me? I was just idly wishing for life to be more interesting! Don't we all do that??? I didn't mean by being given psychic powers, with no instruction manual, and being asked to take on an evil witch!

I don't even know where to begin. What do I do? Who do I tell? Who can help? The fairy who showed me the dream? Even Raven would think I'm nuts. *Who will ever believe me???*

Whoa.

Hold on.

I don't know for a solid fact that all this is true. It's just a dream I had, remember? Sure, it's a dream that corresponds with a lot of coincidences, and it's a dream that explains an awful lot about how I got where I am today, but not one single person has confirmed that Melinda seriously intends to physically harm Raven or anyone else. I'm only assuming this is true because I'm putting what would normally be completely innocent circumstances together with my own madness, and spinning a yarn so crazy that I'd be laughed out of the police station or, worse yet, my own bed.

I can't tell Chuck about this. That's obvious. He already hates that I'm talking about knowing what he's thinking and not being unable to prove it, and that I'm reading all these new books and hanging out at Raven's shop. He's already worried about losing his sensible wife.

What would he say if I told him, "I had a dream about a pretty little fairy and a dancing cloud that gave me magical powers and, oh yeah, our neighbor is planning to bomb Raven's shop and I know this because I can hear her thoughts and walk around inside her body at will."

I'm screwed.

Okay, I've decided. I'm going to mind my own business. This isn't my fight; I barely know these people and I have absolutely no way of knowing that I'm right about any of this. I'm going back to my normal life.

Whew, that feels better. I've learned my lesson. No more playing games with powers I don't understand. No more poking into other people's heads. And, no more assuming that I have any clue what other people have planned with their own lives that are none of my business.

Except that, as I type this, I just now glanced out my window and saw Melinda taking a box of glass bottles and a gas can out of her trunk and into her house.

God, help me.

Journal Entry 8

Thank goodness for Tammy Webster. She has convinced Melinda to back off on the Molotov cocktails.
I'm not getting the entire, verbatim conversation, but Tammy is over there, right now. I can see her through Melinda's front windows. They're arguing, but Tammy is standing her ground. Good for her!
I'm still trying to get the hang of this listening ability I seem to have developed. Sometimes it works and sometimes it doesn't, sort of like spotty cell phone service.
When it is working—if I imagine myself inside someone—I can hear/feel/see what they're experiencing.

Thank goodness for Tammy Webster. She has convinced Melinda to back off on the Molotov cocktails.

I'm not getting the entire, verbatim conversation, but Tammy is over there, right now. I can see her through Melinda's front windows. They're arguing, but Tammy is standing her ground. Good for her!

I'm still trying to get the hang of this listening ability I seem to have developed. Sometimes it works and sometimes it doesn't, sort of like spotty cell phone service.

When it is working—if I imagine myself inside someone—I can hear/feel/see what they're experiencing. This time, though, the 'hearing' part of that isn't working as well. I can only hear both sides if I move back and forth from inside one of them into the other, which is causing me to get an interrupted version of what they're saying. Usually I would be able to stay inside one of them and use that set of ears to hear the whole thing, but not today. The signal is being scrambled and I don't know how to tune it in.

I need to find a way to eavesdrop, for lack of a better word, without actually being inside their bodies to use their senses. Meantime, here's the gist of what I'm half sensing/half hearing. I'll try to keep typing as they talk, but I make no promises that I'll catch all of it. There is no rewind button on real life, so I have to type on the fly:

TAMMY: Shouldn't starting a fire be the last resort? Wouldn't it be better to ruin her reputation, instead? That way you're not committing any crimes.

MELINDA: *(first few words are lost as I move from inside Tammy and into Melinda)* … think the cops will actually catch me? I'm protected by powers greater than any human, remember?

TAMMY: *(words lost as I move again)* … take chances? Wouldn't you rather see her shop fail and her life fall apart instead of making a martyr out of her and her shop? That would just bring the coven more closely to her aid.

MELINDA: *(words lost. damn it, this is frustrating. if only I could be a fly on the wall)* … a good point. What do you have in mind?

How weird. As I type, I have the strangest feeling of being pulled upward and out of Melinda's body, as if by magic … someone else's magic, someone with wings. An angel? That fairy? It's the weirdest feeling, as if I have absolutely no control, but going up, up, up…

… into a fly! Ewwwwwwwwwwwwwwwww!

Oh my God! I have to learn to be more careful about what I say!

Stop! I don't *literally* want to be a fly on the wall! Can't I be *like* a fly? Can't I have a fly's perspective without being inside this …

… that alien, creepy space?

Whew, that's better. I popped out just as quickly as I popped in, thank God, but I also heard high-pitched giggling. Where that came from, I do not know.

I have no idea what I look like right now, but the fly has now buzzed away and I'm still able to view the room from above. I don't think I'll ever stop grossing out about what that felt like. Yech.

I missed some of the conversation, but here's what they're saying:

> TAMMY: … you know how the churches feel about her store.
>
> MELINDA: I think you are definitely on to something. You're not as dumb as you look!
>
> TAMMY: (I sense that she feels a mixture of pride at the compliment and rage at the insult) I'm glad you think it's a good idea. I've already done up a sample flyer. Look.

Tammy then pulled a folded paper out of the back pocket of her faded jeans and proudly handed it to Melinda.

Oh, hell! Chuck is hollering for me! If I don't go, he'll get pissed. This is one of those times where I have to choose between him and the "crazy stuff," as he calls it.

Journal Entry 9

I just reread the tail end of where I had to abruptly leave off last time and, if you don't know Chuck, as I do, that makes him look like a complete jerk. I just didn't have time to explain what was going on.
I don't jump at his beck and call. We don't have one of those marriages, believe me. I may have allowed myself to become a household drone, but I'm not an obedient, subservient wifey. I'm way too stubborn and independent for that.
But this time he sounded like whatever he was calling about was important, and it was. The toilet was overflowing and he was yelling for me

I just reread the tail end of where I had to abruptly leave off last time and, if you don't know Chuck, as I do, that makes him look like a complete jerk. I just didn't have time to explain what was going on.

I don't jump at his beck and call. We don't have one of those marriages, believe me. I may have allowed myself to become a household drone, but I'm not an obedient, subservient wifey. I'm way too stubborn and independent for that.

But this time he sounded like whatever he was calling about was important, and it was. The toilet was overflowing and he was yelling for me to bring in some rags and stuff to mop up the floor while he dealt with the problem.

I was just miffed because I was in the middle of something important, too, and he could have called Amanda to help (although he probably knew as well as I do that it would have taken her at least twice as long to come when called and she would have pretended not to know where the mop or rags were, so she wouldn't have to actually do anything to help).

The problem is that my important issue isn't one

I can explain to him, of course (I'm sure he'd never believe I was inside a fly—I'm not sure I believe it!). At least the bomb scare seems to have been back-shelved for now so I can breathe a sigh of relief, but I need to find a way to learn what Tammy suggested to Melinda regarding how the churches feel about Raven's shop before they do any harm.

So, with Chuck now exonerated, I can continue.

On another topic, I had another one of those not-really-a-dream dreams. I've learned to trust those because they feel different from the dreams I have while I sleep, and the ones that feel this way have always proven to be true in some way.

For example, after wondering whether my dream about the spell Melinda cast was real or not, I had a series of similar, harmless little dreamlike episodes that were all easily proven true—déjà vu type experiences but with a little more oomph. I know this sounds silly, but I 'dreamed' about it raining green peas and at the grocery store that day a bag of frozen peas fell out of the freezer when another customer was reaching in there for some veggies. And, I dreamed lyrics to a song and heard Chuck singing that same song, later. None of these are of any consequence, but they all come true. And they all felt like this kind of dream, as opposed to the kind you have when you're asleep and can barely remember them later.

Anyway, in this dream I was lying in bed, having one of these dreams. It was a dream within a dream, kinda hard to describe.

So, in this dream, I was lying in bed and I saw the fairy from the TV show again. You know how they're usually portrayed as tiny, dressed in green, glowing and with a playful, impish personality? This one was that size, it had wings and it sparkled purple and gold (not glowing, or green), but it was NOT playful and impish, it was kind of testy. It was stomping on and kicking the bridge of my nose, yelling in a thick Scottish or Irish-sounding accent, "Wake up, yeh mithering git! Didn't yeh ask fer help? Well, yeh got it!"

I woke up from that dream but was still asleep within the primary dream, and even there I was a little confused about what that could mean. I know nothing about the symbolism of fairies, or even what they really are. My knowledge of fairies ends with Peter Pan and the Lord of the

Rings. Or are those elves?

See? I don't know much about what kind of creatures they actually are. I'll have to do a little research to find out what this could mean. I guess I'm going to Karma Korner to pick up a book or two on the subject.

And, gee, while I'm there, maybe Raven will feel gossipy and I can get a little more insight into what Melinda and Tammy may have in mind.

Journal Entry 10

I'm going to have to retire the word "weird" from my vocabulary because it's become meaningless, like when you say a mundane word, like "door", over and over and over and over. Eventually it doesn't even sound like a word anymore—it becomes a goofy, meaningless sound. One of these days I'll go back and count just how many times I've used the word "weird" in my journal to describe what my life has become.

However, I insist on one last usage, because today's events were just plain *weird*.

I'm going to have to retire the word "weird" from my vocabulary because it's become meaningless, like when you say a mundane word, like "door" over and over and over and over. Eventually it doesn't even sound like a word anymore—it becomes a goofy, meaningless sound. One of these days I'll go back and count just how many times I've used the word "weird" in my journal to describe what my life has become.

However, I insist on one last usage, because today's events were just plain *weird.*

I was on my way to Karma Korner to get a book on fairies and I had to park a couple blocks away. The construction in that area has done such a number on the neighborhood that there is nowhere to park nearby, so I ended up parking on a street I've never been down. It's a side street, with older shops—the kind that you know before you even enter that they're going to smell close and musty—and a beat-up sidewalk that's all cracked and broken.

I found a little antique shop I didn't know existed. There was a beautiful pendant in the window that caught my eye. I couldn't resist going in.

Another woman happened to come in right behind me, so there were three of us in the shop: me, her and the shop owner.

At first glance, the shop owner looked like a hard-living woman in a sexy, skin-tight dress and ratty mink stole. She had a tattered, Joan

Collins wannabe look (circa 1970s). Her complexion was rough, as though she had suffered brutal acne as a teen, and she was missing some teeth. But she had a killer body. Wow!

It took me a second take to realize this was a man. The woman who entered the store with me must have realized it at about the same time, because she audibly gasped just as it was sinking in to my head that, "I'm looking at a dude in a dress."

The difference between me and the gasping woman is that she was shocked and repelled, immediately writing the story in her head that she would tell her friends later, "You will not believe what I saw in this little antique shop off of Orange Street!" I, on the other hand, knew that this poor guy just wanted to dress like a pretty girl, ever since he was a small child. It wasn't his fault he was too masculine and rough looking to pull it off very well.

I felt his biggest disappointment in life was that his male body came with the societal restrictions that men of our generation deal with, especially in the Midwest—no feminine or artistic expression or flare allowed, without causing raised eyebrows and possible ass-beatings. Most of the time he just wanted to play the role of a gorgeous woman, so he/she could wear lovely things and flip her hair flirtatiously, to drive men wild with desire as they gazed lustfully down her deep cleavage. It was interesting to see the "male gaze" from a male perspective—his desire to be ogled by men was nothing like I've ever felt.

There was a lot to unpack here, but too little time. Never mind all the progress that the LGBTQ community had made—it hadn't yet trickled down to his/her life, which was so filled with pain, with customers in her shop who looked at her like she was a freak. Why couldn't people just accept her as she was inside? She wasn't trying to offend anyone, or shock anyone. She just so badly wanted to express her fabulous femininity, in whichever body shape felt right in that moment. And besides, she was in her own goddamned store, where she should be able to dress however she wants!

I heard myself saying, "What a gorgeous dress!" because it was, and it seemed to be what she most wanted to hear.

She lit up and, for a moment, really was dazzling. Finally! Someone saw her Inner Joan!

It was this moment when I realized how easy it is to not just make or break someone's day, but to deeply affect their life. Not too long ago, I might have reacted like the other woman in the store. We may have even rolled our eyes at each other or whispered about "Miss Thing" when his back was turned. I was ashamed of the memory of who I once was.

This was apparently too much for the other customer, because she huffed a loud "Ugh!" and walked out. That left me with my wannabe-Joan. It was an uncomfortable moment because we both knew why the other customer made such a dramatic exit, and it briefly felt like there was a proverbial elephant in the room. But I sensed that the best way to handle this would be to ignore the discomfort and just be two human beings. Oddly, I sensed, it would give us both a healing and I'm not sure what that even means, as I write it.

So, his/her gender became a non-issue and I asked about the pendant in the window. It was an antique, sparkling white topaz set in sterling filigree, and it was one of the most beautiful things I had ever seen. It was a little higher in price than I can afford right now, but I could save up for it. It might just take a while.

"Oh, it's not going anywhere," she assured me, "It's been in the shop here for six months and I just put it in the window this morning. You're the only person who has ever expressed an interest in it."

"I'm glad to hear that," I told her. I couldn't explain why, but something deep inside me knew that I simply had to possess it. I took her business card from the caddy next to the cash register on my way out and said, "I'll be back as soon as I have enough to pay for it."

She genuinely wished me well, and said, "I hope you'll be the one who ends up with that lovely piece."

I walked down the block toward Karma Korner, feeling good about myself, feeling like I had helped to make someone else feel truly accepted, for the first time. It was deeply moving. I don't know when else I've ever known for a fact that I've done something truly good, a "What Would Jesus Do?" moment.

Then I heard her voice calling me from the shop door, "Ma'am, oh Ma'am, please wait just a moment."

I turned around and saw her delicately mincing down the broken sidewalk toward me, the way anyone wearing such high stilettos would have to walk over such uneven concrete, with something in her hand. I had a brief, silly thought that it was the pendant.

Instead, she handed me a small brown glass vial, saying, "It's rose oil. I bottled it myself. I have a whole side business, blending oils and such for love potions and magical things like that. I want you to have this so it will bring you closer to owning that gorgeous pendant. I'll go ahead and take it out of the window so it won't attract anyone else's attention."

I was so touched that it almost brought tears to my eyes. I took the vial of oil and thanked her, promising her I'd be back as soon as I could. As I turned to leave, I vowed that I would own that necklace—that it would be like a medal of honor that I would wear to remind myself of what happens when you're nice to someone just for the sake of being nice.

When I wandered into Karma Korner, I wasn't paying much attention to what I was doing. I was still thinking about the shop owner, and I had just opened the vial to smell the oil. It was amazing! I've never really liked the smell of rose perfumes or rose scented air fresheners. They remind me of the bacon/perfume stink. But this oil smelled like I was nose deep in a bouquet of real, lush, red roses. It made my scalp tingle and it took me away to another world for a brief moment. Pure heaven, it was.

Raven noticed that I was somewhere else and commented on it. "What do you have there? It seems to have transformative powers!"

I laughed and told her the story. I added, "The shop is just around the corner. I had to park down there today, and I've never seen it before. The owner said that she'd had the pendant I admired for six months." I showed her the business card and the oil.

What she said next was interesting. She told me that rose oil is one of the "highest vibration" oils. She said, "It has properties of pure, essential love and the power of celestial quality magic. This was, obviously, a deeply heartfelt gift."

Strangely, all I could think of was playing one of the *Legend of Zelda* video games where the hero, Link, would be rewarded with a new tool or special power every time he completed a level of mastery. I felt like my vial of rose oil was a magic potion that I received after talking to just the right shopkeeper, or a prize I won for reaching a new level.

However, the reason I was at Raven's shop today wasn't to win potions from gnarled hags who are actually beautiful witch queens under an evil enchantment, rewarding those who see beyond the façade that most people scorn. It was to find out about the symbolism of fairies. This, I didn't mind confiding to Raven, to a certain degree.

"I had a strange dream the other day about a fairy stomping on my nose as I slept, yelling that it was there because I asked for help. Even before the dream, I kept hearing the word 'fairy,' and seeing pictures of fairies.

"Oh, that's an auspicious sign!" Raven clapped her hands with excitement. "Even if you don't believe that fairies are real beings who live in the woods and fields of wildflowers, they symbolize being watched over and protected. They're clever and wise, and they know when they're being fooled with. They are fiercely protective of the ones they love and can be dangerous when crossed. Sounds like you've got a guardian!"

I said, "Well, I don't believe in fairies—I mean, come on. We all know they don't really exist, no matter how cool it would be if we lived in that world, but if I don't believe in fairies then how can this be a good sign? There's not a real fairy hovering over my shoulder, watching to make sure I don't cross the street without looking."

Raven is such a patient person. She didn't even try to make me feel like she thought this was an ignorant statement, even though I could tell she did believe I was naïve. This struck me as odd because she's the one who believes in fairies and is acting like I'm the delusional one.

She said, "You don't have to believe in them because whether they really exist or not is irrelevant. If you have the essence of 'fairy' in your consciousness, then you carry a protective force about you, one that will energetically repel negative things from harming you. Besides, isn't it more fun to live in a world where they might be real?"

I nodded, yes, and she continued, "It's like the rose oil. The oil itself is just oil, even though rose does have high vibration properties and is best used for positive spell work. But the intent with which it was given was more important. You now carry a powerful blessing from someone whose heart you touched. See what I mean? You've been changed, as a person, at a soul level. From here on in, everything you do will be from a new level of consciousness."

It made sense. I bought a book on fairies that Raven recommended because I felt rather silly even discussing the topic. The book spells the word "faery" so I guess I've been corrected. Meantime, I had almost forgotten I wanted to broach the topic of how the local churches felt about her shop, given what I overheard Tammy saying to Melinda.

Without any segue whatsoever, I clumsily came right out and asked. "How do the local churches feel about your shop, with the witchcraft and the coven and all?"

Raven only showed mild surprise at the abrupt subject change— it takes a lot to nonplus this woman—and replied, "I have a good relationship with the more progressive ones, and the middle of the road churches mostly ignore us. They disagree strongly with what they *think* we believe in, mostly because they don't bother to find out exactly what that is. But since Wicca is accepted by the United States military as a legitimate religion, they are almost forced to tolerate us as equals, more or less." She sighed, "There are one or two church leaders who preach against us. They tell their parishioners that we are Satanists which, of course, is ridiculous, and that we should be avoided at all costs."

I was too scared to ask her what she meant by Satanism and why it's ridiculous, but pushed on, "Do you think any of them would ever do more than that? Like try to close you down or hurt you in any way?"

She nodded, and shrugged, "We've had experiences like that in the past, but it's usually just the people who even those churches would call extremists or zealots. No one who takes the time to research us takes them very seriously. The press will cover it for a couple days until it dies down, we get some free media coverage and an explanation about who we really are, and the troublemakers are usually seen for the radicals that they are."

That sounded like it would be almost worth having some minor kerfuffle stirred up, as long as no one got crazy—sort of a "No publicity is bad publicity" kind of thing, so I'm not sure if that's the direction that Melinda and Tammy would go.

I decided that I couldn't let it go, just in case, so I made up a lie. Can she tell I'm lying? I don't know. There are certainly times when I know what others are thinking, so what if she can, too? But I had to take the chance—I'm doing no harm as long as my intent is loving, correct?

"The reason I asked," I lied, realizing this would also explain the out-of-the-blue question I asked earlier, "is because of a conversation I overheard at work. Two people I don't know very well were talking at lunch about their church's plan to stir up some trouble for you. Something about launching a flyer campaign. I'm sorry I didn't hear more of it, but there was no way to do that without it being obvious that I was eavesdropping."

Raven smiled, her eyes twinkling. She really is such a nice woman. She reminds me of my mom's sister, my favorite aunt who was always just nice to me no matter what—she never teased me, she was always glad to see me, and never made fun of me like so many other grownups who think teasing adolescents is fun.

Anyway, Raven thanked me for letting her know and assured me, "It's nothing to worry about, but I appreciate the heads up. I'll spend a little time this week making sure my solid connections to the other churches still stand, just in case. It never hurts to have a safety net. Thank you."

With this, she gave me a big, patchouli-scented hug, which took me aback for a moment. I'm not a huggy person and don't care for touchy-feely demonstrations of affection. But this was such a nice hug that I found myself gladly returning it. I was able to leave the shop with a comforted mind. If this was all Tammy and Melinda were up to now, I felt like I would be okay leaving it alone and going back to my own life. What a relief!

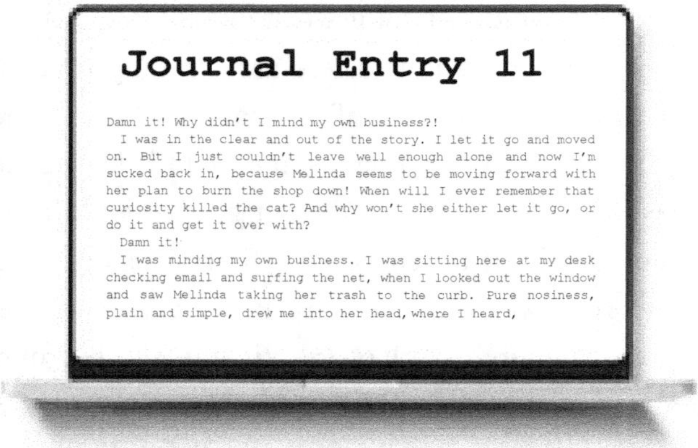

Journal Entry 11

Damn it! Why didn't I mind my own business?!
I was in the clear and out of the story. I let it go and moved on. But I just couldn't leave well enough alone and now I'm sucked back in, because Melinda seems to be moving forward with her plan to burn the shop down! When will I ever remember that curiosity killed the cat? And why won't she either let it go, or do it and get it over with?
Damn it!
I was minding my own business. I was sitting here at my desk checking email and surfing the net, when I looked out the window and saw Melinda taking her trash to the curb. Pure nosiness, plain and simple, drew me into her head, where I heard,

Damn it! Why didn't I mind my own business?!

I was in the clear and out of the story. I let it go and moved on. But I just couldn't leave well enough alone and now I'm sucked back in, because Melinda seems to be moving forward with her plan to burn the shop down! When will I ever remember that curiosity killed the cat? And why won't she either let it go, or do it and get it over with?

Damn it!

I was minding my own business. I was sitting here at my desk checking email and surfing the net, when I looked out the window and saw Melinda taking her trash to the curb. Pure nosiness, plain and simple, drew me into her head, where I heard, "Tammy doesn't know what the hell she's talking about. No one cares anymore about that shop. Raven is so airy-fairy, and love and light that no one would believe us if we say that it's a front for satanic rituals and orgies. If I want this done right, I'm going to have to do it myself."

Then, thoughts without words. I saw, in her mind's eye, the glass bottles in her basement, waiting to be filled with gasoline and rags.

I admit, I started freaking out a little bit. I didn't know what to do, but I obviously can't ignore her. I need help! Why won't the help I've asked for so often ever get here? Raven says we all have spirit guides who are just waiting to assist—ask and ye shall receive, she says—and I'm asking! Where the hell are they???

While I was shrieking internally, watching Melinda arrange her trash cans, she must have heard my thoughts like I can hear hers because next thing I knew she looked up at me through the window and our eyes met. Holy Mother of God, she looked right at me. My heart stopped in my chest.

My head began rushing with a deluge of too much information all at once. I saw that this is very real, and that when I received these powers, she did, too, but she didn't know about me before. She now knows just as much about me as I do about her, as a result of seeing me and hearing my mental panic about her plan. Now she knows that I exist, and that I know what she's up to.

Oh God, now I've done it. *I've attracted the undivided attention of a psychopath who plays with fire. What did I do?*

Raven insists that when you call for help, your spirit guides are always there, but I don't see them and I don't hear them. I think Raven has rocks in her head. I'm very, very alone in this.

Please, God, if you can hear me, if you exist, if I haven't pissed you off too much by playing with things I shouldn't, please help me!

Journal Entry 12

I started reading the book on Wicca because that topic seems the most pressing. I need to understand what Melinda is doing, what she's working with and how, if I'm ever going to stop her. The book about faeries can wait.

Although, come to think of it, I did have another dream within a dream about that same faery. It was that same sort of dream I had recently where I watched, from within another dream, as the little pixie kicked my nose while I slept.

This time, the faery was throwing a tantrum, standing on my forehead, stomping its foot in anger. It was furiously trying to get my attention but, in that facet of

I started reading the book on Wicca because that topic seems the most pressing. I need to understand what Melinda is doing, what she's working with and how, if I'm ever going to stop her. The book about faeries can wait.

Although, come to think of it, I did have another dream within a dream about that same faery. It was that same sort of dream I had recently where I watched, from within another dream, as the little pixie kicked my nose while I slept.

This time, the faery was throwing a tantrum, standing on my forehead, stomping its foot in anger. It was furiously trying to get my attention but, in that facet of the dream, I was again asleep and I couldn't wake up. In my primary dream, I was watching me sleeping with this faery stomping around on my face. It finally stood just below my eye and tried to lift my eyelid to wake me up. It was actually quite comical because she was having a hard time pulling my eyelid open and keeping it open as she peered into my eyeball, yelling, "Oi! Anyone t'home?" She had an adorable but thick accent—I thought she sounded Scottish, sort of, but she also sounded like one of the Beatles, like a cross between the two regions, Scotland and Liverpool.

My dream-self laughed, watching this scene, and the faery must have heard it because she suddenly turned and faced me (in my primary dream) and snorted, "Yeh think it's funny, do yeh? Well, I have better things to do with my time than play sidekick to some daft ha'p'orth!"

Getting the hang of this dual dream conversation, I replied, "I can wake her up. Hold on."

I tried to use my physical hand, in real life, to open my physical eyes to wake up my dream-self. I could feel my hand forcing my eyes open but I still couldn't see anything but the dream scene. The faery just rolled her eyes at me and said, "Yeh really are soft, aren't yeh?" Then the dream faded and disappeared.

I can't wait until I have time to read the book about faeries because they're showing up everywhere I look. Magazine covers, songs, dialog in TV shows—it's bizarre! You know how when you buy a new car and you think it's relatively unique, but then you see nothing but cars just like the one you just bought? It's the same kind of thing. All of a sudden, I'm seeing faeries everywhere.

But, for now, the witchcraft thing is taking precedence because as far as I know the faeries aren't threatening to throw a flaming bottle of gasoline through Raven's window.

What I've learned so far is that Raven was right: Wicca and witchcraft are not necessarily the same thing. Wicca is a religion that honors nature and the natural forces of life. They have way more archetype gods than I could ever keep track of, but primarily they believe in a god AND a goddess, which I think is kind of nice. I've always had a hard time grasping the concept of the one and only Deity being a Man and of human women being an afterthought, just to give Adam a subservient toy. It never seemed right that if God even had a gender, then why wouldn't there be a Goddess, too?

I'm getting off track here. My personal beliefs about God aside, Wicca is not what Melinda is practicing and that's why Raven bounced her out of the coven.

Melinda is practicing the kind of witchcraft that isn't bound by the Wiccan Rede that Raven and this book talk about, "An it harm none, do as thou wilt." Wiccan witchcraft (unfortunate that they are using the same word because people are afraid of it) is about working with nature and the flow of life. It's used to help heal and make things groovy, and their rituals aren't too much different than the kind of thing you'd see in a Catholic Mass. Basically, they're all just calling upon the powers of what they each call "god" to help make their lives better.

Those powers can be used with or without the Rede, because the Rede is nothing more than an ethical framework, albeit an important one. Imagine if we all had unlimited power and could do whatever we want, no matter who it hurt or what it destroyed. That's what Melinda is doing and, again, why Raven threw her out of the coven.

There has to be some set of rules for the use of this power or we'd live in utter chaos, everyone doing whatever they want … and that's what the Rede and any other religion's version of the Golden Rule is designed to prevent. It boils down to the philosophy of Bill and Ted who said, so succinctly, "Be excellent to each other. Party on, dude!"

Plus, the book says that it's important to remember that just because someone is practicing witchcraft and not living under any religious dogma does not mean they are doing harm. They just aren't members of a religion. They can still be ethical and use the forces of Nature. We're all using them, all the time, anyway—even if we're not calling it "witchcraft"—just by living our everyday lives and expressing our will-power.

That's when the laws of karma become important because the way you use the powers that be will affect you as well. For example, I used my powers of empathy (that's what it's called when you can feel what others are feeling—who knew there was a name for it?!) at the antique shop to make the shop owner feel good about herself and was rewarded with a gift of equal vibrational meaning—rose oil. Raven was right about that, too. Rose oil, according to this book, is a very powerful potion and I'm even more touched by the gift, now that I know what it means.

The book does explain a little about empathy and other forms of psychic abilities, but Wicca is its primary focus so I'll have to look more into empathy elsewhere. I suppose I could just Google it, couldn't I?

Later. For now, I'm on the hunt. A witch hunt, as it were, so I'm being careful.

Now, if you recall, I downloaded the whole scene where these powers were transferred to both me and Melinda. I think I understand it better now. She was building what is called a cone of power, which the book says is a "concentration of focused intent, designed to create a specific outcome."

Wow, I just realized something important.

If I'm able to pop into Melinda's mind at will, then she might be able to do the same to me. I just felt her disturbing presence in this room and it scares the bejesus out of me just thinking about her peering into my mind. It reminded me to reinstall the thought-wall that I haven't paid enough attention to maintaining. She probably showed up because I'm writing about her and thinking so hard about what's going on. It's almost like I'm calling her to me.

I don't know for sure if she's here but it doesn't matter in the end. If nothing else, just thinking about her is a reminder to put up a protective thought-wall before I do any more research because that was one creeeeeeeeeepy feeling when she suddenly looked up at me through the window like that. The sensation of her probing my mind felt like swallowing a bucket of worms, like I was filled with slimy, crawling things and could barely keep from vomiting. I do not want that to happen again.

There are a couple of protection spells in this book I might try, although I would feel silly. Also, I'm still not completely comfortable with the whole witchcraft idea. It goes against pretty much everything I was raised to believe. I think it's mostly the word "witchcraft" that bothers me. If they didn't call it that, I wouldn't be so concerned.

I mean, the book sure makes it sound like it's been misunderstood all these years, and I haven't seen anything that would lead me to believe otherwise. The book makes it excruciatingly clear that Wiccans have just as strong a moral code as members of any other religion, and believe in a similar Golden Rule. Raven is a fine person and I would know if she wasn't. I can see inside her, remember?

One of the spells is simple: it's a matter of sprinkling sea salt in a clockwise circle around my house while setting the intent that no evil may cross. It's more like folk-magic than spell casting. Most people would just think it's superstition, creating a placebo effect, and that makes sense.

Gaaah! I have to interrupt to vent for a second. I was looking for a pen to make some notes about the salt spell and, once again, they're all over the floor! It's gotta be Chuck knocking them off the desk, because Amanda hasn't been in my office all day, but Chuck has. I'm gonna wring his neck!

Anyway I can totally understand, now, how believing that "This action will create that result" *can* sometimes bring about that result. If you firmly believe it to be true, you start acting like it's true and before you know it, it is true! Your spell swirls up the ethers, telling them how you want them to solidify. When you end a spell with the words "So mote it be," you're telling the swirling ethers to start firming up into what you've requested, like saying "Amen" at the end of a prayer.

It's like if you Google-search lawn ornaments, you soon start seeing ads for plastic flamingos on every web page you visit and you think, "Hey, that's a coincidence! I was just thinking of decorating my lawn!" Next thing you know, you're pricing fake flamingos on sticks and buying them by the dozen. You're feverishly bidding for great deals on eBay and your lawn looks like a Florida retirement home, and you don't even realize it's algorithms that brought you together.

My vision is expanding these days to where I can see the way things fall together like puzzle pieces. In fact, once I saw a flash of the energy grid, for lack of a better term, that holds everything together, sort of like chicken wire acts as a mold for papier-mâché. I wasn't doing anything, just living life and in a flash I saw this grid made of white light, underlying everything I looked at. It faded quickly, but it stayed long enough for me to understand what it was.

Another time, I was lying in bed next to Chuck, watching his back rising and falling as he snored, drowsily counting his breaths like I was counting sheep. I was dozing in and out, more awake than asleep. Again, in a flash, I could see into his skin, how the cells formed fractals down to a molecular level. I was so startled that I woke up and couldn't see it any longer. It was just a quick flash, but I saw it.

I've found myself drawn to the work of visionary artists like Alex Grey, who paints incredible portraits of what he calls the human energy field. Even though I don't understand what this all means, it makes so much sense, somehow, in a way that I can't explain, I can only comprehend.

So, I guess I'm not so worried about having to "cast spells" or become a "witch" in order to control these new abilities of mine. I mostly want to know how Melinda is doing what she does. I'll still probably go ahead and do the sea salt protection ritual, just to feel safe. Sure, I have my thought-wall that I've put up, but that means I must maintain it and sometimes I forget and let it go. It's hard to remember to do, although I suppose it will become easier if I can tell when she's trying to get in.

Problem is, now that she knows I'm on to her, she's put her guard up as well. She's effectively blocked me from seeing into her so now I'm flying blind. I have no idea what's she up to now. She's had lots of practice with this stuff and I'm a newbie.

I just know I must be very, very careful.

Journal Entry 13

She's good. Melinda is very good at this game.
I was at Karma Korner today talking to Raven and trying to lead the conversation, in order to warn her. Now that Melinda and I have locked eyes, she knows I exist–a fly in her ointment–and she's keeping me out of her head. That's why I finally went to warn Raven: I don't have the luxury of time anymore. I had to take the chance that she might think I'm nuts because I don't know when this is going to happen, just that it is.
'Remember how hard it was for me to hear the conversation between Tammy and Melinda because I had to keep popping in and out of each of them, and then I ended up inside the fly? (Still shuddering in revulsion, by the way.)

She's good. Melinda is very good at this game.

I was at Karma Korner today talking to Raven and trying to lead the conversation, in order to warn her. Now that Melinda and I have locked eyes, she knows I exist—a fly in her ointment—and she's keeping me out of her head. That's why I finally went to warn Raven: I don't have the luxury of time anymore. I had to take the chance that she might think I'm nuts because I don't know when this is going to happen, just that it is.

Remember how hard it was for me to hear the conversation between Tammy and Melinda because I had to keep popping in and out of each of them, and then I ended up inside the fly? (Still shuddering in revulsion, by the way.) Melinda, apparently, has learned how to eavesdrop on a conversation from inside one of the people talking, a trick I'm still trying to learn. I know this because I saw her presence behind Raven's eyes today.

I was asking Raven about the churches again—that seemed like a good way to broach the topic, since I had already insinuated that I work with a religious zealot who wished the store harm. She said, in her warm and loving voice, "I'm happy to report that all is well, and I'm even making a little headway with a deeply fundamentalist church just outside of town. I wouldn't have thought to make the effort right now, if it wasn't for you asking about it, so thank you for bringing it up. They just got a new pastor, who's a little more open minded than their last one, so it was divine timing that led to our conversation."

While I was glad to hear this, I had to now come up with a new way to tell her that someone plans to bomb her store. I couldn't think of anything, and I realized that I would have to trust her and tell her what's been going on with me. Now that I know her well enough, I know that not only will she keep my secret, but she'll—more importantly—believe me. I know that now.

So, I started to say, "Remember when you told me about those threatening emails and phone calls you were getting? I think I know who sent them," but before I had two words out, I saw that Raven was no longer the primary consciousness in her body. Her smile changed to a sneer, and her usually warm eyes transformed into slits of icy hatred. Although her features remained mostly Raven's, I could see Melinda's personality looking out at me through her eyes.

She snarled and said, in frigid tones, "Think twice, bitch. You don't want to be on my wrong side. I know where you live and I know when your brat is home alone."

Words cannot describe how deeply this horrified me. My heart seized up and I now know what the phrase "My blood ran cold" means. Never mind the creepiness of watching Raven's normally serene and lovely face morphing into a mask of black hate. Amanda was home, alone, across the street from Melinda's house. *Now!*

I hurried out of the store and drove home fast, knocking over a couple of construction cones as I pulled out of my parking space. I didn't even say goodbye to Raven because—as I ran out the door—Melinda cackled at me using Raven's melodious voice, which made the scene even spookier.

Of course, Amanda is fine or I wouldn't be calm enough to sit here at my computer typing out this story. But I think I scared the bejesus out of her when I rushed in the door screaming her name, only to find her lying on the couch talking on the phone, elbow deep in a bag of cheese puffs. I was so relieved that I didn't bother yelling at her for getting neon-orange "cheeze" dust on the good furniture.

Through the front window—the same window through which I first watched Melinda chasing Tammy—I once again saw Melinda on her front porch. But this time she was watching me and laughing so hard she was doubled over, clutching her belly.

I hurried over and closed the shades so she couldn't see in, unaided, and reinforced my silent request for a protective thought-wall around my house. Apparently, the sea salt protection circle that I laid out earlier either doesn't work, or I didn't do it correctly. It's time to stop playing. I need help, now. Where the hell is it?

I *demand* help. Now!

If it helps, I'll even spell it out in the kind of language that the book suggests using if you're uncomfortable "invoking the gods" (which I definitely am!):

> *Universal Intelligence is within me and all around me. I am a perfect manifestation of that Intelligence. Therefore, I call upon its power to help me defeat Melinda Underwood.*
> *I beseech this power to protect my family and friends and my self. I have this power within my abilities and will it to be so, according to the highest good of all, harming none.*
> *So mote it be.*

Let's see what good that does.

Journal Entry 14

I had another dream but, of course, it wasn't just a dream. I was told that it was a "conference in spirit".

I was also told (by whom, I'm about to explain) that—since I'm unwilling to accept that this is really happening, for fear of insanity or ridicule—I can't access the information or help that I need, while I'm awake, because I don't want to believe it's possible. That's why it always has to come to me in a dream. Hence, a conference, in spirit.

Also, apparently, I can't consciously access any help—in fact, I'm blocking it—until I accept that our physical reality is just another kind of dream. This bends my mind and makes me want to curl up in a ball, drooling.

I had another dream but, of course, it wasn't just a dream. I was told that it was a "conference in spirit".

I was also told (by whom, I'm about to explain) that—since I'm unwilling to accept that this is really happening, for fear of insanity or ridicule—I can't access the information or help that I need while I'm awake because I don't want to believe it's possible. That's why it always has to come to me in a dream. Hence, a conference, in spirit.

Also, apparently, I can't consciously access any help—in fact, I'm blocking it—until I accept that our physical reality is just another kind of dream. This bends my mind and makes me want to curl up in a ball, drooling.

Let me back up and start at the beginning.

The spell I typed out yesterday must have worked, because as soon as I fell asleep I found myself in a misty, swirling-fog-filled room, all white and hazy. There was a white table, with white chairs, white walls, white curtains with white light pouring in through white window panes. My first thought was, "Boy, could this place be more stereotypical?"

Then I saw a being made of white light—it looked like a hologram. It sat at the table and I felt, more than heard, the words, "Welcome to the newbie room." I also 'felt' that the greeting was in response to my reaction to the room's appearance, to let me know that it looked that way because it's *my* stereotype—it's what many newbies expect, so it's exactly what they get. I, in fact, created the scene myself with my cynical expectation.

Then I found myself wondering why the room couldn't look more like my favorite counselor's office, from when I was in my twenties and a little confused about life. She helped me a lot and I miss her company and advice sometimes. Before I even finished the thought, I was sitting in her office in my usual chair and she in hers. But "she" was the white light-being, wearing my counselor's skin. She said, "This place can look like anything you want—however you're most comfortable."

So, I thought of and immediately appeared at the beach in San Onofre, California that I visited once, long ago, with its high cliffs behind me and the Pacific Ocean before me. The hologram being, this time, appeared as a beefy lifeguard in a Speedo and asked, "Are you done playing around? We have work to do."

This knocked us immediately back to the Newbie Room, because the admonishment made me feel kind of stupid and ashamed that I was wasting his/her time.

"That's okay," it said, "you're allowed to do whatever you want. If you want to play on the beach, go right ahead. There is nothing that you have to do. I just thought that you were feeling some urgency, due to your … ahem … demand for assistance—which, by the way, has been trying to get through to you since you first asked for it."

"What do you mean?" I asked.

"You've been asking for help since the beginning. Requests for help never go unanswered, but you have to let it in."

"Let it in?" I cried, more than a little pissed. "Of course, I would let it in, if it ever showed up! I've been begging for help! I have no idea what I'm doing with these powers—which, by the way, I never wanted—and I'm literally faced with an evil witch who wants to harm me and my child because I accidentally wished I could be more like Gandhi while that crazy dame across the street was trying to take over the friggin' world!"

I realized, about half-way through this breathless rant, that I probably shouldn't be shrieking at an ethereal being who says she/he is here to help, but I couldn't stop myself. Finally, I had someone who was listening to me and to whom I didn't have to explain myself—someone who might have some answers—and I needed to vent!

"Slow down. Have a seat," he/she smiled and gestured at a comfy-looking easy chair that wasn't there a moment ago. "I understand your frustration. It's part of wearing a human suit. It's natural that you're cut off from knowing how to do this, because that's one of the primary definitions of 'human being.' You're playing a game in the physical realm, but with blindfolds on, to make it more interesting. Without the blindfold, there would be no challenges, just eternal grooviness."

"What's wrong with that?" I demanded.

"Nothing," it replied, "but it can get a little boring. You'd never have a problem or puzzle to solve and, even if you did, you'd solve it too easily. So, many of us slip into human suits, put on the blindfold, and let the fun begin. When you're not wearing yours, you look just like me. Your problem is that your blindfold slipped a bit before you knew that you were wearing one."

That analogy made sense somehow so I calmed down and sat, heaving a sigh of relief. I almost expected the chair to dissolve like a cloud beneath my weight but it held and was, in fact, the most comfortable chair I've ever sat in. I asked, "You're here to help me with the Melinda situation?"

"Well," she/he said, "Yes and no. I'm here to help with whatever you need but you've been sent an assistant for that specific task. You've already met a couple times. Last time, as I recall, she was having trouble waking you up by lifting your eyelid because it weighs almost as much as she does."

"The faery?!?" I sat up straight and asked, "That was real? I thought it was a dream, some sort of symbolic message that I had to decipher." I thought for a minute and asked, "What would have happened if I woke up then? Would she have disappeared with the dream?"

"That's hard to say," the being of light said, stroking its nonexistent chin while it pondered. "There are very few absolutes here. She probably would have disappeared because you don't believe in faeries and couldn't wrap your brain around her physical presence in your world.

That's why she's been having such a hard time getting through to you."

"Well," I countered, "in my defense, I didn't believe in all of this other nonsense that's been going on these past weeks, but that didn't stop it from happening."

"That's what I mean about no absolutes," it said. "Normally, you would be right. The enormous psychic download you've received couldn't have happened, all at once and out of the blue like that. Usually this is a gradual process, and only when it's asked for. But conditions 'just happened,'" it explained, using finger quotes, "to be favorable. You were in exactly the perfect receptive state of mind, sincerely wishing for —and open to—a more enlightened state of being, when you drifted off during the movie."

I wanted to ask some questions but the being kept talking, "Melinda 'just happened' to be calling down a tremendous amount of power and got distracted long enough for you to tap in and take a big chunk of it. It was the darndest thing. I've never seen anything like it. True coincidences are almost unheard of."

I didn't know whether to be flattered or terrified.

"So, there is no special reason this happened to me?" I asked, "I'm not supposed to use my powers for good, or to fight crime, or something like that?"

"Do you mean are you a Chosen One? A savior-type?" he/she asked and then stated, "No."

I was briefly disappointed but didn't have time to pout because it was still talking, "What it boils down to is 'you get what you ask for' and, at some level of consciousness, you asked for it. You got it. Just like that. If you're a Chosen One, then wouldn't that make Melinda the same? She got what she asked for and she isn't going to use her new abilities to save the world, is she? She asked for it, she got it. Simple as that."

"Oh, my God!" I said, a thrill of fear shooting through my intestines making me wonder if there was a bathroom nearby. "So, you guys don't care that she's going to start fires and mess with innocent kids?"

The being reached over and stroked my hand—it felt like touching pure static electricity—and said, "Of course we care. We always err on the side of being nice just because it feels groovier. If you want to be mean, that's your choice, even if not our preference. That's the whole basis of the human experience. You get to play with all the colors in your paint box. We stay out of it unless we're asked to interfere. You have free will, in your human suit, and we butt out until we're invited. If you're inviting me, I'd be happy to help. I've arranged a faery for you, haven't I?"

"You have?" I asked, "Where is she? And who are you?"

"It doesn't matter who I am—you wouldn't believe me anyway. And she's around here someplace, I'm sure." She/he called out a long, intricate name that I couldn't understand.

"What kind of name is that for a faery?" I asked. "I always thought they had—well—cutesy faery names."

"You sure have a thing about names, don't you?" he/she mused. "I'm quite sure she'll let you know what her name is." The light-being glanced around and said, perplexed, "I don't know where she is. Could be anywhere, really. The Universe is pretty big."

"Well, if she does show up, will I be able to see her? Will other people be able to see her?" I had horrifying visions of my life becoming like one of those movie plots where no one but me can see the ghost.

He/she pondered my question and finally said, "Hard telling. I assume that it will be a matter of belief. After all, she's been around you for some time now and you've never seen her when you're awake, mostly because you don't believe in faeries. But I bet if you were in the company of a little girl who practically lives in her faery costume and loves Disney movies, she would be able to see faeries with no problem. However, that little girl would never be able to convince her mother that there was a real faery there, and over the years the grownups in her life would eventually train her to stop believing in such things. As an adult, that same little girl would never be able to see faeries, even if one was stomping on her nose or tugging on her eyelid to wake her up."

This brought tears to my eyes. She/he had me pegged. I remember that faery costume. I loved dressing up in that thing, watching movies and reading books about faery godmothers and Tinker Bell. I did, at one time, really believe that—if I only wished hard enough—I could have my own faery to play with and fly with. Peter Pan did it, didn't he? It never happened, I assumed, because I didn't know how to wish hard enough.

"So, that's why I can't see her now?" I asked, thrilled by the implied possibilities. "Are you serious that she's been in the room with me, already?"

"Absolutely. Haven't you noticed how many of your pens are perpetually on the floor? Haven't you actually seen one shoot off the desk for no reason at all?" she/he asked.

I did remember that. Seemed like every time I turned around I was picking my pens up off the floor but I assumed it was Chuck, being his usual slob self. But once, while I was bent over to retrieve my Sharpie, another pen came sailing off the desk and hit me square in the rear end. I didn't see it leave the desk, though, so I couldn't conceive of a way for it to have done that.

This was exciting! I could have my very own faery! I mean, in real life, not just make believe. Fantastic scenarios flew through my imagination as I pictured the two of us soaring on moonbeams and living in a swirl of pixie dust. I giggled, just thinking about it.

"How can I contact her?" I begged the light-being. I wanted to meet my faery!

"Any number of ways. You choose. Remember, there are no absolutes and you're the writer of this play. How do you want to meet her? What would help you to believe that she's really there?" he/she replied.

I thought about this for a moment. A wisp of a memory floated through my head, Peter Pan's instruction that said, if you believe in faeries, clap your hands.

I clapped my hands for all I was worth and the misty, white world around me exploded into shards of multi-colored light. I heard the heavy bands of limiting thoughts that previously restrained my mind snapping as they broke, as walls fell down … down … down … like so many dominoes. I was in a house of mirrors, watching countless images of myself—and this light show around me—bouncing back and forth into each other. I felt myself falling, tumbling 'round and 'round, not afraid of, yet greatly anticipating, the landing. When I did land, it was into something very soft, like a great mound of mown grass.

The last thing I saw, before I realized the mound was my bed, was infinite rainbow prisms shooting across the sky and a thousand tiny faces tee-heeing at my abrupt landing. When I opened my eyes I was in my bed with Chuck snoring loudly next to me. I must have reacted to the dream-landing physically, jarred in my sleep, because he snorted and rolled over, the way he does when I kick him to stop snoring.

I looked cautiously around the darkened room. I didn't see any faeries in here. Dare I clap? I didn't want to wake Chuck and have to explain why I'm applauding in bed. So, I got out of bed, typed up these notes, and gave a couple quick, quiet claps, almost afraid to see if it worked.

Nothing happened, so I'm going back to bed. I'm hoping for a couple hours of dreamless slumber.

Journal Entry 15

I woke up in the middle of the night again. I've been doing that a lot lately, waking up at 3:00 and not being able to get back to sleep until about 5:00. It's almost not worth going back to sleep. The alarm is set to go off at 6:00 and, by the time I finally drift back off, it's even harder to wake up with the alarm, even if it does have the most obnoxious, clanging bell in existence.
Chuck and I both need all the help we can get when it comes time to get up in the morning, so we have one of those windup clocks with the oversized bells on the top–the kind that offers a soothing tick-tick-tick, with a good old-fashioned

I woke up in the middle of the night again. I've been doing that a lot lately, waking up at 3:00 and not being able to get back to sleep until about 5:00. It's almost not worth going back to sleep. The alarm is set to go off at 6:00 and, by the time I finally drift back off, it's even harder to wake up with the alarm, even if it does have the most obnoxious, clanging bell in existence.

Chuck and I both need all the help we can get when it comes time to get up in the morning, so we have one of those windup clocks with the oversized bells on the top—the kind that offers a soothing tick-tick-tick, with a good old-fashioned alarm that rings when the metal clapper goes spastic and wails on the bells.

This morning, though, I did manage to doze a little. Because it's so hard to wake up, I didn't want to fall back into a deep, REM cycle so I just rested and hoped that this would be enough to get me through the day at work. I've learned that this is the best approach to insomnia. Spending any time fretting about being unable to sleep only makes it worse and, even if I don't sleep, at least this way I get some rest.

As I dozed on and off, I heard something rustling around on my nightstand. Afraid to look (was it a mouse? a big bug? something worse? what's worse than a big bug?) I lay there, frozen and listening, to make sure I wasn't dreaming.

No, there was definitely something moving around over there. It took everything I had to not freak out and either start swinging or run screaming from the room.

I opened my eyes and slowwwly rolled over onto my side. A splinter of light from the streetlamp out front shone through the curtained window over the head of our bed. Chuck desperately tries to block all light with heavy curtains and a sleep mask (he can't sleep with even a hint of light in the room). With only this small amount of light, I could see just a trace of something moving but, the more I stared, the more I saw that it seemed to emit its own luminescence.

Cautiously, so I wouldn't startle whatever it was, I reached up to move the curtain above my head just enough to let in a little more light. A triangle of illumination fell on the nightstand, a sufficient amount to let me see her.

It was her! The faery from my dream! The same one that I saw trying to pull my eyes open to wake me up!

Clapping my hands had worked! I had a faery, right here on my nightstand!

She was so beautiful, even more so than any faery artwork that I've seen. Paintings can't do justice to the radiance I witnessed. She was about six inches tall with shiny black hair and dressed in a spectacular frock of purples and blues, which shimmered like a peacock's feather. Her wings were exquisite, iridescent lace that sparkled in the light of the street lamp. And her face—so darling! Exactly what you would expect a pixie to look like, with perfect, miniature features.

She froze in place when the light hit her and she stared at me as I stared back. Not wanting to startle her further, I stayed quiet and just gazed at her beauty, awe stricken that this was actually happening to me. There was a real, live faery on my nightstand!

Just then, the clock struck 6:00 and the alarm bell blasted its horrible, spine-jangling cacophony. The dreadful racket scared the daylights out of my poor faery, who screamed in fright and immediately disappeared!

That was hours ago, and I haven't seen her since. I'm at work right now, on my lunch break. I could wait until I get home and type this stuff out before I go to bed, but I wanted to make sure to get this all down before the memory fades after a long day at work, home life and whatever other crazy stuff might happen, as it does every day now. I'll just email this to myself and paste it into my journal when I get home.

Journaling at work like this makes the whole thing both easier and harder to believe. I mean, at home there's one story and one way of being, and here at work it's an entirely different thing. I'm not the same person here as I am at home. Here, I'm more efficient, more withdrawn, and I don't have many friends.

Well, I guess that's the same at home, too. I only have a few friends, and I'm okay with that. But at least, at home, I feel like I belong. And even if Amanda and Chuck are both completely oblivious to all the effort I put forth to make their lives easier, just like here at the office, at least they love me and I love them. These people, here at work, are another story.

For example, right now, Ron is sitting at his desk surfing porn. He doesn't know I can see it; he thinks he's being sly and sneaky, pretending to be hard (no pun intended) at work. But his monitor is reflected in the window behind him and he's watching a video of a woman—ahem—enjoying some time alone, so to speak.

What a disgusting perv! I just know he's going to walk past me in a minute to go into his private bathroom and I don't even want to think about what he'll be doing in there.

Seriously, that is just wrong! In the privacy of one's own home is one thing, but at the office? Ewwwww! I don't want to be in his presence while he has a stiffy! He is so lucky I need this job or I would report him in a New York minute.

Yep, here he comes. I'll have to switch windows for a second as he walks by …

… and there he goes. Please, God, let the walls be thick enough so I don't have to hear what's going on in there. Wouldn't it be hysterical if he got his thing stuck in his fly when he zips back up? I would laugh so hard, and it would make me so very, very happy.

Ugh! Enough about his revolting antics and his, hopefully, shredded Johnson. I don't want to give either of them any more space in my already overloaded noggin.

So anyway, it's hard to remember, while I'm at work, that this Melinda/Raven story is happening at the same time. My worlds are colliding and it's giving my life a very surreal flavor. Sometimes I think I'm going crazy and other times I feel like this is the most natural thing in the world. Which way I feel is dependent upon where I am and who I'm with. I certainly can't talk about faeries, witches and psychic events with anyone at work. Can you imagine how they'd react? Half would laugh in my face and the other half would try to stage an intervention.

I almost slipped last week when I was gabbing with Alexis, the receptionist. I enjoy talking to her. She's young and seems open minded enough, and she's one of the nicer people here. After all, that's part of her job description—she needs to be able to keep a sunny smile in place for the customers, no matter what's going on behind the scenes.

Alexis was telling me about her upcoming anniversary with her most recent boyfriend, who I've met a couple times when he's picked her up after work (and didn't like much). They've been dating for six months and she was delighted that they've made it this long because she's had an extensive history of losers. She was making plans to surprise him over the weekend with a romantic dinner and a reservation at a swanky hotel. She had the whole thing planned and had been saving up for weeks to pay for it. It really did sound like a nice weekend.

Anyway, as she was gushing over how wonderful it was going to be, I got one of my lightning bolts that told me that it wasn't gonna happen. He was about to break up with her, before the week was out. He, too, realized that it was six months and wanted out before it got any more serious.

Not only could I see that, I also saw that complex energy grid again, the foundational web upon which this whole reality is built, and the pattern that her life story with men was structured upon.

It started when she was very small—she was excited that Daddy was coming home from a long business trip. She was dancing, happily, as only innocent little kids can, thinking about how much fun they would have together when he got back and he swung her up on his shoulders, like he always did when he returned from his trips.

But this time, Daddy only came home long enough to pack an extra suitcase, leaving Mommy sobbing in her bedroom as he drove away with another lady in his car. The trauma of that event caused an unconscious pattern of PTSD so jarring that it short-circuited Alexis's innocent personality.

She was permanently glitched in that moment, psychologically frozen in time. It prevented her from seeing in the men she dated the "fear of commitment" flaw for what it was. All she knew was that these men made her feel like home. Like a CD with a skip in it, that same scenario kept playing itself out over and over and over again, with different men, all throughout her life. She wasn't old enough yet to be introspective and recognize that it was a pattern: All men leave.

And it was about to happen again, leaving her feeling the same way she felt back then—confused, heartbroken and abandoned. The original event was so painful that she didn't even remember it happening, so she had no idea that this is where and when she first got derailed. And no wonder she never gave the time of day to poor Tony in Accounting, who would be a much better match for her, because he's a nice guy who would never do that to her so she didn't feel like she deserved someone like him.

I knew she was going to be shattered and devastated when this latest version of Daddy broke her hopeful, childlike heart. I had to force myself to choke back a sob because I could feel her impending pain so strongly. I felt like I had to do something, say something, to prevent this, so I blurted out, "He's not going to be able to make it this weekend."

Granted, not the best choice of words, but I didn't have time to think about it and I didn't even realize words were pouring out of my mouth until they were halfway spilled.

Alexis glared at me, eyebrows furrowed, and demanded, "How do you know?"

I stammered and stuttered, and finally came up with, "Oh, I don't know. Men are like that, aren't they? Always disappointing you." Blame it on men, rush out the door. Get the hell out of there, Lola!

Oh, now what? Ron is hollering about something, but the hell with him. I'm on my lunch break and I'm not answering.

Except, he's really whooping it up. You don't suppose ...

He couldn't have really caught his thing in his zipper, like I hoped, right? Ha! If only I had that kind of power.

Okay, I can't ignore this. He's really yelling and I'm not that heartless. I'll finish this later.

Journal Entry 16

I.
DO.
NOT.
BELIEVE.
THIS.

Ron actually did catch his penis in his zipper! At first, I thought it was the funniest thing ever. After all, if anyone deserves it, it's Ron. But once I saw how much pain he was in, and it was a lot, I felt small and petty. The poor guy was

I.
DO.
NOT.
BELIEVE.
THIS.

Ron actually did catch his penis in his zipper! At first, I thought it was the funniest thing ever. After all, if anyone deserves it, it's Ron. But once I saw how much pain he was in, and it was a lot, I felt small and petty. The poor guy was crying, for Christ's sake. Now that I'm home again, typing these notes, I'm deeply ashamed of myself for wishing this very thing would happen.

But, holy cow, I didn't think it would!

No, the more I think about it, there's no way I could have caused that. Just because I have these freakish psychic abilities doesn't mean I have the kind of powers that could make something like that happen, just by thinking about it. Maybe I saw it happening in advance and didn't realize at the time that it was a premonition because it didn't come with a lightning bolt.

Besides, what the hell is he doing in there on office time with me right outside the door? He's lucky I don't slap him with a sexual harassment case. It's not like he hasn't made plenty of creepy remarks in the past, or leered down my blouse whenever he gets the chance. He is, after all, the reason I own so many turtle neck sweaters. He deserves everything he gets.

In fact, he's lucky I was even there (although that makes the story creepier) to help and to call his doctor to fit him in for an emergency appointment (he refused to go to the ER). Because of his revolting behavior, I had to miss the rest of my lunch hour and did he even thank me? Of course not.

I also never finished telling the story about Alexis and her boyfriend, because I had to take care of him. The dirtbag did break up with her, and she was so devastated she called in sick Thursday and Friday. I'm the only one who knows why and I'm not bringing it up, especially since she was already so wary of me.

On another note, it just occurred to me that I didn't feel Ron's pain, like I have with other people. I wonder why that is. Anymore, if someone near me is feeling something very strong, no matter what it is, it bleeds over to me. If I don't have my psychic wall up, I'm right there with them.

I wonder if Ron has some sort of unconscious psychic shield up, like I've learned to do to keep Melinda out. A guilty conscience might do that. Or, maybe it's because he doesn't feel emotions, only physical sensations. Maybe that's why he's such a pig—he doesn't allow himself to feel like a human being.

Hmm. Something to ponder.

Well, enough about Ron and his magical pecker. I can't believe he became the big news of the day. He topped, temporarily, the fact that an actual, real live faery was on my nightstand this morning!

It really was there! I checked to see if it came back—it hadn't—but I did see that the curtain is exactly how I left it this morning, pulled back, and I saw tiny footprints in the dust. (Sue me. I don't dust my nightstands very often. Like I don't have enough to do?)

There were adorable teeny-weeny, itty-bitty little footprints that showed where she walked. She seemed to have spent most of her time near one of my rings, where I put it the other night when I took it off before bed. It's one of my favorite rings, but I don't wear it very often because the stone is large and kind of gaudy. I like it because it's sparkly and, every once in a while, I allow myself to be gaudy, like with that topaz necklace. The pendant is a lot larger than I normally would wear, but it's just so glittery that I have to have it.

She must have liked the ring, too, because there were marks in the dust, which showed that it had been dragged. I don't know what she was trying to do. All I can do is report what I saw and wait for her to come back.

Meantime, I finally picked up that book on faeries that I got from Raven's shop a long time ago. I never got around to reading it until now because I was so focused on Melinda and trying to figure out what to do with all that. Today, faeries win the battle for my attention, especially faeries that have apparently been assigned from above to help me battle Melinda.

One of the first things the book says is that faeries are afraid of bells. It says that you should build a faery garden—not sure yet exactly what that means—if you want them to show up in your life, but make sure there are no bells or wind chimes in their garden, because in olden times when people believed in faeries, they used bells to chase away mischievous pixies. That explains why she screamed and disappeared when the alarm bell rang this morning.

Honestly, a month ago, I would have thrown this book in the trash. "Build a faery garden for your faeries." Puhleez. Funny what a difference a few weeks makes.

I'm not very far into the book, but here's what I know so far, aside from the bells. Faeries are spirited, fun-loving and helpful to the people they love, but they sometimes play tricks, for their own amusement. They are offended by greed and lies and, if invited, will assist with magic.

I don't know why anyone would want to scare something like that away. I could put up with a few tricks if it meant that I had a magical helper. And wasn't I told that those pens that I keep finding on the floor are the result of my faery's pranks? If putting up with minor inconveniences like that means getting some help with this Melinda situation, I'll gladly pick up a pen or two.

I hope the alarm clock didn't scare her away forever. I hope she comes back tonight. I'll have to find a way to wake up in the morning without the alarm, because I don't want to frighten her again. Maybe I just won't go back to sleep if I wake up at 3:00, as usual.

Or maybe I'll go to bed now so I get in some extra sleep before then. Why not? Amanda's gabbing on the phone and Chuck is surfing the net on his own laptop (Better not be porn! You know what I do to men who surf porn!) so neither of them even knows I'm alive. Might as well turn in. I'll report back in the morning, hopefully with another faery sighting!

Journal Entry 17

I'm at work again, writing during lunch. Ron isn't here today. Wonder why.
This is the first chance I've had to type up some notes because I had a very busy morning! I woke up at 3:00 again, just as I hoped. At first nothing happened and I had a hard time staying awake, mostly because I was trying to. Don't you hate that? Wanna fall asleep, your eyes stay wide freakin' open. Wanna stay awake, the Sandman dumps an extra load in.

I'm at work again, writing during lunch. Ron isn't here today. Wonder why.

This is the first chance I've had to type up some notes because I had a very busy morning! I woke up at 3:00 again, just as I hoped. At first nothing happened and I had a hard time staying awake, mostly because I was trying to. Don't you hate that? Wanna fall asleep, your eyes stay wide freakin' open. Wanna stay awake, the Sandman dumps an extra load in.

Just as I was drifting off, as I was in that halfway world between asleep and awake, I heard the noises from the nightstand. I was already turned in that direction and had the curtain propped open so I didn't have to move at all. I opened my eyes and saw her again. She was bent over, dragging the gaudy ring as if it were very heavy for her into the pool of light from the streetlamp. I guess—if I were only six inches high—this ring, with the heavy silver and that huge stone, would be a bit of a chore to move.

It dawned on me that she was trying to move it so that it would catch the light. I sensed her desire to watch it sparkle. I debated whether to offer to help and risk scaring her again, or just lay back and watch her struggle. Finally, I whispered, "Do you need some help?"

"Well, I'll be! Look who can finally see me," she declared, in a voice much louder than I expected out of someone so tiny. It was an adorable, high pitched voice, the kind one would expect from vocal cords so miniscule, with a rather thick accent, just like in my dreams where she sounded like a cross between the Beatles, with their famous Liverpool accent, and my Scottish aunt. She had that same lilting tendency to make her sentences sound like questions, with the final words tilted with an upward inflection. Listening to her speak was like listening to music.

Even so, I felt a knee-jerk reaction to shush her. Sleeping with Chuck for so many years has taught me that he is not a person who enjoys being awakened unless it's time to get up. He's a laid-back guy, but a bear if you wake him unnecessarily. She apparently sensed this because she said, "He won't wake up. I'll fix 'im." She pronounced "up" like "oop", like the double oo's in "book".

She flew up above us and, wow, what a sight to see! As she gracefully flitted upwards, I was given my first sight of faery dust—she glowed with it as she exerted herself. It looked like miniscule specks of gold glitter but, unlike glitter, it apparently didn't need an external light source to make it sparkle.

She hovered over us and pulled out (from where I don't know) a sparkling wand that, because of the way it glittered in the small amount of ambient light, appeared to be made of cut crystal. She waved it over Chuck and said a few words that I didn't understand. She aimed it at him and—*ZAP!*—a stream of what looked like liquid faery dust blasted out of the wand. It hit him square in the chest, and poofed up like a mushroom cloud, which spread and covered him in a thin aura of shimmering haze.

While it was beautiful to behold, it made me nervous to see Chuck zapped and trapped inside the cloud. I had no idea what it was doing to him or if he'd be okay. Again, she sensed my concern, because she said, in her lilting accent, "He'll be fine. He'll sleep until I give the word. Now, we can have a nice chat without yeh gettin' so antsy."

Now that I was finally face to face with her, and able to freely talk, I couldn't think of one thing to say. I stared at her, stupidly, my head completely blank.

Finally, she took pity on me and spoke first. "D'yeh have any idea how hard it was to get yehr attention? I've been trying for ever so long!"

"I didn't think you were real!" I stammered. "I dreamed about you, but I thought that's all it was—just a symbolic image or something. I didn't know!"

"Aye, I'm real enough," she replied, dryly, pronouncing it 'enoof'. "And I've been assigned to yeh, so let's get cracking. I've a life to get back to, don't I?"

I swiveled my head to look at the clock. "Now? It's only 5:17."

"Oh, aye? And yehr point is?" she shot back. "Didn't yeh beg for help? Isn't someone yeh know threatening to do 'orrible things to innocent people?" She flitted in the air above me and Chuck, and continued, "Wanna go back to sleep? Go ahead. Like I said, I've got plenty of other things I could be doing."

"Uh …" I spluttered, feeling just as stupid as I must have sounded, "I guess you have a point." It occurred to me that my wish to live in denial allowed me to forget the urgency of my request for help. Plus, the fact that Melinda's taking her sweet old time to actually do anything takes away my hurry.

I got out of bed and threw my robe on. Chuck continued to snooze in his faery dust cocoon. "Come on," I gestured toward the door. "Let's go to my office. We can talk there."

"Yeh want me to leave him like this?" she pointed at Chuck.

I thought for a moment, envisioning what it would be like if he were to wake up to go to the bathroom, find me gone, and come looking for me. I could only imagine what his face would look like if he found me in the other room, talking to a faery. "Yeah, for now. No point in inviting trouble."

Walking through the house to my home office, the one where I type these notes every day, helped to solidify the reality of this bizarre scene. I could be fairly certain that I wasn't asleep, having a very lucid dream about a faery fluttering in the air behind me as I walked to the office. I felt the cold floor on my bare feet and heard the desk chair squeak when I sat down. I saw the faery hovering a foot or so above my desktop, enveloped within a faint aura of shimmering faery dust. I could even smell a residual of the incense I burned last night. Yep, this was real "enoof."

The reality of the scene also helped to bring me out of the excitement about having a faery and back into the urgency of dealing with Melinda. I knew I wouldn't be able to get back to sleep if I tried, so "5:17 AM" was now meaningless.

Of course, now that I'm sitting here at work, trying to stay awake at my computer, 5:17 carries a lot of meaning. But, at the time, I was wide awake and ready to go. The first thing I did, after taking a seat at my desk, was ask the faery, "What's your name?"

In response, she flung out a long string of heavily accented syllables that went in one ear and out the other. I'm not very good at mimicking accents. I can't do a proper "Queen's English" or even a glottal-stopped cockney accent, which pretty much anyone can approximate without embarrassing themselves too badly. But her accent was far more complex.

"Say that again," I begged. "I didn't understand a word."

She rolled her eyes and repeated her name so I tried, hesitantly, to say it back to her, Americanized, "Fellween Glamourtina?"

Her jaw dropped open and she just stared at me. She finally gathered her wits and huffed, "Listen harder, yeh daft git!" Then she said it again, albeit a little more slowly.

"Apple Wine Egg Martini?" I moaned.

She glared and clenched her fists, and stomped her foot in the air, poofing a cloud of faery dust. "Why, you styoopid human! I oughta …"

"I'm sorry!" I cried. "I've never heard of a name like that and your accent makes it hard to understand what you're saying!"

She muttered, "Yeh're the one with the accent," as she flung a pen onto the floor, just like she'd been doing all along. "Fine," she said, still floating in the air above my desk, "I'll spell it out for yeh. Get a pen."

This was the first time I've been able to see how she knocked the pens off my desk. She pulled out her little wand again and made a swoop in the air, almost like a golf swing, and the pen went sailing. I snatched another pen just as she was about to send it flying to the floor.

"What, you're not using faery dust?" I asked.

"Am I 'eck as like! I won't waste dust," (pronounced: doost), "on child's play. Now, are yeh ready?"

I grabbed a scrap of paper and wrote down the letters as quickly as she gave them to me: A-E-T-H-E-L-W-Y-N-E E-G-L-A-N-T-I-N-A.

Then she said it again, slowly, "Ay-*thel*-wine Egg-lan-*tee*-na," in her deeply-accented, tiny little voice.

"I thought faeries had names like Tinker Bell or Twink." I said.

"Cheeky! Do not compare me with Tinker Bell!" she huffed, giving me the talk-to-the-hand gesture, "After that whole brouhaha with the book and the play and the film, that diva's head got so big it wouldn't fit through the door. Even now, she fancies herself as grand as Queen Jennett, herself."

It bummed me out to hear this because I always thought Tinker Bell was adorable. Sometimes it's not a good idea to know too much about your favorite celebs, ya know?

On another note, I didn't realize the implication—at the time—that this means Tinker Bell is real. She was saying that Tinker Bell isn't just a cartoon or a character in a novel or play. There is a living creature named Tinker Bell. That's rather hard to digest.

Anyway, I continued trying to sound out her name to mimic the way she said it, "*Ay*-thel-ween En-*glant*-inna?"

"No, no, no! Pay a-bloody-ttention. Ay-*thel*-wine Egg-lan-*tee*-na!" She was practically shouting now, and it wouldn't have surprised me to see faery dust shooting out of her ears.

"Good God, you're like Alex Trebek, telling me I got the answer wrong just because I mispronounced it!" I shouted back. We stared at each other for a long moment until I finally begged, "Are you sure I can't call you Twink?"

Her raised eyebrows, wide eyes and flared nostrils answered my question, or so I thought, but then she folded her arms over her chest, turned up tiny her nose and sniffed, "You can try, but I may not answer."

I was okay with that and willing to take the risk.

With the preliminaries finally out of the way, it was time to get to work. I didn't know where to begin but she, fortunately, dove right in. "What, exactly, do yeh need help with? Remember what yehr oversoul told yeh, we're only allowed to help when we're specifically asked, so until yeh tell me what yeh want, I'm on me own to entertain m'self." With this, she swung her wand again and another pen shot off the desk.

"You mean the hologram thing in my dream was my oversoul?"

"Oh aye, that's who I mean. One of them, anyway. The one yeh met with is yehr direct, higher Self, the one that's closest to yeh and easiest to connect with. Remember the blindfold she talked about?"

I thought back—the memory was fuzzy—and vaguely recalled the being saying that humans were all wearing metaphorical blindfolds in order to make life interesting.

"What she didn't tell yeh," Twink continued, "is that she is you, without the blindfold. She's no hologram; she's yehr true self—yehr expanded essence, if yeh will ... and even if yeh won't. Ever seen them Russian nesting dolls?"

I nodded. I had a set of them when I was a child, a doll within a doll within a doll, within a doll.

"Right. Think of yehrself as the innermost, solid doll. The oversoul you talked to is the one right outside of yehr awareness, but there are more outside of that one. This one is the closest to yeh, physically, but she's not wearing a blindfold, so she's not restricted by yehr limited view of how this whole thing works. Didn't yeh notice that she even sounded like yeh?"

I had noticed. I even wondered, later, how she/he (I still felt weird calling it "she" even though Twink was doing so) spoke English in the same manner and cadence as I.

Twink explained, "What yeh heard weren't words, it were the essence of her thoughts. Yehr own brain's filter translated it into words that mean summat to yeh. If yeh were French, yeh'd have heard her words in French. Even the way I sound to yeh is modeled after human speech patterns in the area of yehr world that's closest to where I live, so's you and I can communicate."

"Really?" I asked. "Where is that?"

She flew over to the old globe on the top shelf of the bookcase and pointed, "Right around here, I reckon." I got up to see where she was indicating and it was the British Isles. The print was hard to read, because it's a small globe, but it looked like somewhere in northern England.

"Got any more irrelevant questions on yehr chest?" she asked. I shook my head 'no.' "Right, then," she said, "let's get to work. What are we doing here?"

I was torn between asking more about what an oversoul is and talking about Melinda. Twink's snotty impatience nudged me toward the latter, so I said, "I don't know, exactly, what I need help with. All I know is that Melinda and Tammy are planning to throw flaming bottles of gasoline through my friend Raven's shop window and that something even more horrible is going to result from that. And, now, she threatened to hurt my daughter if I don't butt out. I have no clue what to do about any of this. She and I apparently have similar powers but she knows what they are and how to use them. I don't."

"I know all that," Twink snorted, which caused her to bounce a little in the air. "I've been following along with the story, haven't I? But what do yeh want me to do about it? Yeh have to be specific when yeh ask for help."

"What can you do about it?" I asked. "Can you make this whole thing go away as if it never happened? Can you bring me back in time to the day this all started so I can do things differently?"

She shrugged. "No do-overs, I'm afraid. Yeh're too deeply embedded into this life-stream. Too much has happened to go back now and rewrite it without causing disruptive ripples in the continuum. Yeh've already been changed too much to go back without doing damage."

"Damage?" I squeaked.

"Mental illness, yeh'd call it. Making a quantum leap like that causes the average human mind to seize up and yeh might not recover with yehr sanity intact. By the way, I'll admit that I'm impressed with how well yeh've handled the leap yeh did take. Not many humans would be able to do that. That's why yeh feel like yeh're going crazy half the time. It's too much, too fast."

I was feeling too desperate to acknowledge the compliment or to question any of the mind-bending things she just said. "Then what can you do?" I cried.

"Calm down and think," she said, enunciating clearly, as if speaking to a child. "What do yeh need the most help with?"

"Well," I said, after deliberating for a moment, "right now my biggest obstacle is that I don't have access to the inside of her head anymore, now that she knows about me. She's shut me out. So, I don't know when she plans to attack Raven, or even if she'll really go through with it."

"Oh, she'll go through with it, alright. I can tell yeh that much," she said, casually.

"Well, why doesn't she just do it and get it over with? The suspense is killing me!"

"Because, for her, revenge is a dish best served cold. She's relishing the plotting and planning. For her, that's the fun of it. She doesn't even care who she harms anymore, either her roaming man or yehr mate, Raven. In fact, she's forgotten about him, now that she has you and Raven to toy with. Either one'll do. She just wants some action. She's lived her whole life brewing up one vendetta after another. Yeh're just witnessing her most recent adventure."

That made so much sense. I know a lot of people who live for the drama and, therefore, spend all of their time creating more of it. Reality TV shows create many a career riding on the backs of people like that.

"The problem is," she continued, "yeh're also witnessing the most violent one. She's finally stepped over the line into being dangerous, instead of just a hateful bint. One advantage yeh have over her is yehr willingness to ask for help. So … ask for it," she hinted, in a mildly condescending voice.

I was frustrated beyond measure. "For crying out loud, just help already! Help me figure out what to do!"

"What," she iced back at me, "do yeh think I'm doing? And I would watch my tone, iffen I were you." She pulled out her pretty little wand and brandished it at me.

I quickly apologized. "I'm sorry. I'm just feeling so stupid and lost, and out of my element. It wasn't too long ago that my life was normal. I'm not cut out to play cops and robbers. I just want my old life back." I was close to tears.

Apparently taking pity on me, she relented. "That bus has left the station, as I've already told yeh. Yeh're in this up to yehr ears, and that's the truth, so yeh'd better pull yehrself together and think. I'll ask yeh again. What ... do ... you ... need ... help ... with? Y'were 'this close' to saying it."

I tried to remember what I had said. "Was it that I don't know what she's thinking anymore?"

"Bingo!" She shot a puff of faery dust into the air with her wand, just for effect. "So? Let's try it again. What do yeh need help with?"

"Knowing what she's thinking?"

"Uh huh. Come on, you can do it. Ask ..." she encouraged.

"Will you help me to get past Melinda's psychic thought-wall?"

"I thought she'd never say it!" she cried to the heavens, dramatically raising her arms above her head. "Aye. I will help yeh to get past Melinda's defenses. Any particular method, or would yeh like for me to devise my own?"

"Oh, your own is fine!" I said, happy to leave that up to her. Her fiendish giggle, in response, was a little alarming but I didn't want to know what she had in mind. It was such a relief to know that I had someone to help me, someone who actually could help me, that I didn't care how she did it.

"I'll be back when I know summat." And, with that, she disappeared in a puff of faery dust, which reminded me of poor Chuck, frozen in sleep under his own cloud of dust. So, I checked on him, and he was fine. The sparkling slumber-cocoon was gone.

I knew I wouldn't be able to get back to sleep, so I just stayed up and got ready for my day. It was almost time to get up anyway and I needed at least a pot of coffee. And now, I need to grab some lunch while I've still got a little time on the clock.

I can't wait to see what happens next!

Journal Entry 18

I didn't realize how hard on me this whole thing had become until Twink came along to give me some relief. I feel like a huge weight has been lifted off of me, knowing that I have an expert in my corner. For the first time in weeks (months? how long has it been?) I feel like I can breathe again.
Now I understand what Chuck meant when he said I was neglecting him and our home. I guess I was. Unintentionally, of course, but I must admit that my focus wasn't on them. How could it be? He has no idea what I've been going through!
Today I made a point of trying to be back to normal so I threw on my comfortable weekend grubbies (jeans and a t-shirt) and we all went to the mall, just to hang out and spend some

I didn't realize how hard on me this whole thing had become until Twink came along to give me some relief. I feel like a huge weight has been lifted off of me, knowing that I have an expert in my corner. For the first time in weeks (months? how long has it been?) I feel like I can breathe again.

Now I understand what Chuck meant when he said I was neglecting him and our home. I guess I was. Unintentionally, of course, but I must admit that my focus wasn't on them. How could it be? He has no idea what I've been going through!

Today I made a point of trying to be back to normal so I threw on my comfortable weekend grubbies (jeans and a t-shirt) and we all went to the mall, just to hang out and spend some time together. Chuck needed some new khakis and Amanda is always willing to spend the day at the mall, even if it is with her parents. I didn't plan to buy anything because I'm saving up for that white topaz pendant at the antique shop.

Come to think of it, I never did see the antique store again after that first time. I've parked down that street since then but haven't seen it. Granted, I wasn't looking for it, but I'll make a point next time I'm in the neighborhood to find it. I still have the business card with the address on it. I'll look this week.

Anyway, our trip to the mall was an eye opener. It's been a while since I've been there with my brood and it demonstrated how much I've changed. The last time we were all there together, it was just mindless, consumer-driven fun, punctuated by food-court gluttony. Chuck is one of those rare men who likes shopping, so I've always enjoyed going to the mall with him.

In contrast, today, I found being amid the crowds to be stifling and I could barely wait to escape from the humanity overload. The noise and the chaos as desperate people tried desperately to feed their desperate needs—spending spending spending—and the profit-driven chain stores with their overpriced items made by underpaid, third-world sweatshop workers, made me physically nauseated. I've never thought about it this way before and I had to sit down for a while because I was so overwhelmed by it all, so we grabbed a table at the food court.

Chuck bought me a cola and a burger after I told him that I was feeling like my blood sugar was low, since I skipped breakfast. I've consumed thousands of these burgers and sodas over the course of my lifetime but, today, just seeing it on the table in front of me made me almost hurl right there.

I glanced around at the other fast food joints to see if there was anything that wouldn't make me sick but many places felt the same—as if their food was heavily processed and artificially flavored by corporations who had no concerns for animal rights or human health.

God, I hope I'm not becoming a vegetarian. I have enough to do, without learning a whole new way of shopping, cooking and eating—not to mention the fit Chuck would throw if I was spending more on the grocery bill for special food. No way is he about to give up his steaks and burgers.

In a tucked away corner of the food court, I spotted a place that didn't feel nauseating, a shop that sold those fruit smoothies that my family and I make fun of because who would want fruit in a blender when you can have a greasy hamburger, dripping with grilled onions, crisp bacon and cheese? Right? However, this place felt like a beacon of hope, drawing me inwards. I told Chuck I needed to walk around a little and that he could have my burger and pop. He immediately began scarfing it down, so I wandered to the smoothie shop.

The closer I got, the better I felt—rejuvenated, even. My eyes, which I hadn't realized felt heavy until they didn't anymore, were now wide open and awake. Colors seemed brighter and my energy levels shot up. The cute young guy behind the counter, with wild hippie hair and lots of ink, asked what he could get for me. I had no idea what to order, so I asked him what his favorite was.

"Excellent question!" he enthused, almost seeming phony in his gusto. I peeked inside his head, though, and saw that he meant it, sincerely. He told me, "My favorite is the Organic Orgasmo," as he pointed at a colorful cartoon poster, reminiscent of R. Crumb's *Mr. Natural.* On it, all sorts of fruits were climbing into a blender, with ecstatic looks on their orgasmic faces.

"Only the best, non-GMO, organic fruits," he said, "mixed with our magical blend of nutritious stuff and feel-good mojo. It'll only take me a minute to whip one up. Whaddya say?"

He was so adorable that I couldn't pass up his sales pitch. I nodded my consent and he got to work. While he made my Organic Orgasmo (can they use that word in places where kids work? I guess so, but times sure have changed, haven't they?) I read some of the posters on the walls that said that a portion of all profits go toward rainforest preservation, that employees are shareholders and that the company believes in something they called "conscious commerce," whatever that means.

Whatever it was, the place seemed to agree with me, because I felt better in there than I had in a long time, especially better than I had just a few minutes ago. I paid for my smoothie, which he handed to me with a dramatic bow, saying, "Voila, Madame."

I took one sip and, oh my God, I was in heaven. The drink was bright green and the taste was a strange combination of pineapple, freshly mown grass, and other vibrant flavors I couldn't name.

As soon as that first swallow hit my gut, it was as if my chest burst with joy and all my cells began to sing that same angelic tone from my Gandhi dream, so long ago. Even my nipples were hard. Organic Orgasmo, indeed! Who knew food could do that? (Okay, chocolate is a sexy bitch, but this was fruit!)

I thanked him profusely, and he smiled and winked knowingly. And here's where it got weird (uh huh, that wasn't the weird part). As I exited the smoothie shop, pretty much right where their tile ended and the food court tile began, it felt like I had to push my way out. There was a resistant force discouraging me from leaving—the air was thick out there —like I was now moving through water.

The noise from the food court, which I hadn't even noticed while I was waiting for my smoothie, was a wretched, cacophonous din that hurt my ears—cell phones ringing, children running amok and screaming for attention as their parents ignored them with their faces buried in their screens, couples arguing—it brought back that nausea that drove me into the smoothie shop in the first place.

Knowing I couldn't stay in the smoothie shop for the rest of my life, I forced myself forward, back toward my family, who were busy munching away at their burgers. By the time I got back to our table, I was woozy and lightheaded, exhausted from the effort of pushing through the thickened air. Amanda was texting away on her phone, and Chuck was almost finished with his second burger. "Whatcha got there?" he asked.

"An Organic Orgasmo," I said. "It's very good. Wanna try it?"

I offered him the cup and he gave it a quick slurp. Before the concoction even hit the back of his throat, he dramatically bugged out his eyes at me and spit the glorious nectar into his empty soda cup.

"Oh my God, it tastes like mulch!" he said. Unimpressed and shuddering, he went back to his burger.

"All the more for me," I said and took another sip. Once again, I felt that explosion of pure, raw health surging through my body. I noticed, as I drank, that the thick air around me became a little less oppressive. So, I tried another sip and the same thing happened again, as if my aura was expanding—I finally understood what that oft-used phrase meant. I sucked so hard on that straw, drinking so fast, that I ended up with brain freeze and had to slow down. By the time I drained the paper cup, I felt right as rain and back in the game.

I glanced back toward the smoothie shop, as Chuck and Amanda picked up their trays and garbage to clear the table, and saw the young man leaning on the counter, watching me, smiling. He winked again and waved, as if he understood what was happening to me. I can't explain why, but I burst into tears of joy mixed with sobs of deep sorrow as if, once again, two worlds were colliding—two worlds that were so far apart that soon I would be forced to make a choice: in which world would I live?

Alarmed by my out-of-left-field weeping, Chuck demanded, "What is wrong with you today?"

"Must be hormones or something," I lied.

A little more sympathetic now, but hoping I wouldn't elaborate on my 'women's issues,' he asked, "Are you okay? Do you want to go home?"

I told him I'd be fine. I didn't want to upset them or ruin their day, which they were apparently enjoying. Oblivious to my mini-meltdown, Amanda grabbed Chuck's hand and tugged him toward one of her favorite stores, "Come on, Dad. I want to go in here. See the top in their window? Can I have it pleeeeeze?"

They threw away their garbage and put away their trays while I looked again toward the smoothie shop. The young man was watching me, holding up a large plastic jug, nodding and gesturing as if to say, "You want this, don't you?" I told Chuck that I would meet them at the store and went back to the smoothie shop.

"I knew I recognized a kindred spirit," he said as I walked back into the safe haven of his shop. He handed me the plastic jug. "This here is the magic mojo mix that we put into our Organic Orgasmos. We sell it so you can make them at home if you want. The recipe is on the side. Just pick up some fresh, organic fruit at the health food co-op." He pointed at a plastic business card holder next to the cash register and said, "There's their address. Plus, when you're ready for a refill, just wash the jug and bring it in, and we'll fill 'er up. That way you don't have to worry about recycling it. You just keep reusing it."

I took a business card, thanked him, paid for my magic mojo powder and met up once again with my family. I'm looking forward to experimenting with making my own smoothies here at home. The co-op is only a couple blocks from Raven's shop, so I'll check it out next time I visit her.

One more strange thing happened at the mall today. I don't even want to think about it but if I don't get it out, I'll start obsessing, which will make it worse.

Chuck and I were in Amanda's posh store, holding her gotta-have top—she was in the dressing room trying on a dozen others—when a sales girl approached us to ask if she could help us find anything. We both said, "No, thanks."

She was a very pretty young woman, probably mid-twenties and obviously childless, with those perky boobs and flat stomach. She looked Chuck in the eye and I heard her thoughts, loud and clear, "What are you doing with *her*?" Then she looked at me and silently sneered, "I could easily take him away from you."

All this, of course, without opening her mouth, but I *heard* it. I was so shocked that my jaw fell open and I must have gasped out loud because as she walked away, Chuck asked me what was wrong.

"That little bitch!" I said, "I'll slap her face off!"

"*What?*" He cried, dumbfounded, "She just asked if she could help! Why would you want to slap her?"

I knew there would be no way to explain this one, so I made something up and indignantly replied, "Did you see the way she looked at me? Like I'm not good enough to be in her store?"

Chuck looked me up and down, "Well, you could have dressed up a little. This is kind of a swanky store and you're wearing … that." He gestured dismissively at my jeans and t-shirt.

This stung. Chuck and Amanda both looked nice today, and I did look like a shlub. Plus, the fact that I couldn't step inside his mind—and, believe me, I tried—meant that he was thinking something he knew would hurt my feelings and built a psychic-wall. He had, intuitively and without realizing it, learned at some point in his life to keep some thoughts to himself, and this was apparently one of them. But, even without my psychic abilities, I could see he was embarrassed by how I was dressed.

It just doesn't seem fair, does it? Women have to bust their butts to cook, clean, raise a family, work outside the home, stay sane and still look sexy in order to keep their man from wishing they looked like some minimum wage tart in a Midwestern mall. And I'm not slut shaming here, because this had nothing to do with how she was dressed, this was totally about how she acted, completely disrespectfully toward another woman.

Men, on the other hand, just have to throw on a pair of Dockers and have money in their wallets for the aforementioned tarts to throw themselves at them. Never mind that their wives are standing right there!

Seriously, is there ever a time when I don't have to worry about what I look like? Can I never just relax and lose the underwires and tight waistbands without being concerned about the loss of my happy marriage? Do I always have to worry about being on display for Chuck's eye-candy pleasure, for fear of someone younger and prettier taking away my man, the same man whose crunchy socks I pick up off the floor?

We were supposed to have a date night tonight because Amanda is sleeping over at Kirsten's house, but now I don't even feel like it. I feel old and ugly, and I'm sure he's going to be fantasizing about that girl while fondling my saggy middle-aged boobs, wishing they were tight and firm like hers. And there's not a damn thing I can do about it.

Great. Now I feel like curling up in a ball and sleeping the rest of the day. Maybe I need another Organic Orgasmo. Too bad I have no organic fruit in the house. I guess I'll just go take a nap. I'll write more when there's something to report.

Journal Entry 19

Twink came back today, finally. I was beginning to think she wasn't going to, that she was just a figment of my imagination because it's been almost a full week since I saw her last.

In the meantime, it was nice to try to live a normal life again, even if last Saturday was spoiled by that mall hussy. Chuck and I did have sex that night but it wasn't very good because I felt so lousy about myself. I had to fake it just to get it over with and there was none of that connecting with God stuff going on. I wasn't able to feel that soul mate thing again because I'm sure his mind was elsewhere, just as I expected it would be.

Twink came back today, finally. I was beginning to think she wasn't going to, that she was just a figment of my imagination because it's been almost a full week since I saw her last.

In the meantime, it was nice to try to live a normal life again, even if last Saturday was spoiled by that mall hussy. Chuck and I did have sex that night but it wasn't very good because I felt so lousy about myself. I had to fake it just to get it over with and there was none of that connecting with God stuff going on. I wasn't able to feel that soul mate thing again because I'm sure his mind was elsewhere, just as I expected it would be.

But I did get a lot accomplished this week. The house needed a serious cleaning, which I haven't been doing much of lately, and the laundry had been piling up. It cleared my head as I cleared the clutter.

Amanda and I had a nice time Tuesday night when Chuck worked late. It was girls' night, and we made cookies and gossiped. She told me about a boy at school she has a crush on, and I told her about what it was like when her dad and I were first dating in high school. It was a sweet time and she's a good kid.

Sometimes I don't give her enough credit for having a good head on her shoulders, because I'm so focused on her getting her homework done and keeping her room clean. She reminds me so much of me when I was that age. I hated when my own mom nagged me like that, but honestly, if she hadn't, I probably would have never picked up a sock off the floor or wasted time on my homework. I had better things to do (Chuck, being one of them).

I also managed to get to the co-op and bought some organic produce. I've been making my own Organic Orgasmos and, while they may not taste exactly like they did at the smoothie shop, they do still have the same effect. I feel great whenever I drink one, so I have one before work every morning. It helps me get through the day, to more easily ignore Ron and his repulsive ways, and concentrate on work.

My sleep patterns are still screwy but I'm used to it by now. Plus, I've been deliberately trying to stay awake just in case Twink came back, which is what happened this morning. I was lying there, waiting for the alarm to signal it was time to stop lying there, when I heard her, again on the night stand. This time she was trying to turn the alarm off.

I gestured at her to meet me in the office. We had a little time before Chuck had to get up, and I wasn't comfortable with the faery dust coma she put him in last time.

Once we were in my office, I apologized for the alarm clock ringer being turned on, "I forgot that bells scare you. I'll see if I can find one with a gentler tone."

"They don't scare me, yeh twit! Whatever gave yeh that idea?" she scoffed, floating in the air above my desk.

"Well, the last time you were there when it went off, you screamed and disappeared. And the book said faeries are afraid of bells, that they can be used to scare mean ones away." I explained.

"You humans." She rolled her eyes. "Bells don't scare us, they're just jarring. They break the connection between the worlds, don't they? Isn't that what you use them for—to bring yeh out of the dream world? Do they frighten yeh, or do they startle yeh?"

She folded her arms across her chest and continued, huffily, "That's why I screamed, not 'cause I were scared. I were startled, it were so 'orribly loud. That bloody clock's as big as me, innit? Wouldn't you scream, too, if a bell as big as yehr head, a foot away, suddenly blasted an alarm?"

Apparently, I hit a nerve. She was pretty ticked off, and her accent thickened as she cussed me. I guess I can't blame her because what she was saying made perfect sense. I've tried meditating a few times because Raven has recommended that I try it, and if the phone rings somewhere in the house I am immediately snapped out of whatever relaxed mindset I was able to attain. I told this to Twink, after I gave her a little time to calm down.

"Oh, aye. That's good because yeh're trying stay awake as yeh fall asleep. That's when our worlds merge and we can communicate. That's why yeh can only see me when yeh're dreaming, or still half asleep, before yehr alarm bell scares yeh. Perhaps yeh could practice doing that, so I don't have to work so hard to get through to yeh."

"Have you been trying to contact me?" I asked.

"Well, not so much lately, as I've been busy with yehr mate across the street. But before, when I were still trying to break through …"

I interrupted, "When you were knocking the pens off my desk to get my attention?"

She nodded and, just for fun, sent a pen sailing across the room.

"Well, why don't we make that a signal that you're trying to get ahold of me, until I can learn to meet you halfway, on purpose?"

"Right. That would work," she said absently, knocking another one to the floor. "Don't yeh want to know what happened with Melinda?"

I had almost forgotten. "Yes!" I cried. "Tell me!"

She savored my curiosity, enjoying knowing something I didn't. "Well, she doesn't have a date yet for her Molotov cocktail party, so yeh've got a little time. She doesn't yet have Tammy convinced to help her, and she needs an accomplice who'll risk the drop for her. I'd say yeh probably have a week or two before yeh have to worry about that. But yeh better start brushing up and training because she's gonna give yeh a fight. Besides, she's working on another project, first."

I ignored the dire warning, temporarily, because it scared the life out of me, and asked, "What other project is she working on?"

"I can't say, can I? It's not summat yeh've asked me for help with. You only asked about the bomb threat." I rolled my eyes and she continued, "I'll take pity on yeh and give yeh a clue. Yeh've seen a hint of it in action, already."

"Oh, you're not going to make me play Twenty Questions, are you?" I begged. "Can't you just tell me?"

"Sorry," she swung another pen to the floor. "I'd like to help, but yeh have to play by the rules. Ask a proper question, yeh'll get a proper answer."

Frustrated, I turned to another issue. "Did you figure out a way to get me past Melinda's shields so I can see inside her again?"

"Not yet," she said, as she landed on my desk and sat down. She was out of pens to fling. "That's what took me so long to get back to yeh. She's determined and that strengthens her power. I spent my time watching her, picking up yehr information and a little extra. That's the part I can't tell yeh about unless yeh ask ..."

I interrupted again, "Well, how about if I ask you to tell me what you learned?"

"Nice try. But I'm not here to do it for yeh, I'm merely here to assist. Yeh'll have to puzzle this out for yehrself. I'm only here to make sure yeh don't blow yehrself up, or worse."

"Okay, fine," I said. "Can you at least give me a hint about what I already saw?"

"I guess I could give yeh a tiny clue." She thought for a moment. "What happened recently that bothered yeh the most? Did anything unusual happen?"

Well, shoot. Pretty much every day something unusual happen, these days. But which instance bothered me the most? "The salesgirl at the mall?"

"Now yeh're thinking. Has it occurred to yeh ..."

Just then, the alarm clock in the bedroom blasted and, even this far away, it was enough of a jarring noise to startle both of us into losing the connection. Damn it! Why hadn't I turned it off when I got up?

Well, at least I know that I have some time before Raven's shop is under threat and Twink is on the job. She'll let me know if anything changes. Meantime, I'll have to either figure out what her clue means, or the right questions to ask her.

Maybe both.

Journal Entry 20

I needed some time alone to puzzle on Twink's reluctant clue, so I shooed Chuck and Amanda out to pick up a pizza. I just finished reading my most recent journal entries here to see if there's something I've missed, perhaps something I wrote and forgot about or that didn't seem important at the time, and a couple things have sprung up with big, red "Pay attention to me!" flags.

First, I need to check back with that antique shop, because Raven did say that the rose oil is powerful and the shop owner told me that I could use the oil to get the pendant. I'm not sure how, but that's what she said and I'm fixing to find out.

I needed some time alone to puzzle on Twink's reluctant clue, so I shooed Chuck and Amanda out to pick up a pizza. I just finished reading my most recent journal entries here to see if there's something I've missed, perhaps something I wrote and forgot about or that didn't seem important at the time, and a couple things have sprung up with big, red "Pay attention to me!" flags.

First, I need to check back with that antique shop, because Raven did say that the rose oil is powerful and the shop owner told me that I could use the oil to get the pendant. I'm not sure how, but that's what she said and I'm fixing to find out.

I also mentioned, back then, that it felt like the pendant would be like a Nintendo prize that means I've moved up a level, like it felt when she gave me the rose oil. I wonder what I have to do to get to the next level to earn the pendant. I think that maybe using the rose oil, which has been sitting on my dresser gathering dust, might not be a bad idea.

Second, and more importantly, Twink's questions made me think about what happened at the mall with that shop girl. And the more I think about it, the more I wonder if that wasn't Melinda's doing. Remember when she somehow entered Raven's body and threatened me and Amanda? What if that was her, inside the shop girl? I can't say for sure, because the moment has passed, but it felt like a presence like Melinda's.

If it was her, what was she doing there? Why would she do that? What would she have to gain?

Hey, a pen just fell on the floor. I wonder if Twink is here. If only I knew how to meet her halfway. She said—wait, I'll scroll back up and copy and paste it here …

> *"(Meditation) is good because yeh're trying stay awake as yeh fall asleep. That's when our worlds merge and we can communicate."*

I'm going to try that. I'll be back in a minute.

###

It worked! Twink just left, so I can tell the story now.

I tried meditating but that doesn't seem to work for me. I think I must be doing it wrong. I just can't seem to reach any kind of—well, anything. I'm not sure what exactly I'm trying to do, and maybe that's the problem. If only I knew what it was supposed to feel like, I'd know when I was there.

Instead, I took her words literally and tried to "stay awake as I fell asleep." I went to my room and lay down, trying to let myself drift off, but it was hard because I was also trying to stay awake. I think I was too nervous about not being able to do either, because I felt like I was bouncing around like a pinball, too awake, too asleep, too awake, too asleep, and I couldn't find a balanced center.

Finally, I think Twink took pity on me and I heard her moving around on the nightstand. She said, "Can yeh hear me now?"

I opened my eyes and slowwwwly sat up, careful to not jar either of us out of the connection.

"Yes," I said, "I did it! You're here!"

"Yeh did nowt," she replied, haughty as usual, "*I* did it, and I've *been* here. I got tired of watching yeh flailing about in the astral and stepped over the veil to meet yeh. But at least yeh got close enough to the edge to see me. Hooplah to you!"

I was so glad to see her that I ignored the sarcasm. "Hey, help me figure this out, okay?"

"Why d'yeh think I threw the pen? I can see yeh're on the verge of getting it. Do yeh have some questions for me? Hopefully the right questions?" She casually floated above the nightstand, back and forth, like she was in an invisible little boat, riding invisible little waves.

"Okay. This is what I was thinking. You said that my clue had something to do with the incident at the mall, but the girl in the store …"

"Oh aye, yeh're nary calling her a tart n'more?"

I brushed that aside, "The poor thing probably didn't even know she was doing it. I think it was Melinda inside her body, like that time with Raven. Melinda looked me dead in the eye, through Raven's eyes, and talked to me. This felt the same, like a foul, wicked presence snarling at me."

"Go on," Twink encouraged.

I took this as validation because one thing I've learned about Twink is that she lets me know, in no uncertain terms, when I'm wrong.

"So, my first question is, was that Melinda? Am I right about that?"

"Yeh've got it. Give 'er a prize!"

I was right! So, then I asked my next question, "If it was her, then what was she doing there? Why would she do that? What would she have to gain?"

"Eh up, now yeh've broken the questions rule."

"Which rule?" I asked. "I can't keep track of them."

"Yeh've asked too many at once. One at a time."

"Okay," I tried to remember what I had asked first. "What was she doing there?"

"You tell me. What were she doing there?"

Sometimes I don't like this game. This was one of those times. I sighed, "Messing with my life? Making me feel horrible about myself?"

"Nay, don't ask me," Twink shrugged, "tell me. Is that what she did, made yeh feel bad?"

"Well, yeah, at the very least! I spent all day Saturday feeling awful, and it even affected …" I stopped short of telling her about the lousy sex Chuck and I had that night because I didn't want to talk about my sex life with a faery, especially a faery that I was beginning to feel isn't the friendliest one they could have sent. I stammered, "… well, it affected my marriage."

"Does that answer yehr question? What she were doing there?"

"I don't know if that's what she meant to do, but that's certainly what happened. So, yeah, I guess that's the best answer I can come up with for that question."

"Okay," Twink goaded, "What were yehr next question?"

"Why would she do that? What does she have to gain?"

"That's two," she said, "but essentially the same question so I'll allow it. Tell me, Lola, why would she do that? What does she have to gain from making yeh feel awful about yehrself and affecting yehr sex life?" She winked at me—not in a friendly way, but in an "I know your secret" way.

I'm sure I blushed, even though I desperately wanted not to. I felt my face grow hot but I ignored it and charged forward. "I don't know what she would have to gain from this. How can this help her blow up Raven's store? But wait," I remembered, "You said she had a new project, right? And this event was a part of that, not the bomb threat."

My mind felt like it was full of steel wool, too many sharp threads all jumbled and tangled up. Too much to unravel. I finally had to admit to Twink, "I don't know. Can you help me at all?"

She grinned and said, "Yeh're so close to gettin' it. I wouldn't want to rob yeh of the good feeling yeh'll have when yeh figure it out for yehrself. Yeh have a bit of time to play with, but not much. I'll check back with yeh in a couple days, unless an emergency comes up. But I doubt it will."

With a flash of faery dust, she disappeared, leaving me with another uncomfortable puzzle to solve, just as Chuck and Amanda returned with the pizza.

Journal Entry 21

I must admit that I'm stumped. I can't, for the life of me, figure out what Melinda's new project might be, if all it involves is playing mind tricks in the mall. Chuck didn't even see the same thing I did, so it obviously wasn't for his benefit. In fact, he didn't seem to notice the girl was there, beyond a cursory "no, thank you" when she asked if she could help us.

I'm going to have to mull this over, because nothing is coming to mind. Meantime, I did want to make a note that I tried to find that antique store on my way home today. I drove up and down the street that I parked on. I even

I must admit that I'm stumped. I can't, for the life of me, figure out what Melinda's new project might be, if all it involves is playing mind tricks in the mall. Chuck didn't even see the same thing I did, so it obviously wasn't for his benefit. In fact, he didn't seem to notice the girl was there, beyond a cursory "no, thank you" when she asked if she could help us.

I'm going to have to mull this over, because nothing is coming to mind. Meantime, I did want to make a note that I tried to find that antique store on my way home today. I drove up and down the street. I even checked the next blocks over on either side and it was nowhere to be found. Granted, I didn't have the business card with me, so I didn't have the exact address with me. I must be mistaken about where it is.

I even scrolled back up in this journal to find out if I said anything about where it was. All I said was that it's off of Orange Street, but I was reminded of what the shop owner said when she gave the vial of oil to me.

> *"It's rose oil. I bottled it myself. I have a whole side business, blending oils and such for love potions and magical things like that. I want you to have this so it will bring you closer to owning that gorgeous pendant."*

I have no idea what that's supposed to mean, except that Raven told me rose oil is one of the highest vibration oils. She said that it had properties of pure, essential love and the power of celestial quality magic. She said it was a deeply heartfelt gift.

I wish I knew more about how to use things like rose oil or magic. I'm afraid to fool around with it because what if I do it wrong? What if I turn Chuck into a newt? Or, to be serious for a moment, what if it's just plain wrong, no matter what Raven says or what my intent is? What if we're all just lying to ourselves into believing it's okay to play with, in an effort to rationalize the lengths we're willing to go to in order to get what we want? What about God's will?

I've had this same conversation over and over with myself here, but the topic is in no way resolved, is it? I've never been able to feel solidly okay with what I'm involved in. I really need to figure this out.

Let's go back to what Raven said about the oil: *"... rose oil is one of the "highest vibration" oils. She said that it had properties of pure, essential love and the power of celestial quality magic. She said it was a deeply heartfelt gift."*

I wonder what would happen if I just open the bottle and take a whiff while thinking about all this. Raven did say that inhaling it has transformational qualities. Back in a sec.

###

I opened the bottle, closed my eyes and took a deep sniff of the oil. I then 'saw' a mental image of myself as a kid, taking a bubble bath in an all pink bathroom. The tub was pink, the tiles were pink, the towels were pink, and the bubble bath was rose scented. Then, the scene faded to where I was my grown self, surrounded by pink clouds. When I exhaled, I was back here again. Strange. I didn't expect anything like that!

Then I tried it a second time and it felt like my Grandma popped into the room with me for a second, and then popped away.

'Wait a minute,' I wondered. 'Where is my Grandma? In heaven. What's in heaven? Clouds.'

Not pink clouds, of course, but I wondered if that's what Raven meant by rose oil having the power of celestial quality magic.

One more deep inhalation just now made the room feel like it was filled with light-beings, like the one I talked to in my "spirit conference" dream. I think I'm on to something. I'll write more in a minute, after I play with this for a bit.

###

WOW! This is very cool. I've now found a new way to contact another light-being. The rose oil, combined with the method I just stumbled upon, is like a key to the door.

Here's what I did. I held the opened bottle of oil under my nose and kept inhaling it while keeping in mind that I wanted to know the meaning of "celestial quality magic." Next thing I knew, I was in a room similar to the Newbie Room that I saw before, only this time it was all different shades of pink! When I saw the pink clouds during my first sniff, that was just a glimpse of the place, almost like I was bouncing on a trampoline and my head poked into the room for just a sec before I came back down.

Sniffing the rose oil continuously like that—sustained, intentional inhalation—helped my consciousness to float upward, like I left my body and my spirit floated up. That's probably not the most accurate way to describe it, but it's the best I can do while writing this so quickly. I want to make sure I capture all of it before I lose the memory.

Anyway, inhaling the rose oil helped me to mentally 'float' upward into the Rose Room. It felt like the Newbie Room, which was all white, except this was pink and flavored, for lack of a better word, with rose essence. It filled all my senses: like real roses, the scent was almost too thick and intense, with an exquisite yet almost overpowering aroma.

It made me so woozy I almost lost physical consciousness, but I forced myself to stay awake so I wouldn't forget what happened. Is that what Twink meant when she said try to stay awake while I fall asleep?

Another holographic light-being was there, this one pure white but tinged, like a partially dyed rose, with the most beautiful shades from fuchsia to the palest pink. I gasped at the exquisite beauty of the colors, they were so deep and rich—so vibrant and alive, their intensity causing me to weep. I'm still tearing up from the memory.

The light-being spoke to me first, in a voice so overflowing with love that I almost couldn't bear it. To use the word 'love' does it injustice. I was so overwhelmed by the sound of its voice that I felt like I turned inside out and became a hologram, myself, for a moment. That passed quickly because I once again had to force myself to maintain awareness. It would have been easy to just let go, but I wasn't sure if I would ever come back. Is that what it feels like to die? I don't know, but that's the closest I've ever come to even wondering.

The pink-tinged light-being didn't say much or, if it did, I don't remember because I had such a hard time staying connected to my conscious self. What I did hear—not in words, but in essence—was this:

"You have nothing to fear from Raven or the new path you're taking. Adhere to the truth and you can do no wrong."

I could feel myself fading and sensed that I had time to ask only one question before I lost focus. There were so many to ask that I had a hard time coming up with the right one, so I just asked the first thing that came to my head, "How will I know the truth when I see it?"

The light-being exuded the essence of a smile (it didn't have a mouth—its features came and went—I didn't see the smile as much as I sensed it) and placed one hand on its chest in a Sacred Heart gesture. A spot of pink light began glowing there, getting brighter and brighter.

The light-being bowed and gestured, toward me, with its other hand. I put my hand on my own chest and felt the same thing happening there—a glowing spot of beautiful, white-tinged-with-rose light. But as soon as I looked downward to see what was happening, I lost my connection and fell back into my body.

I repeat: WOW!

I think I need to stop writing for a while so I can think about this. Later, dude.

Journal Entry 22

I don't know if I want to do this anymore. Ever since I got back from the Rose Room, I've been achy and sick to my stomach. I'm on edge, my chest hurts and I started crying while watching the news last night because all the stories were so upsetting. "Man's inhumanity to man" is such a deep reality. I almost threw up at work because I so desperately do not want to be there anymore, working for such an awful man. The contrast between where I'm going and where I've been is too great. The pain and ugliness I see all around me is overpowering and it's affecting me, physically.

I don't know if I want to do this anymore. Ever since I got back from the Rose Room, I've been achy and sick to my stomach. I'm on edge, my chest hurts and I started crying while watching the news last night because all the stories were so upsetting. "Man's inhumanity to man" is such a deep reality. I almost threw up at work because I so desperately do not want to be there anymore, working for such an awful man. The contrast between where I'm going and where I've been is too great. The pain and ugliness I see all around me is overpowering and it's affecting me, physically.

I wish I'd never had that damned dream. I'd gladly trade all the abilities I've gained just to have my life back. What good are they if I can't function in the everyday world anymore? They're doing more harm than good.

Of course, this is causing the wedge between me and Chuck to grow larger. He doesn't understand what's happening to me. (How could I expect him to? I don't even understand!) He knows that I've changed and he hates it. He's taken to working later and later and he barely talks to me. He's civil, but there's no warmth there. I miss him.

Even Amanda is treating me differently. I don't know whether it's normal adolescence or a reaction to me and what I'm going through. All I know is that she seems to be avoiding me and keeps telling me that I'm getting weird.

I don't understand how I can have such incredible, uplifting, ecstatic experiences and feel so awful the rest of the time. You'd think that such marvelous visions and feelings of such intense love would bleed over into my real world and help me to feel better. Instead, it's just the opposite and the contrast is stark. As good as it did feel then is as bad as it does feel now.

Looks like Twink wants to talk to me. A pen just rolled off the desk.

You know what? Screw her. I'm tired of her games, her snotty demeanor and her refusal to help in a way that actually is helpful.

Come to think of it, the hell with all of them. Raven, too. What has she done for me that makes me so gung ho about stopping Melinda from blowing up her stupid misspelled shop? It's not my business, it's not my problem. Have at it, Melinda baby.

In fact, I'm not going to write any more tonight. There's a chocolate cake downstairs just waiting to be eaten and that's what I'm gonna do. Maybe if Amanda and Chuck are lucky I'll save some for them, but they better not count on it after the way they've been treating me.

Screw 'em all.

Journal Entry 23

I hate Melinda Underwood. If it weren't for her, my life would be normal. If it weren't for her, none of this would have happened. And if it weren't for her, my marriage would still be intact.

I don't know where to even begin. It's been several days since I've written and, quite frankly, I wasn't planning on writing anymore. I had washed my hands of the whole thing and did my best to go back to my life. I went out of my way to make Chuck happy and to convince Amanda that I'm the same mom she's always known. I knew it would take more than a couple days to undo the damage, but I didn't realize that so much

I hate Melinda Underwood. If it weren't for her, my life would be normal. If it weren't for her, none of this would have happened. And if it weren't for her, my marriage would still be intact.

I don't know where to even begin. It's been several days since I've written and, quite frankly, I wasn't planning on writing anymore. I had washed my hands of the whole thing and did my best to go back to my life. I went out of my way to make Chuck happy and to convince Amanda that I'm the same mom she's always known. I knew it would take more than a couple days to undo the damage, but I didn't realize that so much damage had been done. For crying out loud, Amanda practically hates me and Chuck has started flirting with other women, right in front of me!!

Yesterday afternoon, I called Chuck at work and tried to make a midweek date, like we used to do when we were still young and in love. I thought maybe it would help to patch things up. He agreed, grudgingly, but probably only because I wouldn't take no for an answer. I'm rather ashamed to admit that I got a little whiny and had to lay a guilt trip. Not my most attractive behavior but I didn't know what else to do. He was doing everything he could to get out of it.

My first red flag should have been when he suggested we meet at one of those chain restaurants that hires pretty, young girls with perfect bodies to wear tiny shorts and tight t-shirts, and then pretends that the restaurant's "coincidentally" sexist name has nothing to do with the waitress' barely covered chest. I won't even mention this place's name because they don't deserve the space in my mind or on this page.

Chuck knows how I feel about places like these—that they are just as damaging to the human psyche as using T&A to sell beer, cars, or any of the other countless advertising campaigns that somehow equate a semi-nude female with their product. I know it's my issue to deal with, but that doesn't make it any easier to accept that this is where Chuck suggested we go.

Besides, would he want his own daughter to work at a place like that? I'm sure he'd throw a fit if Amanda even suggested it.

First and foremost, I consider myself to be a feminist, even if I don't always act like it. So, for Chuck to even consider that we meet there for a date tipped me off that things are worse than I thought. Talk about a deliberate jab!

Of course, I covered my hurt feelings and suggested another place, one with a more suitable, romantic adult ambience. He reluctantly agreed, so we met there after work.

Well, we might as well have gone to the other place, because our waitress was just as young and pretty, and was wearing a just as tight and low-cut top as the beer 'n' wings waitresses. I had half a mind to complain to the manager. After all, this is a respectable place for couples to have a nice, romantic meal without the threat of having a waitress like Tits McGee leaning down in front of my husband's face as she placed the menus on the table, giving him a glorious and gratuitous cleavage shot. I didn't need this damned intuition to know that he was deeply enjoying this. I could see it in his eyes, the bastard.

By the way, I'm fully aware of how old, grouchy and insecure I sound. I can't help it—that's how I feel! I feel like my whole life is slipping away and there's nothing I can do to stop it. And I know that the more insecure I feel, the needier and clingier I'm acting, and that's chasing Chuck away just as much as his annoyance at my new interests.

I tried—really, I did—to act cheerful and unbothered by his

suddenly apparent interest in ogling other women right in front of me. After all, he's a man, right? Men are supposedly "visually stimulated," right? (By the way, in my opinion, that's a load of rationalizing garbage if I've ever heard it: "We have to look! It's the way we are!") As long as he's coming home to me, I should be grateful he's still got a working libido, right?

Wrong.

I don't know what happened, but he used to keep this kind of thing to himself. He used to respect me enough to not let me know when he looks at other women. Now it's as in-my-face as I can allow without filing divorce papers. Okay, maybe not divorce papers, but some other dramatic response that I haven't come up with yet.

See, he knows how I feel about stuff like this. We've been married long enough for him to know all of my knee-jerk issues, just as I know his. Part of what made our marriage a happy one is that we have learned how to live together without pushing each other's buttons. We don't rock each other's boats. And now, he's damn near capsizing mine!

Anyway, I tried to ignore Tits McGee's humongous boobs in our faces. In fact, in an effort to appear light and airy, and attractive to Chuck, I was especially friendly to her, even though I wanted to scratch her eyes out (and his, too) and pop those over-inflated balloons with my fork. Trying to pretend that nothing is wrong while one's world is falling apart is no easy task. I deserve an Oscar.

It just got worse from there. Chuck wouldn't look me in the eye unless he had to, all evening long. It was like we didn't even know each other. I tried to ask him what's going on, why he was being so cold to me, but couldn't get the words out.

Honestly, I don't understand. Yes, there has been some tension, but not any worse than a few other times over the years, the typical kind of stuff that every marriage goes through. This is the first time things have gone this far awry. I don't know what I've done to turn him so far away from me, and me from him. I don't even like him anymore.

I could barely choke down my meal. I ordered my favorite, but every bite of food stopped at my throat. I should have ordered a salad or something light. This damned intuition let me know that he was seeing me as gluttonous—shoveling trowels of cheesy pasta into my fat face—while our lovely young waitress, with her slender waist and gargantuan breasts, captivated him with her every lithe and supple move.

Finally, we just went home, nothing resolved. We haven't spoken much since then, beyond civil "pass the salt" types of conversation.

I don't understand why I can't figure this out. For the past couple months, I've had to deal with these lightning bolts and intuitive flashes when I don't want them, but when I could use one, when it would actually be helpful to know what's going on in someone else's head, nothing happens. It doesn't work. It's just like when Melinda blocked me from her head. Now I can't even see into Chuck's.

Hey, wait a minute. I wonder …

Two pens just shot off my desk, and one of them flew all the way across the room. Twink is back. That usually means I'm on to something. I wonder if Melinda is behind this, as well!

Another pen just went sailing, only this one did a loop in the air. Impressive!

God, what a relief! If this is Melinda's doing, then at least I know it's not mine! I'm going to see if I can connect with Twink. I'll write more when I know something.

Journal Entry 24

Oh, thank God for faeries! I was ready to write her off because she's been such an unobliging pain in the butt, but I take it all back now. I'm on track again!

First, before I tell what happened, she and I finally came up with a way to communicate without having to try so hard. It's much easier to connect now, thanks to her great idea.

Once I managed to find my way into the proper mindset between asleep and awake, while sitting at my desk—no small task, by the way—Twink came through.

Oh, thank God for faeries! I was ready to write her off because she's been such an unobliging pain in the butt, but I take it all back now. I'm on track again!

First, before I tell what happened, she and I finally came up with a way to communicate without having to try so hard. It's much easier to connect now, thanks to her great idea.

Once I managed to find my way into the proper mindset between asleep and awake, while sitting at my desk—no small task, by the way—Twink came through.

"Eh up," she said, "I had a thought. Where's that lovely stone yeh purchased at yehr mate's shop?"

I opened my desk drawer and pulled out the quartz crystal that I bought from Karma Korner during one of my first trips there. "This one?" I asked. "I don't know that I'd call it lovely. It's not very clear—it's kind of foggy." I held it up and showed it to her. Instead of being transparent, like glass, it has what looks like of a cloud of mist inside.

"Oh aye," she said, "That's called faery frost, innit?

"I don't know. Is it?"

She ignored my question and said, instead, "Hold it in the palm of yehr hand."

As I held my hand out flat, with the crystal in the center of my palm, she fluttered down and landed on my hand, standing right next to the stone. My hand began to buzz from the contact with her feet.

What a feeling! An actual faery was standing on my palm. I had never touched Twink before (the dreams of her standing on my face don't count because I didn't know she was real at the time, plus it was in the dream world, not the physical world). She weighed about the same as a parakeet and her tiny feet emanated miniature electrical zaps as she walked.

She put one minuscule hand on the crystal and pulled out her sparkling wand with the other. Saying a few unintelligible words, she swirled the wand in the air and then let loose with a charge of faery dust, aimed at the crystal. It lit up with a glorious inner light. It was spectacular!

"As long as yeh have this crystal on yehr person, either in yehr pocket or worn as a charm, you can call for me more easily."

I was more excited by this than by any present I've ever received in my life. This glowing, magical crystal is the kind of thing I used to pretend I had, when I was little, when I still believed magic was real. I had a toy scepter, which had a big, gaudy rhinestone on the end, and I used to pretend that it was my magic wand. This crystal was even better than that, because it was really magic! It was all I could do to not giggle like a schoolgirl, even as the glow faded.

In fact, I'm still so excited about it that I almost forgot to mention what Twink found out, regarding Melinda!

Remember that I was trying to figure out what's going on between me and Chuck, and how I can't see inside him, like I can't see inside Melinda? And how the light suddenly dawned that it might be Melinda's doing? I was right!

Twink told me (after a stern lecture about ignoring her the other day—she tried to get through, then, to let me know, but I was too angry to listen), "I've been trying to tell yeh, but yeh wouldn't listen, that you are that colicky bint's new project!"

"Well," I asked, a little defensive, "why are you now able to tell me about it without my having to ask specific questions?"

"Because," she gritted her teeth with annoyance and explained, "the level of threat had reached a point where I can no longer withhold the information from yeh, simply for my own amusement."

She admitted that she had been toying with me because there was no imminent peril, and the rules that she is bound to allow her to tell me only what I either need to know or specifically ask about. "I didn't volunteer for this assignment, yeh know," she continued. "I'm under orders and I daresay I don't half resent yeh for it. But I finally took pity on yeh and decided to stop mucking about."

I was too excited about my new crystal light to care much that she had been such a little brat.

OUCH!

Sorry, but she was!

Okay, now I have to watch what I type about her, because she can apparently read human words. She just kicked me in the ear. You wouldn't think tiny little feet like that would make so much of an impact, but she packed a wallop behind her kick.

Anyway, I didn't even care that she's been screwing with me for her own perverse pleasure. I'm just grateful to know she's back and that the hell I've been experiencing these past weeks has been of supernatural origin. Melinda has been casting spells against me. She's been deliberately messing with my head.

When I pressed her for more information, Twink said, "Melinda's trying to distract yeh from paying attention to what she's up to. If yeh're too busy with yehr own problems to care about hers, she can do whatever she wants. Yeh're out of the way."

It took Twink so long to find this out because Melinda's psychic thought-wall is powerful, too strong for either Twink or me to permeate. Melinda has also begun building one around Chuck so I couldn't see inside of him unless she wanted me to see what he was thinking. I knew that something was different! When Melinda saw the reaction that her mischief at the mall caused between us, when she saw that chink in my armor, she knew she had found a weakness so she used it against me.

Of course, my knowing this doesn't mean that she's been stopped. She doesn't even know that I'm on to her. Plus, I have no clue how to counter her actions. But it does help me to know that there's more going on here than meets the eye so, if it happens again, I'll be prepared to deal with it, and not take Chuck's behavior personally.

I need to figure out how to fight her at her own game whether I want to or not, since she's apparently unwilling to leave me out of it. I was ready to walk away—in fact, I already had—but she pulled me back in.

Twink said, "Melinda still plans on torching Raven's shop but she still doesn't have a set date. She was waiting until she had yeh securely tucked out of the way."

I wondered aloud, "Should I let her know that her plan failed, or should I continue acting as if I don't know anything?"

"That, I couldn't tell yeh," she said, "but I'll keep my ear to the ground and let yeh know if answers to that question are forthcoming. Meantime, keep playing dumb."

By the way … funny story … I also asked Twink how she knows all this, without being able to penetrate Melinda's thought-wall. Remember when I asked her to do that and she asked if I had a preferred method or if I wanted her to use her own? Remember how she giggled when I told her to do it her own way? Well, that little pixie is hell on wheels and I hope to never really get on her bad side.

At first, she thought it would be a breeze. After all, what human could possibly keep her out, especially if that human was completely unaware of her existence?

Apparently, Melinda could. She is evil enough to be extra paranoid, because only someone with ice in their veins could even imagine the kinds of things Melinda has protected herself against. Her thought-wall is a thought-fortress, according to Twink.

This is almost too gross to describe but, as Twink says, if you need to get in, you need to get in, and the best way into a fortress is where it's unprotected … through the sewer system.

She sent a doodlebug (that's what she called it) up Melinda's tail pipe, so to speak, to distract her in much the same way that Melinda distracted me.

While Mighty Melinda was busy fighting off an almost constant attack of explosive diarrhea, she was too sidetracked to keep energizing her protection as much as she should have and Twink was able to get the information she needed.

I wish I could have been a fly on the wall to see that.

NO, WAIT! I DON'T MEAN THAT!!!!

I have got to stop using that expression. I'm learning just how important it is to be careful what I wish for. Lately, I've been getting it.

Journal Entry 25

Words can't express how relieved I am. I was 'this close' to caving in. Not that I want a fight—God knows I'm too chicken for that—but knowing that all is not lost makes the idea of fighting back palatable.

I'm not sure where to begin, so I'll summarize here to see if there's something I haven't thought of yet:

a) Melinda drew down the power we accidentally shared in order to get revenge on a cheating boyfriend, Raven and anyone else who pisses her off.

Words can't express how relieved I am. I was 'this close' to caving in. Not that I want a fight—God knows I'm too chicken for that—but knowing that all is not lost makes the idea of fighting back palatable.

I'm not sure where to begin, so I'll summarize here to see if there's something I haven't thought of yet:

a) Melinda drew down the power we accidentally shared in order to get revenge on a cheating boyfriend, Raven and anyone else who pisses her off.
b) Tammy has been drafted as her stooge. Tammy isn't happy about it, but is too weak to say no.
c) Raven has no idea (or refuses to believe) that anyone wants to harm her. I tried to warn her, but was stopped because …
d) Melinda knows that I know about her plan and that I have the same powers.
e) Melinda has FAR greater knowledge about how to use them, but she doesn't know that I have Twink on my side.
f) Melinda has begun a full-blown psychic attack against me, to distract me. But, she doesn't know yet that I'm on to her.
g) Melinda plans to bomb the shop once I'm successfully out of the way.

So, it would seem that I have two options:

1. I can pretend to go along with her plan, pretend that I'm out of the way, laying a trap for her to go ahead and commit her crime. Twink can continue monitoring her actions and let me know when it's time. I could possibly call the police with a tip when I know for a fact that she and Tammy are on their way to Karma Korner to do the deed.

   OR

2. I can confront her and challenge her to a duel of powers.

Obviously, I'm hoping for Option 1. I wish I had some way of knowing the best thing to do. Without access to that information, it seems to me that Option 1 is the smarter and safer way to go. Can you say "No brainer?" I knew that you could.

###

Will wonders never cease? I had to stop writing for a while because the most amazing thing just happened. I know I say that a lot lately but, just now, as I was typing I had the strangest feeling that someone was in the room with me.

It was me!

I looked up from my computer monitor and saw a ghostly, holographic image of myself standing in the doorway, watching me type.

The sudden apparition scared the daylights out of me, much the same way it startles me if a face suddenly appears in a window. (That used to be Chuck's favorite game when we were first married and our kitchen window was right above the sink—he loved to sneak up on the window from the outside and scare the life out of me when I was doing dishes. He thought it was hysterical to make me scream like a girl. He finally quit doing that the day he startled me into dropping and breaking his mother's heirloom Depression Glass platter.)

I admit that I screamed—a little—and the other Me immediately disappeared. Then I recalled what Twink said about bells and the myth that they scare faeries away: it's not that they are frightened away, it's that the connection is broken.

I assumed that's what happened and that I could bring "Me" back if I tried. So, I backed up to what I was doing when it happened and tried to recreate the scene.

I centered myself in an approximation of that "'tween sleep and wake" state, and reread what I was typing when "I" appeared:

> *"I wish I had some way of knowing the best thing to do. Without access to that information, it seems to me that Option 1 is the smarter and safer way to go."*

I closed my eyes and give it a few seconds. Then I slowly reopened my eyes, and there I was!

"Very good!" the other Lola said to me. "You're really getting the hang of this!"

I was pleasantly surprised to see that it worked. I really am getting the hang of this! One other thing I've gotten the hang of is not assuming that I have a clue what I'm getting the hang of, so I didn't presume to know how or why I was standing there, talking to me. So, I let her do the talking, after an initial greeting of, "Hi. I can't wait to hear what you have to say."

She laughed. It was strange hearing it, because people have always told me over the years that I have a very distinctive laugh, but I never notice it because I'm too busy laughing.

But here it was, my familiar laugh coming out of my face, and it did sound—well—different. Sort of like notes running up and down the scales; I can't describe it. It was just as bizarre hearing my voice coming out of her, because it sounded like I do on recordings, not like it sounds inside my own head. Funny.

"I remember being where you are right now," she said, "and wishing that I had the answers I needed. That's why I'm here."

All right! Answers delivered on a platter! It's about time some help came to me with that specific intent, instead of leaving me to figure out some cryptic meaning.

"I'm all ears," I told Me. "I'm about worn out and could really use a little assistance."

She smiled, kindly, "Yes, I can see that. I'm here at this moment because you're at a very important crossroad. You said that you wish you knew the best thing to do, but you've only thought of two options."

"There's another?" I asked, hopeful.

"At the very least," she grinned. "There are infinite probable futures, an unlimited number of possible timestreams, each created with every different decision you make. If you decide to wear the green shirt instead of the red one, you might elicit a different outcome—perhaps an ordinary conversation about that specific shirt—which subtly steers your life in a direction that would not have happened if you'd worn the red. Do you see?"

I was unsure why she was talking about what color shirt I might wear, although I did love the green top with the sparkly buttons that she was wearing, but encouraged her to go on. "Sure. That's pretty elementary. What's the point?"

"The point," she explained, "is that all timestreams exist in parallel universes. In one timestream, you wear the red and nothing remarkable happens. In the other, you wear the green and your life is bent down a slightly different path. While your immediate future may not be varied much, ten years down the road those paths could be vastly different. There are endless numbers of parallel timestreams, all existing at once."

My brain hurt. "Thanks for the information, I think. How is it relevant?"

"I'm getting there. I remember what it was like to be where you are now and how hard it was for me to grasp these concepts, so I'm trying to explain in a way that will help."

She sat down and made herself comfortable in the rocking chair I keep in the office because Amanda used to sit there sometimes while I was working (she hasn't done it so much since she's getting older, but I like to keep the chair there, just in case she ever wants some Mom-bonding time). The chair rocked back and forth, making a squeaking sound as the floorboards creaked under the weight. Odd that a holographic, ghostly being could make this happen.

She continued, "In case you haven't figured it out, I'm you, from the future. One possible future, that is."

I raised my eyebrows. "Did this happen to you when you were me? I mean, did you have another You come and talk to you?"

"Not at the exact same point in time as you are right now, so our futures are slightly different. Not enough to make a huge difference in this situation, though. Because I know now that I can, I'm coming to you at the point in time when I remember wishing most desperately for some guidance."

"Do tell."

"I will," she grinned. "You were about to limit yourself to only two options in dealing with Melinda. I'm here to tell you that you haven't even come close to considering what else you can do. Who can blame you? You have no idea, at this point, what you can even do. And one thing you can do is to anchor into the future you desire and pull yourself toward it. That's what I'm here to teach you to do."

I felt brainless. I didn't get it. "Huh???" I asked, stupidly.

"I know," she commiserated. "But it's easier than it sounds. Just suspend your disbelief for a little while and it will all become very clear."

She waited to see if I had any questions. My silence informed her that I did not, so she continued.

"As I've already explained, there are an infinite number of possible futures ahead of you, each dependent on the decisions you make now. There are some futures that you will thoroughly enjoy and some that you will not. I think it's a safe bet that you would like to find yourself in one that you will enjoy. Yes?"

I nodded.

"Any idea what that will look like? What are the circumstances you would like to find there?"

"Well," I pondered for a moment, "I would like for my family to be healthy and well, and together."

"Okay, that's good for starters," she said. "What about Melinda?"

"Oh, of course I want that situation resolved," I replied. "I assumed that was obvious."

"Never assume," she said. "What else? Go ahead and brainstorm a little. Just throw ideas out there. Draw me a picture. Let me hear it."

"Give me second to think." I begged. She nodded and rocked, waiting patiently. "Okay, like I said, I want my family to be happy and well. I want these problems behind us. I want Melinda out of my life, crisis solved, no fire bombs through windows, no harm done to Raven's shop."

A pen shot off the desk. The other Me guffawed, "I forgot she used to do that!! Twink, you crack me up!"

With this, every pen in my pen cup (I have a dozen or so because half of them don't even work but I can't make myself throw them away) flew upward and into a formation like the Blue Angels performing at an air show. They looped and soared and put on one helluva display. The other Me clapped with delight, while I sat dumbly in my desk chair, jaw on the floor. Who knew Twink could do that?

"I think she's trying to tell you that you're leaving something … er … someone out of your future storyline," Me suggested.

I didn't know what to say. Was Twink still there, in my future? I rather thought she was a temporary aide, as fleeting as my visits to the Newbie Room or the Rose Room. It didn't occur to me that she'd be part of my life for that long. She's certainly made it plain that she's not here by choice and can't wait to skedaddle.

"Um," I stammered, "can I make wishes for her? I don't know what she wants."

"Twink is here to help you to get your sea legs with the powers you've recently received. And I know that right now you wish like hell that this had never happened. But believe me, in the future you're going to be very glad that it did. That event was a major pivot point in your life, one that wiped out a huge number of miserable possible futures. But since it's such a large change, the 'gods,' so to speak, took pity on you and assigned Twink to help you for as long as you need her."

I didn't know whether to be distraught or relieved. It's nice to have the help, but Twink didn't seem to like me much. I think I would prefer someone a little nicer to me in my corner. Then, it dawned on me …

"Okay, I would love for future-Me to have a mutually beneficial working relationship," I quoted from my knowledge of business letter negotiation jargon, “with Twink for as long as it serves both of us.”

“Nicely done.” Other-Me told me. “Now, do you have a pretty good feel for what you’ve described? Can you feel what it would be like to actually be in those circumstances?”

I tried. “Not really. I’m not sure what you mean.”

She gave a thoughtful frown. I recognized it as the face I make when I’m trying to figure out a problem. This was an interesting experience, watching myself in action.

“Okay,” she said, “just go with me on this. Close your eyes and listen, and follow along with what I tell you to do.”

I closed my eyes and got comfortable, ready and listening.

“Imagine what it will feel like when you’re, say, six months down the road, with this whole thing behind you. Melinda and her plan are just a memory. Raven’s shop is safe and sound, and you and Twink get along beautifully. She helps you as much as you help her and you enjoy hanging out together.”

Her voice was soothing yet animated, expressing perfectly the excitement and contentment I wish I could feel in my everyday life. Up until now, however, I always thought of “contentment” as meaning nothing hurts, I’m not hungry, no one is mad at me and I don’t have to go to the bathroom.

“Your family is healthy, happy and together. You and Chuck have mended all fences and are a happy couple once again. Amanda is a well-adjusted girl, who respects her parents, cleans her room …”

I couldn’t help laughing at this last. Amanda? Respectful and tidy?

The other Me laughed as well, “Hey, a girl can dream, right?”

“Right,” I agreed, “but you lost me as soon as you said that. I don’t believe that will ever happen.”

“Okay, maybe I got carried away. But you get what I’m saying, right? Were you able to deeply sense how happy that future will feel?”

I could, and I said so. “If only I knew what to do to get there ...”

She interrupted me before I could say any more. “No, you’re missing the point. It’s not a matter of knowing what to do to get there; it’s a matter of learning to be it before you get there.”

“You lost me again.”

"You were able to feel that future, right? Well, keep that feeling in mind whenever you are faced with a decision. Ponder each option that you have and choose the one that feels most like that future."

I was beginning to understand. I felt like a light bulb was literally flashing over my head.

"I get it!" I cried, "Is that the future you're from?"

"Sure is," she beamed. "Another trick you can use, and this has become my own personal favorite, is this: remember that there is a future 'You' in every one of these possible futures, good and bad. And, just like you're connecting with me, you can connect with them. Sometimes they're very far from where you are now, because a lot has to happen between now and then before you can get to them, so it won't be so easy to meet up like you and I are doing now. But you can signal your intent to become that Future-You and anchor into it so you can more easily pull yourself toward that future."

She paused, to make sure I was following her line of reasoning, and I waited expectantly. I was following.

"What I like to do is throw a rope, so to speak, to that future Self. You don't have to have a real rope, just use the one in your imagination. Signal to that Future-You that you want to connect. It's easier than it sounds. Just state your intent and it's done."

Again, she waited to make sure I was with her. Again, I was.

"Once that connection has been made," she said, "and Future-You has a hold of the rope, you now have something to pull yourself forward with. This is the straightest, most efficient path to that future, by keeping this rope in mind and making all of your decisions based on how close to the rope they are."

"Huh?" I felt stupid again, trying to take this all in.

"See, you're free to do whatever you want. If, by making a misaligned decision, you veer off the direct path to that future because you get distracted, or want to try something else for a while, or you forget to keep the future in mind when you make a decision, you are absolutely free to do so. But when you want to get back on the path to that future, just remember that rope and begin again making decisions that pull you forward until you connect to that Future-You."

"You just blew my mind," I said, reeling with all the possibilities she had just presented.

"I know. I'm trying to keep this simple, because it can get complex. Just remember to keep your eye on the prize and your gut at attention. When you feel a warning in your gut, pay attention. Remember to check how closely your choices resonate with how your desired future feels, and choose accordingly."

I had a question, though. "You said that I can veer off the direct path from here to there, but didn't you also say that every decision I make changes my future? How can I ever get to my desired future if I make changes along the way?"

"I had the same question—go figure, since I'm you," she laughed. "If you veer just a little bit off the path, you can get there with your initial intention intact. The further you go away before you come back, the more things change and the longer it might take to get you back there. You might have to jump through a few extra hoops along the way. It might not look like anything you would recognize, but it would still have the same essential feeling of your original desire."

I was fascinated, but noise from outside distracted me. I looked out the window and saw Chuck in the process of dragging the garbage cans at the curb. I love watching him do "man stuff." Even though I hate the concept of gender-assigned housekeeping tasks (i.e., all housework is "woman's work") there are some things he does because they require brute strength. Plus, I do love to watch his muscles ripple as he lifts heavy things.

The other-Me caught what I was thinking and said, "Right there. Notice how warm and affectionate you feel for Chuck right now. That is part of your future scenario, too, right? Isn't that how you want this story to end up? Happily ever after?"

"Of course it is," I replied.

"Then remember what that feels like, always. Even when you're mad or upset, or afraid it won't work. Keep your eye on that prize."

Just then, Chuck came back out with the second can. By coincidence (???) Melinda came out from behind her house with her own trash can. Rather, she came out "struggling" with the weight of her own can.

Chuck, ever the gentleman, immediately put our can in place and rushed across the street to help her.

I didn't need my intuition to know Melinda did not need help. She could bench press that can and two more like it. For crying out loud, she could probably bench press Chuck. But all that Chuck saw was a damsel in distress.

It made me sick to my stomach to see her smiling demurely and batting her eyelashes at his offer of assistance. I wished, too late, that I could turn off the intuition that told me what Chuck was feeling at that moment. He was turned on! She wasn't even all that pretty, and she had that weird red hair, yet here he was flirting back!

As he lugged her trash to the curb, muscles rippling, I saw her surreptitiously unbuttoning her shirt's top button. She waited until he set the can in place and then she bent as if to pick something up off the ground, pretending something she held in her hand had fallen out of the can. As she bent over, her top fell open, giving Chuck (and me!) a clear, unobstructed view of her braless boobs.

Instantly, he was rock hard and she knew it, too. She made a point of looking straight at his crotch, letting him know she saw the physical affect her flashing had created. I couldn't hear what she said because of that damned psychic thought-wall but I saw her intentionally pull her blouse open just enough for him to take another peek, which he did, the bastard! Again, I could feel his physical reaction and he was almost woozy with lust. It took everything he had (including the fact that he was in front of his own house) to not act on it right then and there.

I felt like I had been kicked in the chest, punched in the teeth, dragged through the mud. You name it, I felt it. I was woozy, myself, with jealousy. That bitch! That whore! That … that cunt! How *dare* she!

Then I heard my own voice, calling out, "*Stop right there!* Don't let her get to you. Melinda is manipulating you both! Are you going to let her win, or are you going to grab that rope to pull yourself through this?"

I shook myself back into the room with Me and asked, "What? What did you say?"

"While I'm sorry you had to experience that, this was a perfectly timed illustration of what I'm trying to tell you. You were absolutely centered and standing in your power. You were connected to the future you desire and heading straight for it."

I nodded to show I was following along but asked, disgruntled, "What do you mean, 'standing in my power'?"

She rolled her eyes and grinned, "It is an annoying expression, isn't it? It's New-Age-speak and, basically, it means that you felt like you were right where you're 'supposed' to be, no doubt about it, and you weren't going to be budged from standing your ground. You felt powerful."

I nodded my understanding and she continued, "Then, enter Melinda, stage right. You chose to place all your attention, all your consciousness, all your passion, on the scene playing out in your front yard. You jumped in, feet first, into a feeling that was entirely different from your desired future, which is exactly what she wants … you under *her* power."

"Oooh," I said as the light dawned.

"Now," she continued, "you can follow that path if you want. You could run outside and make a scene or you could start a fight with Chuck when he comes back in. Those and a thousand different other scenarios are yours for the choosing. But who's making that decision—you or Melinda?"

This was really making sense.

"So," she paused dramatically, "you can choose to stay connected to what you want your life to feel like. You can go downstairs and meet Chuck at the front door, treating him like you were feeling about him before Melinda flashed her sizable boobs at him. You can thank him for taking out the trash, and make him feel loved and welcome in his own home. Remember, *Melinda set him up*. He didn't seek a peek at her tits; she deliberately maneuvered the situation to control you both. You don't think she knows you were watching? That entire performance was for your benefit, not Chuck's."

My jaw dropped as it sunk in—Melinda is an evil genius.

"So?" she asked. "What are you going to do? Who's going to win?"

I immediately ran downstairs and met Chuck at the front door, just as I/she suggested. He was surprised and guilty to see me because he had an erection and didn't want me to know about it. I decided to use his discomfort to my advantage.

"Did you take the trash cans out?" I flirted, "Thank you, so much, my big strong man." I laid it on thick, teasing like I used to when we were younger.

He didn't know how to respond. Torn between his lust for our neighbor (that skank!) and his wife, who was suddenly acting strangely —again—he chose to just stand there, not reacting at all.

I remembered what Future Me had told me, upstairs, so I focused on how much I love this man and the warm way I was feeling for him, just a few minutes ago. I felt this outpouring of love soften my face and my heart. I put my arms out and hugged him around the waist ignoring, with gargantuan effort, the erection that pressed against me. "Have I told you lately how much I appreciate you?"

This was such a change from the way we had been acting toward each other recently that it was difficult for me to maintain, and he was obviously uncomfortable, too. He was deeply angry at me, for reasons in addition to what Melinda had been manipulating within him, so this was a difficult shift in gears for him as well.

Strengthening my resolve to concentrate on the future I want with him, I centered myself back into that sensation and said, "Look, I know that things are weird between us. I don't understand what's going on any better than you do, but I know we'll get through this. We always have, haven't we?"

I saw a flicker of conflict in his eyes. He was on the verge of letting me back in. I felt such relief. We were so close to losing a good thing.

Then, *she* showed up. That damned Melinda came to *my* door, where I stood with *my* husband, with her blouse not just unbuttoned, but with the button now missing. She must have pulled it off in the interim.

"I'm sorry to bother you," she simpered at me, pretending that we had just met—in actuality, this was the first time we talked face to face, "but do you have a needle and thread, and maybe some scissors I can borrow? I can't find my sewing kit and, as you can see, my button has come off. I'm afraid I just flashed your husband while he was helping me take my garbage can to the curb!"

She locked eyes with Chuck and gave him a smoldering look that sent him back over the edge of lust for her. I couldn't believe it but he pulled away from me, as if embarrassed to be caught hugging me! He looked straight down her top and said to me, "Why don't you run upstairs and get your sewing kit? It's the least a neighbor can do, right?" He couldn't wait for me to leave.

It took all the strength I had inside me to remember that she was using sorcery on him, that under normal circumstances this is not how he would be reacting, and that these were not normal circumstances.

Problem is, no matter how hard I tried, I simply couldn't win this situation. I don't know how to fight against someone so—I don't even know the right word for what she is—truly selfish and hateful, I guess. It goes against my upbringing. I was raised to be polite and not hurt people's feelings. I've never known how to react when others don't live by those same rules. I usually just retreat and let them win.

So, she won this one. I'm ashamed to admit that I went to get the sewing kit because I couldn't think of a way to say "no" without being rude in front of Chuck with no explanation. As far as he's concerned, she's just a neighbor in need of a favor and, as far as he knows, I have no idea what just happened across the street, other than what Melinda just told me. What good reason could I possibly have to not lend her some minor sewing supplies? Fortunately, I was only gone a short time. Not enough time for her to do too much damage, I hope.

I guess that remains to be seen.

Journal Entry 26

I'm not sure what I should be doing at this point. I don't know if there is even anything that I can be doing. I hate the "hurry up and wait" feeling that has become the undercurrent of my life. It's hard to decide what to do when there's no decision to be made.
I think that bothers me the most … the fact that I must wait for others to act before I can move forward with my life. Melinda, of course, is a prime example, but it's the same with pretty much everyone who is directly involved in my existence.

I'm not sure what I should be doing at this point. I don't know if there is even anything that I can be doing. I hate the "hurry up and wait" feeling that has become the undercurrent of my life. It's hard to decide what to do when there's no decision to be made.

I think that bothers me the most … the fact that I must wait for others to act before I can move forward with my life. Melinda, of course, is a prime example, but it's the same with pretty much everyone who is directly involved in my existence.

With Chuck, even though (as I've mentioned several times) we have a fairly equal relationship, he still feels like he's the one in charge. We had a conversation once about how some religions still believe that the wife must submit to her husband. I was laughing at how old-fashioned and out of touch with reality that mindset is, and he stunned me by saying that he believes that a wife should submit to the man! Flummoxed might be a good word to describe my response. I still have to fight the reflex to drop my jaw to the floor when I think about it. Submit? Me? When pigs fly!

He said that he believes that one person should be the ultimate decision maker. He says, under normal circumstances, a husband and wife are equal in a marriage, but when it comes to major decisions, the man should be the one to make them because the Bible says so and it just makes good sense. At that moment, I wanted to smack him in the head with a cast iron skillet. Isn't that convenient for him? I'm sure he wouldn't feel that way if he was the woman and I was the man!

What if the man is an idiot? What if his decisions end up spending the couple's earnings on popcorn and pony rides?

Plus, what about gay couples? Who makes the final call when there are two men in the equation? Do they never stop arguing? Do lesbian couples go their entire lives without ever making any decisions? Imagine the chaos! I thought about asking Chuck's gay brother, Derek, but how does one broach a subject like that?

Funny how a man who never goes to church feels free to pull out Scripture when it makes his life more pleasant.

I was infuriated to hear that my own husband feels this way and became even more determined to never submit to anyone. But then when I look at the history of our marriage, I can see that I usually do cave in and submit. Not because he's the man, however, but because he acts like a big baby and throws tantrums to get what he wants and I give in just to shut him up. Yeah, that's real manly behavior, isn't it?

Even Amanda runs her own show. She gets whatever she wants, for the most part. Being an only child, she's naturally spoiled rotten and is prone to tantrums. She's also learned to push my buttons and play on my guilt. She knows, because I was stupid enough to tell her—in what I thought was a moment of human bonding—that I'm terrified of making a mistake, of being a bad parent. The biggest mistake I made, long ago, was treating her like she was my friend, instead of my child. I wanted her to like me, so I let her get away with too much and now she walks all over me.

For crying out loud, even Ron, my boss, has more power over my life than I do! If I'm one minute late, or need time off for a doctor's appointment or whatever, he lays guilt trips and throws a tantrum.

Hey, that's the third time I've used that phrase: "throws a tantrum." I didn't realize how manipulated I've allowed myself to become. Is that all it takes? All someone has to do is throw a hissy fit for me to roll over? Am I that big a wuss?

Come to think of it, Twink is that way, too, and I don't care if she does kick me in the ear or fling pens at me! I said it! Twink can be a real brat sometimes!

I've got to do something about this. I can't ignore what I've just learned, that I'm a great big chicken and all anyone has to do to get their way is push me around because I want to be liked. How could I have gone so many years without realizing this?

Hold on a minute. Is that Amanda out front, talking to Melinda? It sure the hell is!

###

Well, that was certainly a prime example of "be careful what you wish for" (or should it be "be careful what you witch for"?) I wasn't even finished typing my thoughts about not being such a pushover when I was given an immediate opportunity to act on it. Good thing I was already fired up, or I don't know if I could have done what I just did.

That was Amanda out front, with Melinda. She was getting something out of the car and Melinda crossed the street to talk to her. All my fears about appearing irrational when dealing with Melinda in front of someone else flew out the window. I didn't care what Amanda thought because I knew that Melinda had threatened her safety, had exposed herself to my husband and was a serious menace to my happy home. Mess with my kid and I become a tigress!

So, I charged down the stairs and out the front door, asking, "Can I help you?" in what I hoped sounded like a stern voice. Melinda just looked up and smiled, pretending that there was nothing wrong.

Amanda turned toward me, smiling as well, "Have you met Melinda? She's lived across the street for months and this is the first time we've met! Isn't that weird?"

"Hi, neighbor," Melinda waved, cheerily.

"Yes, we've met," I said, civilly. No point in being obviously snotty if it wasn't necessary. I'm tired of having to come up with excuses for my seemingly odd behavior. "Amanda, don't you have homework to do?" I nodded my head toward the house and gestured for her to go inside. I could feel her desire to give me a fight but she didn't want to look immature in front of our neighbor, one she looked up to.

This tidbit of intuitive info dumbfounded me. Amanda looks up to Melinda? What the hell? Amanda and Chuck are both dazzled by her! What does this woman do to people to make them react like that?

"I was doing my homework but I left one of my books in the car. See?" She held up a textbook. Saying goodbye to Melinda, Amanda turned and walked in a deliberately adult fashion toward the house, instead of taking the steps two at a time like she normally would.

As soon as Amanda was inside I turned to Melinda, who was still smiling cheerfully at me. This chick deserves every acting award on Earth. I was fuming and couldn't hide it. "Do me a favor and stay away from my family," I said, through gritted teeth.

"Why on earth would I do that?" she laughed, almost flirtatiously, in a perfectly reasonable, relaxed tone. "I'm having *so* much fun with them. And I love having my own little puppet. All I have to do is talk to them and you start bouncing around on your little strings." She moved her hands in the air like she was working a marionette and laughed again, like a delighted child. Anyone watching from their windows would get the impression that she was the sweetest woman in the world and I was the crazy one. And I wouldn't blame them. She was entrancing.

Well, I may be new at the no-longer-a-pushover role, but she had pushed me hard enough. I pretended to be fierce when I smiled back and said, "Don't mess with me or you'll be sorry." In retrospect, I can see that it probably wasn't the scariest thing I could have said to her, but I'm a newbie. Give me a break.

I turned and walked toward the house, striding up the steps two at a time. I ignored her sweet call of, "Buh-bye, neighbor!" I refused to dignify it with a response.

Now that I'm typing it out, I can see that I wasn't very forceful. But at least I didn't cower and submit, right?

###

I just reread today's writings to make sure I didn't leave anything out, and was struck by something. I started out by talking about being unable to decide if there wasn't a decision to be made, and was immediately offered a decision: stand up for myself, or wuss out.

I'm beginning to see that "be careful what you wish for" is important to remember as a constant rule of thumb. I used to think it was one of those cute sayings one throws out occasionally, to explain a coincidence. I do have to start being careful what I wish for, because now that I'm writing things down, I'm seeing a pattern of almost immediate responses to my wishes.

That would be great, but most of the time they are wishes for things I don't want—they're just me grumbling and complaining, and then being rewarded with a real-world model of what I was moaning about.

God, I'm almost afraid to think. What kind of monster will I unleash next? Wait! Cancel, cancel, cancel! I'm not unleashing any monsters! I'm unleashing fluffy, cute little bunnies into Melinda's garden!

Journal Entry 27

Okay, this has gone too far. Melinda's garden is literally filled with rabbits. Even though I find it comical, I seriously was not wishing for her garden to be overrun by fuzzy, cute little bunnies.

I'm afraid to think! Is every little thing I allow to pass through my mind going to start happening like that? For crying out loud, do I have to learn how to be brain dead? Whoops, cancel that extreme example—do I have to learn to not think at all?

Isn't that what Buddhists do? I think they strive toward a state of nothingness, but I don't know what that means. Maybe this is it. Maybe I need to learn to not think.

Okay, this has gone too far. Melinda's garden is literally filled with rabbits. Even though I find it comical, I seriously was not wishing for her garden to be overrun by fuzzy, cute little bunnies.

I'm afraid to think! Is every little thing I allow to pass through my mind going to start happening like that? For crying out loud, do I have to learn how to be brain dead? Whoops, cancel that extreme example—do I have to learn to not think at all?

Isn't that what Buddhists do? I think they strive toward a state of nothingness, but I don't know what that means. Maybe this is it. Maybe I need to learn to not think.

###

Okay, tried it, it didn't work. All I kept thinking was that if I stop thinking, I stop being. The only thing that exercise did was increase my already high level of existential angst. Plus, the fact that I kept thinking about not thinking, and then thinking that I was thinking about not thinking was making me think and all I thought about was thinking. I feel like I've grown a tail and now I'm chasing it. It's like if someone says, "Don't think of a zebra." All you can think about is a zebra.

The whole time I was trying to think about not thinking, I kept hearing a distant voice echoing, “Be careful what you wish for,” so then I’d think about being careful what I wish for, and start freaking out about that, because what if I wish for something I don’t want, so I better not wish for anything, not even to not think because if I got that wish and stopped thinking, I’d die.

That’s when I finally said “screw it,” and gave up. Apparently thinking about not thinking is a shortcut to death, and who needs that, right?

Journal Entry 28

Even though I was completely turned off by the no-thinking experiment, the concept has been bouncing around in my head, coloring everything I do. I've been so busy thinking about not thinking that I haven't had it in me to write. Nothing much interesting happened anyway, other than one conversation I had with Twink, so there wasn't much to talk about except not thinking about having nothing to talk about.

At first, I was afraid to think about anything because I was somehow creating every scenario I thought about and it always ended up being in a way I didn't like. I spent a lot of time "canceling" thoughts that I didn't want to come true. If

Even though I was completely turned off by the no-thinking experiment, the concept has been bouncing around in my head, coloring everything I do. I've been so busy thinking about not thinking that I haven't had it in me to write. Nothing much interesting happened anyway, other than one conversation I had with Twink, so there wasn't much to talk about except not thinking about having nothing to talk about.

At first, I was afraid to think about anything because I was somehow creating every scenario I thought about and it always ended up being in a way I didn't like. I spent a lot of time "canceling" thoughts that I didn't want to come true. If I didn't, I would be immediately pelted with some unpleasant or uncomfortable situation, like someone was throwing darts at me, just for fun.

It did occur to me to wonder if Twink was behind this. I did call her a brat the other day, and that's never a good idea. So, I asked her. That's something the old Lola would never do, come right out and confront anyone. I pulled out my crystal and signaled my intent to communicate by holding it in my palm and thinking of Twink.

She instantly appeared and said, without my having to ask, "Nay, 'tisn't me causing yehr instant karma attacks, though I'd be justified, being such a *brat!*"

I had to laugh, because I could tell that—while she wasn't happy about my careless name calling—she wasn't too mad at me.

"I s'pose I owe yeh an apology," she said, "but just a wee one. I shouldn't have been so mean to yeh at first, but yeh don't know why I'm forced to be here. You'd be snippy, too, if yeh had to knock about in my clogs." With this, she flew in a lovely circle trailing faery dust in her wake, just to amuse herself.

"So, tell me what happened," I suggested. "I'll never know if you don't tell me, will I?"

"Point taken," she said. "Someday I'll tell the whole tale, but today I'll give yeh the short version."

I got comfortable, ready for a story.

"Yeh must understand," she sat on my desk and began, in her tiny, lilting voice, "you and I live worlds apart. What you humans think of as 'Faeryland' is not quite the way things really are. Here, in yehr world, yehr separate personalities run rampant and, in my world, we keep loyal to our clans. We're a collective. We each have our own thoughts, of course. We're not tied in together like a flock of birds or swarm of bees —but we're much more in tune with nature and, therefore, each other. Our physics ain't the same as yehrs, neither. It's as challenging for us to function in the human world as it is for you to do in ours."

"Well, like, what's so different?" I was intrigued.

"For example, yehr greed makes no sense to us. Humans, with yehr egos, seem capable of nowt otherwise. Yeh're always thinking 'me, me, me, mine, mine, mine.' Yeh read about this in yehr book on the Fae, yeah? I don't like everything the book says—it was, after all, written by a human," she said with a curled lip, "but that much, it got right."

I prepared to defend myself because I think I'm just the opposite. I'm too giving, and probably not egotistical enough. But she continued before I had a chance to interrupt.

"Yeh've probably read that yeh shouldn't accept food or drink in my land …"

I didn't remember reading that but it didn't matter. She was telling me, now.

"That much is true. When yeh eat or drink there, yeh're planting roots in our realm. Yeh're ingesting our physicality, yeah? Yeh become solid there from the inside out. Like tipping an hourglass, the sand gets heavier on our side than on yehrs. It gets harder for yeh to leave. Eventually yeh forget that yeh ever wanted to. Some never do."

This sounded like what I felt in the Rose Room. I briefly allowed myself to become such a part of how beautiful it was, and I was afraid that I'd never want to come back.

"So, what happened that made you come here?" I asked.

"Truly, it's a long story with many twists and turns, but the upshot is that …" she hesitated and shrugged, "… I were just having a little fun, toying with an obnoxious human who fancied himself a 'wizard' after reading too many books—somehow, he managed to cross through the veil. I were just trying to show him that he's not as clever as he thinks, so I set him up a challenge. He got stuck over there, didn't he? And now he can't leave, even though he wants to."

Her tiny face glowed red with frustration and her voice got a little louder, her accent thicker. "I were banished while Queen Jennett figures out how to get rid of him. I were forced to leave the realm and come work here for a while, to develop compassion for humans," she snorted. "The sooner I do that, the sooner I can go back. So, make all the mistakes yeh want. I'm here to forgive 'em."

I couldn't help laughing. Her logic was convoluted, to say the least. But at least now I understand why she's here and why she treats me with such contempt sometimes. She'll just have to get to know me. Like I said, my ego is not my problem. If anything, not having enough ego is what I need to work on.

Come to think of it, I wonder if my major malfunction is that I don't have a high enough opinion of myself. God, even writing that makes me feel like I must shrink back down and apologize for even thinking it.

That's worth thinking about, especially considering what I've come up with. During the last few days, when I've been playing with not thinking, I discovered an interesting phenomenon. After lots of practice, I reached a place that might be called Nothingness. Could this be what meditation is supposed to do? There was nothing there but me—no light, no dark, nothing to see, hear or feel. I just was. I was still thinking, because of the abovementioned fear of dying if I stopped, but the noise in my head finally quieted.

I didn't hear any mental chatter, no voices from the past telling me I'm not good enough, or not doing enough, or worries about the future with all the uncertainty in the world. I thought of none of that and just thought about being in that one, safe moment, where nothing bad was happening to me.

While I felt safe in that moment, when nothing bad was happening, I could further it one moment at a time because I was safe in this moment. Nothing bad was happening to me, right now. And if this moment is safe, then so is this one, and so is this one, and the next and the next for as long as I choose to sustain it.

I then realized that, as long as I consciously and deliberately continued to stay in that safe moment—because it's an exact duplicate, a flowing replication from each moment to the next—I would always be completely safe.

Therefore, the only way to create something that wasn't safe was to think about something unsafe—or become afraid that it won't last—and be instantly pulled toward a circumstance that reflected the fearful flavor I added to the formerly safe moment.

So, if I want to remain in a safe place, but add a different flavor, all I have to do is think in that direction and I will be magnetically pulled toward that circumstance. The lapse of time it would take for that to become physical is directly related to how strongly I believe it to be true. If I already feel it's one hundred percent true, I'm there, with no effort. If I feel it's only ten percent true, then I need to bring excited thought about that experience into my "safe" sphere of influence.

I feel like I'm talking in circles. I don't know if I'll even understand what I just wrote when I read it later, but it made sense as it was flowing out of me.

In essence, if I stay centered in the present moment, I am in control of my power. What I create will be my choice and my doing, but a purely ecstatic creation can only come from a place of no ego. Otherwise, whatever existential angst I'm thinking about will be included into the mix and the result will be no bueno.

It's like in the movie *The Fly*, when Seth Brundle gets into his teleporter by himself, he teleports just himself. But when he accidentally adds the fly into the mix the end result is Brundlefly, a horrible combination of him and something he didn't intend.

So, it's not that I shouldn't think, it's that when I am thinking, I need to make sure that it's conscious and deliberate, and focused on my clear intent or my result will be a hybrid of what I really want and whatever else I'm worrying about at the time.

The hard part, I think, will be remembering all of this. Old habits die hard. I must find ways to remind myself to remember.

Journal Entry 29

I saw Melinda talking to Amanda, again. Apparently, I wasn't scary enough for her. I'm going to have to ramp it up. Not that I have any idea what that even means, but there is no way I'm going to tolerate that heifer messing with my kid after I told her to stay away from my family.

I was just pulling up in front of the house after work and saw Amanda crossing the street, toward home, from Melinda's front yard just as Melinda was going in her front door. So, this time Amanda was over there.

As soon as we both were indoors, I let Amanda know that I didn't want her at Melinda's house. "She's too old for you to hang out with. She's at least ten years older than you."

I saw Melinda talking to Amanda, again. Apparently, I wasn't scary enough for her. I'm going to have to ramp it up. Not that I have any idea what that even means, but there is no way I'm going to tolerate that heifer messing with my kid after I told her to stay away from my family.

I was just pulling up in front of the house after work and saw Amanda crossing the street, toward home, from Melinda's front yard just as Melinda was going in her front door. So, this time Amanda was over there.

As soon as we both were indoors, I let Amanda know that I didn't want her at Melinda's house. "She's too old for you to hang out with. She's at least ten years older than you."

Instantly bristling, as she does any time I act like a good parent, she rolled her eyes and said, "Oh, Mom, age has got nothing to do with it. She's cool and she's got a great house, and a pretty cat named Onyx. She let me feed him."

"Don't blow me off," I answered, sternly. "She's too old for you. I don't trust her. I don't want you over there, and I don't want her over here." I couldn't say much more than that. What was I going to tell her, that Melinda is going through her to get to me? That Melinda has been flashing Daddy? That Melinda is psycho?

"Whatever," Amanda said, as she grabbed a bag of chips from the pantry and flounced out of the room. 'Whatever' is right. She can be as snotty as she wants, as long as she does what she's told.

Even so, I followed her to her bedroom, the one we so carefully redecorated just last summer to reflect that she is no longer a little girl but a young woman (even though she insisted on keeping it all pink and a few of her favorite stuffed animals are still hanging around). She threw herself face down on the bed, careful to not let her shoes touch the beautiful new bedspread. Instead of kicking her shoes off, she bent her knees and waved her feet in the air. "What?" she demanded.

"What's her house like?" I asked.

"I told you. It's cool. She's got a cat." She ripped open the bag of chips and began munching.

"But how is it decorated?" I don't know why I was asking this, except to keep the conversation going. She was in Melinda's house, talking to her. I wanted to know what they talked about.

"I don't know," she whined. "Nothing matches and it's kind of messy, but it's comfortable. You feel like you can put your feet on the furniture there." She gave me a sour puss, with that one. She was in a mood! Wow!

I dove right back in, though. Beating around the bush was getting me nothing but attitude. "What did you talk about?"

In exquisite teenage form, she screeched, "God! Leave me alone! We didn't talk about anything! She let me feed her stupid cat!"

My patience was at an end, so I shot back, "Oh, so she just opened her front door, you walked in, put your feet on her sofa and fed her cat. That's the entire story?"

"For crying out loud!" she said, "Her cat was in the yard and I was petting him! She came outside and invited me in to feed him. Happy?"

"You don't have to be so pissy, little miss," I said. "Just don't go over there anymore." I thought twice about leaving it at that, and continued, "And don't talk to her over here, either. Just stay away from her. There's something not right about her."

"Fine! God!" She grabbed the TV remote and turned it on, volume blaring.

Realizing this was going nowhere, I dropped it and left her to her hormone-driven little world. I made my point. I'll have to do something about this, above and beyond forbidding Amanda to talk to Melinda, but at least I've done something about it from this end. It has now been made clear that she is to have nothing to do with Melinda, even if she doesn't understand why.

Now if only I could make the same point with my husband.

Journal Entry 30

It may be too late to make that point with my husband. Oh God, I don't know what to do. He let his guard down, must have gotten lost in lust or something, but I just caught Chuck fantasizing about Melinda *while we were having sex!*

It was awesome sex, too, at first. He was on fire, like a wild man, and we were both going crazy on each other. I thought I would offer yet another olive branch toward healing the breach that has developed between us, so I made a deliberate effort to connect with him sexually, like I have learned to do—to make that soul mate connection. I allowed myself to enter his body, to feel what he was feeling, to think what he was thinking, to respond to him in a way that would make him insane with lust and desire for ME, his wife!

It may be too late to make that point with my husband. Oh God, I don't know what to do. He let his guard down, must have gotten lost in lust or something, but I just caught Chuck fantasizing about Melinda *while we were having sex!*

It was awesome sex, too, at first. He was on fire, like a wild man, and we were both going crazy on each other. I thought I would offer yet another olive branch toward healing the breach that has developed between us, so I made a deliberate effort to connect with him sexually, like I have learned to do—to make that soul mate connection. I allowed myself to enter his body, to feel what he was feeling, to think what he was thinking, to respond to him in a way that would make him insane with lust and desire for ME, his wife!

Instead I found him obsessing about Melinda flashing him, and how exciting and naughty that felt. And I was finally privy to what happened when I went upstairs for the sewing kit and left them alone. She pulled her top all the way open and said, "Quick, before she comes back, I want to feel your hands all over me." And he did it!

He felt her up! He reached inside her shirt with both hands and ran them over her skanky boobs, rubbing her stiffening nipples with his thumbs. Meanwhile, she reached down and grabbed his crotch, to give him a squeeze. And he was replaying this scene over and over in his mind, while he was having sex with me!

This hit me like a punch to the gut. He wasn't fantasizing, he was *remembering*! I almost threw up, right there in the throes of this raw, animal sex we were having. Dear God, what a betrayal! How could he?

I couldn't go on. I pushed him off me and pulled the sheet up to hide my body from him. I didn't want him even looking at me. She's younger, pretty in a weird way and obviously wants him. What better aphrodisiac for a middle-aged, married man?

He, of course, freaked out, shouting at me, "What the hell is the matter with you? What? *What?*"

I started crying, which I hated myself for. I didn't want to cry, I wanted to be pissed! I wanted him to apologize, to make it all better. I wanted him to have not groped her. I wanted this to not be real. I wanted him to hold me and be the old Chuck who used to laugh and joke with me, his best girl.

Instead, he got up, grabbed his robe and stormed off to the bathroom where, I'll wager, he finished things on his own. Me, I just lay there curled up in the fetal position, bawling my eyes out.

Now, I'm at my desk, still fuming and he's dead to the world, sound asleep. But I couldn't sleep. I'm way too upset. I can't believe he can sleep after all that, but sure enough, he's in there snoring his stupid head off. God, I hate him so much right now. I wish I could scream!

I can't obliterate the image of how turned on he was by her, how badly he wants to give it to her, the feeling of her heavy breasts in his hands, her nipples hardening at his touch, and how he was pretending that I was her. I don't know whether I want to kill him or myself. Or her!

All I keep thinking is how I wish none of this had ever happened. And why isn't that the thought that comes true??? That red-headed cow has turned my whole family against me! Even Amanda barely speaks to me anymore.

What am I going to do? I don't think Twink or Future Me or any of them can help me with this. After all, Future Me said that everything would be okay if I just kept focusing on being happy with Chuck. That's what I was trying to do and look what happened.

Hey, there goes a pen. Just a sec. Let me see what Twink wants.

###

I don't understand what has happened, but she has become so much nicer to me lately. At first I didn't like her, mostly because she obviously didn't like me, but I'm beginning to see a new side to Twink. She did help me to feel better.

She said, "Don't take any of this personally. Melinda enchanted Chuck by casting another spell. He's completely spellbound and she's started working on yehr bairn, Amanda."

After I recovered from my initial rage, I was relived because that explains the extra aloof behavior and dirty looks Amanda has been giving me. I couldn't understand why she was so snarly all the time and I chalked it up to teenage hormones. Who knew it was the witch across the street ensorcelling my husband and child?

I suppose I should have figured this out because Twink did tell me that I was Melinda's new project, and that she was working on distracting me so I wouldn't be in the way when she does the dirty deed at Raven's shop. It just never occurred to me that this is how she'd do it.

I asked Twink, "What about the protection spell I did with the sea salt? Wasn't that supposed to keep my home safe and sound?"

"Oh, aye," she said, "if yeh do it right and take it seriously, and if yeh're not battling summat like that cow! Her spells pack a bigger punch because she's so filled with rage. She means to harm yeh, no doubt about that."

That's when it really sunk in—I'm in over my head, big time, with these powers and Melinda is a pro. I'm afraid to use them and she pushes the envelope to see how far she can take them. This ramped up set of powers that we've both received is like a new toy for her.

When I tried the salt spell, I only thought of it as quaint folk magic and didn't believe it would do very much. Also, I performed it with an air of fear and desperation. That's exactly the result I got.

Meantime, crazy Melinda is across the street planning mass destruction. I'm totally out of my league here.

But Twink did make an excellent point. She reminded me, "When

Melinda received her powers, so did you, in equal measure. Yeh're as powerful as she is, yeh just don't know it."

So, apparently, the only thing that differentiates who is more powerful is the strength of the intent. Since Melinda is so angry and hateful, she has been able to overwhelm me because I haven't been pushed hard enough and because my "power" is being diluted by fear and disbelief.

Well, she may not realize it, but she has just officially pushed me hard enough. That witch wants a fight, I'll give her a fight. With a little help from my friends, that is.

Journal Entry 31

I just had another conversation with Twink, to follow up last night's. She informed me that Melinda assumes I'm finally too broken up about my broken home (she was apparently watching the whole scene last night, from inside Chuck) and therefore plans to go ahead with destroying Raven's shop. Tonight!
Just knowing that she was watching us from inside of him, probably laughing at me and my humiliation, makes me so furious I could strangle her! I swear to God, I could smack her with a spiked bat!

I just had another conversation with Twink, to follow up last night's. She informed me that Melinda assumes I'm finally too broken up about my broken home (she was apparently watching the whole scene last night, from inside Chuck) and therefore plans to go ahead with destroying Raven's shop. Tonight!

Just knowing that she was watching us from inside of him, probably laughing at me and my humiliation, makes me so furious I could strangle her! I swear to God, I could smack her with a spiked bat!

But vengeance must wait. I can't just sit back and let Melinda's plan to hurt Raven happen anymore. I know that I've said that very thing many times in the past, but I only half meant it. Circumstances have now reached a point of no return. Melinda may have stopped me from telling Raven before, but that was then, when I was afraid of her. I'm too angry to be afraid, now.

I called Raven and told her I need to talk to her on my way home from work (I'm on my lunch hour right now. Twink and I talked, for the first time while I'm at work, in the bathroom. Hey, if Ron can use it as a masturbatorium, I can use it as a faerytorium.).

Twink said she'd back me up on helping me to build a stronger protection wall, because mine have been amateurish. That way, I can talk to Raven without Melinda knowing or interfering. I've decided to tell her everything, no holds barred. All my lame excuses are obsolete and I'll be damned if that skanky ho is going to win.

Meantime I've got the rest of my lunch hour to kill. Ron is gone to a lunch meeting, so I can either play solitaire or plan what I'm going to say to Raven this evening. Maybe both. I think I'll go ahead and email this file to my home computer and I'll tell you what happens at Raven's when I get there.

###

Oh, my God. Raven wasn't there. She's in the hospital. She was hit by a car this afternoon after a lunch meeting, down on Chagrin Blvd. near the freeway. I've always hated driving in that area because the traffic is insane, so I'm not surprised that a pedestrian got hit. She'll be okay, thank goodness, but she's laid up for a few weeks.

This can't be a coincidence. What are the odds of her being hit by a car on the same day that Melinda plans to blow up her store? Is there no depth that Melinda will not sink to? Dear God! What kind of monster am I dealing with?

Even worse, I heard this news from Tammy, who works at the shop now! I didn't know that until today, because I haven't stopped in to visit Raven for a while, but Tammy applied for a job and Raven hired her!

If only I had found a way to tell her sooner. Now, she's laid up in a hospital bed, drugged, with the enemy working her cash register! If Melinda really does go through with this tonight, and Twink assures me she plans to be there at 1:00 AM, then she's got a wide-open field with an inside assist.

I need to gather my thoughts and my assets and make a plan. My assets are:

- I know what Melinda plans to do and when; she is, hopefully, unaware that I know and, therefore, isn't expecting any resistance from me—especially since she thinks I'm distracted.
- Twink has offered to help in whatever way she can.
- Melinda and I have equal powers and I'm fired up enough to try

using them.

- Future Lola has assured me that I'll know what to do and that I will succeed (even if I haven't a clue how!) as long as I keep my desired future in mind.
- I have the rose oil, which will help me power up, for lack of a better phrase. It will also help me to stay focused on the desired, loving outcome.
- I have the power of good on my side. (I don't know if that's really an asset, but it sure can't hurt!)

For now, I think it would be wise to go get some rest and prepare for tonight. Chuck and Amanda aren't home anyway. I don't even know where they are. I just have to hope that they will be okay and push forward, because as long as Melinda is allowed free reign, my family isn't safe.

I pray that this all works out.

Journal Entry 32

Oh, my God, it's over. It's really over. The fire trucks are gone and maybe now I can stop to take a breath. The sun is coming up and I want nothing more than to go to bed, but I know that I should write this all down while it's still fresh in my mind. At least I showered and changed my clothes. They reeked of smoke and gasoline.

It's bizarre how still everything is now, after such chaos. No birds are singing—it's as if Nature has been thumped into stunned silence. Even so, it's a beautiful, sunny morning. The contrast is almost laughable.

Oh, my God, it's over. It's really over. The fire trucks are gone and maybe now I can stop to take a breath. The sun is coming up and I want nothing more than to go to bed, but I know that I should write this all down while it's still fresh in my mind. At least I showered and changed my clothes. They reeked of smoke and gasoline.

It's bizarre how still everything is now, after such chaos. No birds are singing—it's as if Nature has been thumped into stunned silence. Even so, it's a beautiful, sunny morning. The contrast is almost laughable.

I didn't get any sleep last night before heading out, which isn't surprising. Who could sleep knowing what lay in store? So I meditated, or tried anyway. Mostly I prayed for guidance.

Wait, come to think of it, I must have dozed off because Twink woke me up at midnight. Chuck was sound asleep next to me. I forgot about that. Oh well, no matter.

I left the house at about 12:30 (the shop is only a few minutes away), quietly sneaking out of the house to my car. Melinda's house was dark and her Camaro wasn't parked out front, so I assumed she was already gone. I wanted to beat her there, so that was disappointing, but at least I knew in advance to watch out for her in the vicinity.

I still had no idea what I was going to do when I got there and this drove me crazy—I much prefer to plan things, especially dangerous things, in advance. All of my meditating and praying didn't help me to formulate that plan. All I kept getting was an image of Future Me saying, "You'll know what to do when the time comes." Big help, right?

I parked a couple blocks away from Karma Korner and walked down the side streets to scope the place out from a distance, to see if I could spot Melinda before she saw me. Oddly, I finally saw the antique shop again! Doesn't that figure, that I find it when it's closed? But it reminded me of the rose oil and pendant, which gave me strength.

I took it as a sign that I'm getting close to earning my sparkling up-level badge. I made a mental note of the location so I could find it again in the daylight and continued toward Karma Korner.

I found a recessed shop doorway across the street and a couple doors away so I ducked inside to hide. It was so quiet I could hear the waterfall, blocks away, that the town of Chagrin Falls is named for.

Eventually, I saw the two dark figures from my long-ago dream, both wearing black hoodies and dark pants. The rush of déjà vu was almost overwhelming. The taller one was pulling something out of the trunk of Melinda's red Camaro, which was parked a few doors down from the shop in the other direction from me.

I had no doubt it was Melinda and Tammy. I would recognize them anywhere, even cloaked in black with their faces obscured. I don't know if that would hold up in a police line-up, but I knew it was them—big, beefy Melinda with her crazy red hair poking out the sides of her hood and scrawny little Tammy, pushing stray strands of long, blond hair back under her own hood.

I reached into my pocket to make sure that I hadn't left my Twink-o-phone crystal in the car. It was there, so I gave it a squeeze and called her. She was there, instantly, floating over my right shoulder.

The faery dust that she's always surrounded in let off a beautiful glow, so I whispered, "Won't they see you?"

"Nah," she said, "Melinda can't see me. Didn't I just spent the past few weeks snooping around her house?"

We got quiet and went back to watching. I was so scared that I thought I might pee my pants. I should have gone before I left the house, I know, but I wasn't thinking about that at the time.

Part of me was petrified that all hell was about to break loose, and another part desperately wanted to get it over with. I thought, this must be what soldiers feel like right before they go into battle, when they hear the first rumblings of enemy gunfire and know there is no turning back now. Let's just rip off the damned bandage and do it.

Tension kept me on my toes as Twink and I watched from across the street. Melinda and Tammy approached the shop, each holding a bottle of gasoline with a rag wick. I heard Melinda say, in a stage whisper, "Be careful once you light it. Don't drop it, or you're dead. The gas will catch fire and you'll be standing in a puddle of flames. Just throw it straight at the center of the window and run like hell, that way." She gestured in the opposite direction from the one her car was facing. "I'll hop in the car and pick you up around the block."

Tammy only nodded dumbly. She had to be dumb because even I knew Melinda was going to drive off without her. Maybe she had cast a spell over Tammy, too.

They both stepped into the center of the street to get a little further from the store window, but they moved a little too close to me for comfort. I ducked back further into the shadow of the doorway. I heard a lighter clicking and Melinda swearing, "Damn it! My lighter won't work. Give me yours."

Tammy reached into the pocket of her hoodie and handed Melinda a lighter. Just as she was lighting it, Twink whispered, "You take Tammy, I'll take care of Melinda." God, I was so relieved the she offered to take the big one. I could take care of Tammy. Melinda, not so much.

Melinda lit her wick and quickly handed the lighter back to Tammy. She drew back her arm like a baseball pitcher, preparing to throw the bottle, when Twink yelled, *"NOW!"*

Now … what? I didn't know what Twink expected me to do so I screamed like a lunatic and ran at Tammy to tackle her. She was fumbling with the lighter and hadn't managed to light her wick. As I plowed into her, knocking her to the ground, I saw a huge flash of light and heard the heartbreaking sound of shattering glass. Melinda had succeeded—she had broken the window and the bottle of gasoline exploded.

But wait. No. The window wasn't broken. The sound of breaking glass was just the bottle shattering. It had bounced off the window and landed on the sidewalk in front of the shop, where it broke. The gasoline had spilled all over and the front of the building was engulfed in flames.

Tammy's bottle hadn't been lit, but it did break when the two of us hit the ground. Both of us were splashed with gasoline and I panicked, knowing I had to get the hell out of there or I was going to go up in flames as well. Just as I got up to run, pulling Tammy with me, I saw flashing red lights, through the smoke, and heard the sirens of several police squad cars as they screeched up in front of the store. They were closely followed by fire trucks.

Escaping from the flames was too important for me to, rationally, consider what the police would assume when they saw me running from them. I was only worried about not burning up but, as far as they knew, I was a fleeing arsonist. I heard Tammy's voice, shouting, "There they are, officers, you're just in time!"

I don't even know what thoughts were running through my mind other than *'What the hell?'* but I heard several authoritative voices commanding, "Freeze!"

I froze.

An officer grabbed me from behind and hustled me away from the flames. He forced my hands behind my back to handcuff me when I heard Tammy say, "Not her, officer, she was trying to stop them."

The cop looked unsure about what to do, so he led me to a police car and put me in the back seat. Just then, I saw Melinda's car tearing away, squealing the tires. Two of the three police cars took off in hot pursuit, as the fire department personnel hosed down the storefront.

My mind reeled with confusion. Tammy was here, next to the squad car, talking to the cop who put me in the back seat. But his partner was over there, leading the girl who I thought was Tammy back toward us. If Tammy was over here, explaining to the officer that I shouldn't be arrested, then who was that?

The second officer pulled off the girl's black hood, and scolded, "You're lucky you didn't burn up, little lady!" The girl burst into tears. So did I. It was Amanda.

###

I had to stop writing because I was too emotional to go on. It was a horrible scene and I hope to never go through anything like that again, to see my poor little girl so scared and confused. It made me sick to think of how Melinda had used her.

Thank God, once again, for Tammy. I had no idea she had turned against Melinda. All this time, I thought she was plotting with her against Raven, when she was actually working to save her. She called the police and told them about Melinda's plan (my idea, too, remember?). She showed up at the same time they did, to watch.

She knew that Amanda had been bewitched, and that no one would believe her if she said so. So, she told the police that Melinda had threatened to harm Amanda if she didn't help. It was a lie (or was it?), but I'm grateful for it anyway.

Amanda was crying too hard to talk to the police, so she didn't say anything to implicate herself and I have watched enough cop shows to know that you don't say a word without a lawyer, especially if your story includes witches and faeries.

I'm sure Twink must have manipulated the officers somehow (I'll have to ask her later) because they let us go home after only delaying us for a short while. But we never anticipated the scene that awaited us when we got here!

We pulled up and found our own street filled with more fire trucks. Melinda's house was on fire! I don't have any idea what happened, but I heard a fire department official tell the TV news crews who gathered in my front yard this morning that they suspected arson, in connection with another fire downtown, last night. The air reeked of gasoline and Melinda was nowhere to be found.

Chuck was just coming out the front door to watch—the sirens woke him up—when we pulled up. He started to angrily ask where the hell we had been, but watching a house burn down was more interesting so he dropped it, weirdly. We'll talk later, after I get some sleep.

In retrospect, I'm a little surprised that I didn't use any magical powers while playing the superhero. That's what I thought I was gearing up for!

Wait, Twink is whispering in my ear. She's saying, "Who says you weren't using your power? You were standing in it!" So that's what that stupid expression "standing in your power" means! Perhaps not so stupid, after all.

Journal Entry 33

It's been about a week since I've written anything. It feels good to not have to write anymore. The problem is solved, the show is over, life goes on.

Well, maybe not exactly over—I still have the extreme psychic abilities and I still wish they'd go away—but the crisis has certainly passed. Melinda is history and all is well. No one knows where she is, but it's obvious that she skipped town. The police and arson investigators are assuming that she set her own house on fire to destroy any evidence before she skedaddled, or to distract anyone from following her for a while. Personally, I have a gut feeling that she did it out of pure spite, but they can't put a gut feeling in a police report.

It's been about a week since I've journaled. It feels good to not have to write anymore. The problem is solved, the show is over, life goes on.

Well, maybe not exactly over—I still have the extreme psychic abilities and I still wish they'd go away—but the crisis has certainly passed. Melinda is history and all is well. No one knows where she is, but it's obvious that she skipped town. The police and arson investigators are assuming that she set her own house on fire to destroy any evidence before she skedaddled, or to distract anyone from following her for a while. Personally, I have a gut feeling that she did it out of pure spite, but they can't put a gut feeling in a police report.

They've released her name and photo to the news outlets and other law enforcement agencies. She's all over the internet. They say it's only a matter of time before they pick her up … because she's not a career criminal, she'll probably make a mistake before too long and get caught.

I disagree. She's smarter than they realize and she's probably on the other side of the country right now, lying on a beach somewhere.

It's strange looking out my window at the burned-up rubble where Melinda's house used to be. Work crews can't get started yet because it's a crime scene. It's such a huge mess that it may be a while before it's all cleaned up.

Neither Chuck nor Amanda has much memory of what happened. I don't know if that's because of traumatic shock or because they were entranced. Perhaps it's a combination of both. I may never know for sure, because we don't talk about the elephant in the room. I'm just happy to have my family back and that maniac outta here.

It's funny how the people at work are treating me now. I was all over the news for a couple days: "Housewife Defeats Arsonist" was the headline in the News Herald. Twink was a miffed that I got all the glory but I was irked that they called me a housewife.

And get this! Ron is treating me with a little respect! Is it because I've decided to not take his crap anymore, or because he's afraid I'll tackle him and bring him down, too? Either way, it's fine with me. I finally realize that I don't need him or his lousy job to feel like I'm contributing to the world. "Standing in my power" feels good.

In fact, I turned in my notice and I'm looking for a new job. I'm not comfortable at the office anymore. I've changed too much, and no one there knows how to act around me. I'm not the same Lola they knew, or I knew, for that matter. I think it's time for a fresh start, a clean slate, with people who don't know who I used to be.

Raven is on the mend, thank God, and the shop was undamaged because it's a brick building and the window was never broken, just a little scorched. The decorative paint bubbled and peeled off so the beautiful window needs to be repainted, which is a doggone shame.

I visited Raven in the hospital and told her my whole story, even about Twink. She was scandalized when I told her that I was calling Twink by that name, and said, "You call a Wee One by a name like Twink? When she has such a glorious Faery name?" (I could tell by the way she emphasized those words that they should be capitalized.)

"I tried, but I couldn't pronounce it!" I emphatically defended myself, "She has such a thick accent and it's such a weird name. I didn't see what the big deal was but, boy howdy, was she fuming!"

She burst into laughter, holding her ribs and wincing at the pain the exertion caused, and said, "I'll bet!"

"In fact," I forced myself to admit, "speaking of names, I must confess that I'm uncomfortable calling you 'Raven Starcloak', when I know that your real name is probably something normal, like Mary

Smith." I quickly added, just in case, "No offense."

"None taken," she said, shifting in her bed. "But, have you honestly never heard of a Craft name?"

I shook my head, 'no'.

"Think of it this way," she explained. "One's preferred name is an expression of their true self and to deny someone's name is the same as denying their existence. You told me, long ago, that you can't stand your given name, that Lola is the nickname you prefer. I changed my name to Raven for the same reason you changed yours from Dolores to Lola. My birth name didn't fit me anymore. Doesn't that make sense?"

"Of course, it does," I acquiesced. I felt petty for making fun of her, here in my journal, but at least she never knew about it. Fortunately, she's not that psychic.

"Now that you mention taking offense," she said, "poor 'Twink' is probably reeling with insult every time you call her that. You really ought to learn how to pronounce her name."

I asked Twink about it later, and she confirmed that this was one of the reasons she didn't like me much at first, because I started out our relationship disrespecting her so greatly. She said that eventually, however, she realized that I'm just a 'stupid human' so she cut me some slack. How very … generous … of her.

I agreed to try to learn to pronounce her name, and she agreed to allow me to continue calling her Twink, as a sort of a term of endearment. (Thank God, because I don't know if I'll ever be able to wrap my tongue around all those twisty syllables!)

I also asked her, "Why didn't either of us use our powers to battle Melinda—I mean, aside from 'standing in it'—after all that build up?

She rolled her eyes at me and said, "Speak for yehrself! D'yeh think that window stayed unbroken from sheer luck? That blast of light yeh saw weren't flames, it were from me and my wand. I changed the window into shatterproof glass, didn't I?"

I'm half tempted to ask Raven if the window was already shatterproof, but I guess it doesn't matter in the end, does it?

I never got a chance that night to thank Tammy for her help. She quit working at Karma Korner as soon as Raven got out of the hospital and came back to the shop. I think Tammy went back to work at the library. She told Raven she wants nothing more to do with hocus pocus. Next time I see her, I owe her a big hug.

Whoops, I have to get going. I didn't realize it was getting so late, and I want to try to find that antique store again and pick up that pendant. I have finally saved up enough money and, besides, I've earned it, don't you think?

Journal Entry 34

I found the antique shop with no problem, this time. How weird is that? Every time I've tried to find it before now I either got lost or turned around, or it just wasn't there where I thought it would be. But today, I found it with no effort at all, on the first try. Maybe that means it's finally time for me to own that pendant, like it really is a reward for leveling up.

Of course, I did make that mental note of its location the night of the fires, when I saw the store after hours, but something tells me that, even so, I wouldn't have been able to find the shop before it was the right time. I was almost ready, but not quite, or it would have been open when I saw it again.

I found the antique shop this time. How weird is that? Every time I've tried to find it before now I either got lost or turned around, or it just wasn't there where I thought it would be. But today, I found it with no effort at all, on the first try. Maybe that means it's finally time for me to own that pendant, like it really is a reward for leveling up.

Of course, I did make that mental note of its location the night of the fires, when I saw the store after hours, but something tells me that, even so, I wouldn't have been able to find the shop before it was the right time. I was almost ready, but not quite, or it would have been open when I saw it again.

The shop owner was such a hoot. She recognized me, which was kind of nice. She must have seen me approaching from my car because she came rushing out of the back room of the store, teetering on her stiletto heels, as soon as I opened the door, with the pendant in her hand.

"I hope you're here to claim this beauty!" she gushed.

Once again, I felt a wave of physical desire—like I just had to possess it—as soon as I saw the pendant. The way it caught the light and dazzled, it simply took my breath away. "Yes," I said, "I'm here to finally claim my prize."

"Well, honey, I am so happy it's you who gets to take it home. It suits you." She got busy writing up a receipt as I pulled out my wallet.

After I paid for it, she helped me put the chain around my neck by holding my hair up so I could fasten the clasp. "Isn't that just perfect?" she asked, as I admired myself in a gilt-framed mirror she had hanging on the wall.

"It is!" I said, and thanked her again for setting it aside for me. She gave me a warm hug before I left. What a nice person! This whole experience with her has been wonderful.

I took the pendant off once I got home and it's sitting here on my desk, right in front of me, as I type. I almost don't want to wear it because then I can't see it. It's so gorgeous that I just want to watch it sparkle. If I hold it up to the setting sun—which I can see through the window—it looks like a mini kaleidoscope.

This is strange, feeling so drawn to a piece of jewelry. I feel like it's a part of who I am and it has finally come home. It's soooo pretty! I'm going to take it off the chain it came with, though, because that one is far too short. It's too close to my neck and I like a longer chain.

I have a long silver chain that I can use, which will bring it down to the center of my chest, where I prefer. That way I can tuck it under a shirt, if I want, or lift it on its chain and stare into it in the light. The clasp on the longer chain is difficult to work—it's one of those fasteners that you need strong fingernails and good vision to open—but the chain is long enough that I can slip it over my head, with a little effort.

###

Well, that was strange. Chuck just came into my office and beckoned me to the window. "Come here," he said, gesturing urgently. "When did that happen?"

I got up and hurried to his side, curious as all get out. What on Earth could possibly be wrong now? All I saw, when I looked where he was pointing, was the same old burned-out mess in Melinda's yard. "When did what happen?" I asked.

"That!" He pointed again.

"What?"

"You don't see that the house across the street has burned down?"

he asked, incredulous, as if I had gone blind, or insane.

I narrowed my eyes and peered into his, tapping in to his psyche. He had no protective wall up. He didn't need one. He honestly didn't remember anything about the fires or Melinda, or my wild psychic abilities, and felt no need to be defensive. He was genuinely puzzled that something as obvious as the house across the street burnt to the ground had escaped my notice.

What bothered me even more than the realization that he didn't remember the night when our world literally exploded, was that he also didn't remember seeing the charred rubble every day since then.

Then, it got worse. He called to Amanda, "Honey, come in here!"

"What do you want? I'm busy!" she whined from her bedroom.

"Come here and I'll show you," he said, more sternly than before.

"Fine!" Amanda came slumping into the room, passive aggressively displaying her pique at being pulled away from whatever important thing she was doing in there. "What do you want?" she asked again.

"Look out the window! The house across the street has burned down. You didn't notice?"

Interested now, she rushed over. I stepped back to my desk so there was room for her next to him. "No!" she exclaimed, "Oh, my God, when did that happen!?"

Shaken and dismayed, I watched them gabbing about their 'news.' When they had shown signs of mild amnesia immediately after the fires, I wasn't worried. We were all in shock, and they had both been under Melinda's spell, so it was no big surprise that they might not remember everything. Even Raven said so. But I thought that would fade as time passed and that their memories would begin to come back. Instead, the amnesia was getting worse.

I had incorrectly assumed that we weren't talking about what had happened because we all silently agreed to put it behind us and not bring up everyone's horrible behavior. But that wasn't the case at all. They literally didn't remember, and couldn't retain any new memories about the fires, since then.

"Ewwwwww!" Amanda squealed. "He killed it!"

I hurried back to the window and asked, "Who killed what?"

Chuck pointed across the street again to Melinda's yard. "That cat. It nabbed a squirrel just as it was about to leap onto the tree and get away. You should have seen it. What a hunter!"

It was Melinda's cat, Onyx, tearing into that poor squirrel, its tail still twitching. "Oh God!" I said, and covered my eyes. "I can't watch."

"That is one hungry cat," Chuck said.

"Awww," Amanda crooned, "the poor thing. Thank goodness, he didn't get killed in the fire! I'm gonna go make sure he's okay."

She turned to leave the room but I stopped her and said, "Oh no, you're not, young lady! Don't you go anywhere near that house!"

She looked at me like I was crazy then turned to Chuck. "Dad, tell her to let me go! I just want to make sure he's not hurt."

Thank God, he backed me up. "No, your mom's right. It's not safe over there. See the caution tape? We'll take care of it. Don't worry."

"Oh, alright," she moaned and stomped back to her room, muttering, "You guys never let me do anything."

"Thanks," I said to him. "Should we bring him something to eat?"

It was his turn to give me the stink-eye. "Pffft! No." He pivoted and left the room. "That cat'll be fine on its own. They're born hunters," he said, his voice trailing down the stairs behind him.

I shook my head at both of them and looked out the window again. As much as I hated Melinda and everything about her, I did feel bad for that poor creature. It wasn't his fault he belonged to a psychopath. He had devoured as much of the squirrel's meat as he could find and now lay on the grass with the carcass between his front legs, licking it clean. He was, clearly, starving.

And then I thought, what kind of person torches their own house and leaves their pets behind to starve? I sincerely hoped that—bare minimum—she made sure to let the cat out of the house before she lit it up and was immediately granted a vision of Onyx escaping the flames through the cat hatch, which was built into the kitchen door. So, no, wretched Melinda didn't even bother to make sure her pet was safe, first. I didn't think I could hate her any more than I already did, but I have found within me a new depth of disgust for her.

###

I waited until Chuck and Amanda went to bed and went across the street with something for the cat to eat. I had emptied a can of tuna onto a paper plate and brought some water in a disposable storage bowl. The street light partially illuminated her property, so I could see where I was going as I ducked under the caution tape, but there were a lot of shadows in the yard from the trees and what was left of the skeleton of the house.

It was creepy and I entered the yard with the tape's advised caution so, when the cat leapt out at me from behind a bush, I screamed a little and almost dropped the plate of tuna.

Onyx snaked around my ankles, purring and yowling. I was his new best friend. I set the food and water down, and he dove into the fish right away, gulping it down so fast that he made choking sounds.

As he finished the food and turned to the water bowl, I heard Chuck's voice from across the street. He had opened the bedroom window and was calling to me, "Lola! What are you doing over there?"

I shushed him—it was late and the neighbors were probably sleeping—and gave him a one-finger 'just a minute' gesture before heading back across the street.

I found him back in bed when I got upstairs, waiting for me. "What were you doing?" he asked again.

"Just making sure the cat's okay," I said. "I know you said to forget about it, but I couldn't just leave it there to starve," I explained, as I put on my nightgown and climbed into bed.

"What cat?" he yawned.

I sighed and said, "Never mind. We'll talk about it in the morning," knowing that, by then, he would have forgotten about it. Again. Once he fell asleep, which didn't take long, I got back up to type up these notes. I get the feeling the I'll need to keep track of and pay careful attention to the chain of events again, because the devil is in the details. Literally.

Journal Entry 35

Sure enough, Chuck didn't remember anything about the house fire, or the cat killing the squirrel, or even me feeding Onyx last night. And now, I'm not just worried, I'm getting scared. What the heck is going on?

I tried calling Twink with my crystal but she didn't answer. Then I tried to deliberately tune in to whatever etheric bank of psychic information might be out there–using the half awake/half asleep method–to see what I could see. Nothing. Bupkis. Nada. I'm not surprised, though. I don't even know if I can do that or, if I can, that I'm doing it right.

Sure enough, Chuck didn't remember anything about the house fire, or the cat killing the squirrel, or even me feeding Onyx last night. And now, I'm not just worried, I'm getting scared. What the heck is going on?

I tried calling Twink with my crystal but she didn't answer. Then I tried to deliberately tune in to whatever etheric bank of psychic information might be out there—using the half awake/half asleep method—to see what I could see. Nothing. Bupkis. Nada. I'm not surprised, though. I don't even know if I can do that or, if I can, that I'm doing it right.

Finally, I called Raven and asked if I could set up a Tarot reading with her. I need help and I'm willing to pay for an uninterrupted chunk of her time and occult knowledge. She's still on crutches, but she told me she's well enough to do readings again.

I've never had a Tarot reading before, so I didn't know what to expect. I was a little spooked by the idea because, as I've already said, I was always taught that you should stay away from Tarot cards.

I was nervous, even after Raven's explanation that the cards are just a tool to help an intuitive person explain the otherwise unnamable energy patterns of one's current life-stream.

It didn't make sense when she explained it that way, but I understood better when she suggested that I recall the dream I had about the dancing cloud, so long ago. At the time, I had no idea what that dream was or what the dancing cloud represented. But now that I've lived into the future long enough, I can see that even though the cloud was meaningless to me when it was a current energy pattern, now I have a story to help define what it was—a mass of pure potential energy, like raw clay just waiting to be molded.

That's what the cards do, in advance of the future. You don't need to wait to live out the story to know what current patterns mean. The pictures on the cards help to tell a metaphorical story in a way that the psychic and the client can understand—even if the exact details aren't the same, the pattern that plays out will be.

When I asked her, again, to reassure me that it's not evil, she said, "It's not much different from intending to ask 'God' a question and opening a book to a random page to see what kind of answer you get. It's a matter of who you're asking to speak with. When you ask for a divine connection, whether it's Tarot cards or using a book as an oracle, you're asking the Divine Spirit for help and guidance. I have many Christian friends who use the Bible like this, all the time. How can that possibly be evil, especially if you're not using the information to hurt anyone else?"

After that reassurance, I asked for an appointment and she was able to fit me in today, after juggling her schedule a little. I just got home. I want to type out as much as I can recall while it's still fresh in my mind. I scribbled out some notes at the time, longhand, but I can barely read my own writing.

I don't know what any of the Tarot cards mean but she said the Queen of Swords indicated that Melinda was the cause of Chuck and Amanda's continual memory loss. She couldn't see how Melinda was doing it but the next card showed it was something physical that Melinda had in her possession which used to belong to them.

Raven told me that Twink would be playing a role in the never-ending Melinda saga, so I shouldn't worry that she's not responding—she'll show up when she's needed.

Then Raven said something that scared the life out of me. She said several of the cards indicated that I was going to be tested—physically, mentally, and spiritually. Because so many of the cards delivered that same message, she had no doubt that's what they meant. And because quite a few of them were upside down, she said, it's not going to be easy.

I'm so over this. I don't want to be tested anymore. I've been through enough already! Knock it off, please God?

Seriously, I just want my normal, boring life back. I didn't sign up for this, and I'm sick and tired of these psychic shenanigans. Why can't that lunatic just leave me and my family alone, and go away? I'm willing to let bygones be bygones. Why can't she?

Looking out the window, I see Onyx across the street laying near the rubble, apparently waiting for his owner to come for him. It breaks my heart. I almost want to go get him and bring him home with me but, to be quite honest, I've had enough of Melinda's pussy in my life.

Sorry, I know that was supremely crude, but it's true. I hope that I never experience her in my bed, in my husband's head, again. I don't know if I've ever felt so hurt. Thank God I know now that it was all her doing, and that Chuck was just her puppet, just like she said I was, that day out in front of my house, when she pretended to play me like a puppet on strings. She's quite the puppet master.

Hey! A pen just flew off my desk! Back in a mo'.

###

It wasn't just a pen that landed on the floor. There was a book on the floor, too, over by the bookshelf and the pen rolled all the way across the floor until it stopped near the book. The pen was pointing right at it. It was the book about witchcraft that I bought when this whole thing began, and it had somehow ended up on the floor.

I remembered Raven telling me that sometimes answers can come to you just by opening a book to a random page, so I did that. I decided on a generic question, because there were far too many specific questions to choose from. "What do I need to know?" I asked, and flipped the book open.

Right there, on page 67, a word caught my eye: poppet. I was literally just typing about Chuck being her "puppet" when the pen flew off my desk. I continued reading and saw that a *poppet* is sort of like a voodoo doll, and it can be made from all sorts of different materials. As I read, I started getting those mini lightning bolt flashes of a vision, but the vision kept flickering in and out so I put the book down and focused.

I closed my eyes and concentrated on tuning in. It felt like I was turning a radio knob in the center of my brain—I heard static and "saw" the kind of snow you see on a no-signal TV channel. I realized that, as I tried to mentally tune in to the channel that carried the vision I had been briefly shown, my eyeballs were rolling back and forth and this gave me the idea to use them as my "fingers" on the radio knob. As I moved my eyes slowly and deliberately, I found that the signal was getting stronger or weaker, depending on how I moved them.

I got so excited with this new discovery that I accidentally overshot the signal with too much eye rolling, so I had to go back and fine tune it again. Finally, I locked in on the scene I was looking for and I saw Melinda holding three rudimentary dolls, each made of white tube socks.

Then the vision fizzled and changed, even though I was holding my eyes still. This wasn't my doing. I saw that she had two of the poppets lying on a bed with a tacky green bedspread. It looked like a hotel room, with the heater/air conditioner unit under a wide window with heavy, blackout curtains. I also saw a dresser with one of the drawers open and clothes hanging out of it. What a slob she was. Anyway, those two dolls had snippets of hair—one blond, one auburn—attached to their heads, almost obscured by a piece of cloth tied around each of their faces, which covered their eyes and ears.

She was about to tie a strip of cloth around the third doll's head. I didn't see any hair glued to that doll. Then the vision went blank, as she covered that doll's eyes and ears, as if the TV I was watching the scene on had been turned off.

I'm assuming that the first two dolls are for Amanda and Chuck, and the third doll must represent me. Otherwise, it's an amazing coincidence for the vision to stop flowing at the exact moment that the third doll's face was covered. And didn't one of the light-beings I talked to say that there is usually no such thing as coincidence?

Because I could no longer see nor hear inside her hotel room, and I wasn't done snooping, I tried something new. I tried to feel into the scene I was just watching. I pretended that I was inside the blindfolded doll and used my other senses. After all, they say that the other senses become heightened when we lose access to one of them. I had lost two, so my other senses might be in hypersensitive-mode.

First thing I noticed was the intense hum of the air conditioner. I didn't hear it, because my "ears" were covered, but I felt the vibration. I recognized it because this is one of the things I dislike about staying in hotels, the disruptive presence of a compressor in such close proximity. I felt this way before I became so sensitive, so I can't even imagine how it would feel now.

The more I vibed into the hum, the more it rattled my bones, so I pulled my attention back a little until I was more comfortable with the level of the buzz. I did this by rolling my eyes back, as if I was pulling back on the throttle in a cockpit. I was having a lot of fun learning to use my eyes like this, to steer the experience.

Then I felt the cool air blowing out of the AC unit on my sock doll's "skin", for lack of a better word, and I smelled the room funk. Just like all hospitals smell the same, so do hotel rooms, but this one was also old and musty. I knew now, for a fact, that she was in a hotel—not that this information helped much. She could be anywhere in the world.

So, I decided to expand the sensory experience to see if I could figure out her location. By using my breath, I pretended that I was enlarging the doll, like inflating a balloon. With every in-breath, the doll got larger and larger, until it was too big to fit into the room. I visualized the doll growing beyond the physical structure of the building, its molecules passing right through the empty spaces between the building's molecules.

Soon, I was outside of the hotel, my essence no longer contained by the doll, but I was still unable to see or hear. My consciousness was there, above the building in which she was staying. That much I could feel. I sensed a lot of water nearby. Her hotel room was right next to a pool, or perhaps even a lake.

Then I got it. Just like that, in a flash of insight with no reasoning behind it, I knew she was near Lake Erie. She hadn't gone far … she was up in Cleveland—no, it was further east than that, but somewhere right along the shore, in some lakeside motel with beach access. I wasn't getting enough information to nail her exact location, but at least I knew she was still in northeast Ohio and, therefore, still dangerous to me and my family.

And she had three poppets, made to represent each of us. No wonder Amanda and Chuck can't remember anything. She's still working them, like puppets, and now she's working on me.

I brought my focus back into her room and kept feeling into whatever I hadn't noticed yet. I sensed that she put my doll down on the bed, between Chuck and Amanda's—I could feel their dolls' arms touching my doll's, and the nasty, spooge-stained bedspread on my doll's back. Then I remembered what Raven had said during the Tarot reading, about Melinda possessing something that belonged to them. It was their hair, which she had attached onto their dolls' heads.

She must have stolen a lock of hair from each of them when she got close enough—probably got Amanda's the time she went over to Melinda's house to feed the cat, and God only knows when she stole Chuck's. Maybe when she was pretending she needed to sew a button on her shirt and borrowed my scissors, and made Chuck feel her up. I could stab her eyes out with those scissors. God, I hate her, *so much!!!*

No, don't go there, Lola. Focus.

Damn it, letting her scheming rattle me like that caused me to lose the connection and I can't seem to get it back, no matter how hard I concentrate and roll my eyes around.

Lesson learned: Zen or else.

Well, at least that explains why they can't see or hear or sense—or even remember—anything about her anymore. She doesn't have any of my hair, so maybe that's why the third poppet is not affecting me quite so strongly, nor in quite the same way. And, maybe the fact that she does have their hair helps me to tune in, because I'm connected to them more intimately than she is. Plus, maybe because my abilities are almost equal to hers, that helps me to stay somewhat aware of her hijinks, despite her best efforts. So, I guess I should be grateful for that much, instead of being angry, especially since my anger helps her.

Now the question is, what do I do about it? I wish Twink was here. I mean, I appreciate the pen and the book that she directed me to, but I'd feel a lot less alone if I could talk to her directly.

I need to learn to do this on my own. I can't run to Raven and Twink every time I have a question. Twink hates that and Raven has enough on her mind.

In any case, it's late and I'm tired. And Melinda's poor cat is across the street yowling for her. I gave some thought today to calling the animal shelter to come get him, but I don't know if they'll put him to sleep or not, and he doesn't deserve that. I'll feed him—across the street, of course, so he doesn't think he lives at my house—until someone else takes him in. I picked up a few cans of cat food today, so I'm going to go feed him real quick and hit the sack. See ya in the morning!

Journal Entry 36

I've been giving this a lot of thought and it seems like the best thing would be to find a way to get those dolls away from Melinda. Deciding that was the easy part, even though it's a terrifying prospect. The hard part is figuring out how.

I don't know where she is and, even if I did, she ain't gonna give them up willingly. She's dangerous and I do not want a face-to-face confrontation, so I have no clue what to do about that. I guess I'll cross that bridge when I come to it. The first thing to do is to find her and the dolls. All I know is that she's in a hotel or motel on the shore of Lake Erie, somewhere east of Cleveland.

I've been giving this a lot of thought and it seems like the best thing would be to find a way to get those dolls away from Melinda. Deciding that was the easy part, even though it's a terrifying prospect. The hard part is figuring out how.

I don't know where she is and, even if I did, she ain't gonna give them up willingly. She's dangerous and I do not want a face-to-face confrontation, so I have no clue what to do about that. I guess I'll cross that bridge when I come to it. The first thing to do is to find her and the dolls. All I know is that she's in a hotel or motel on the shore of Lake Erie, somewhere east of Cleveland.

I did a Google map search and found that the most likely place is Geneva-on-the-Lake because it's the only town I could find with hotels/motels right on the shoreline. The rest are too far inland to have the close proximity to water that I sensed last night. It's only about a one-hour drive to Geneva-on-the-Lake, so I'm going to take a drive up there today once Chuck goes to work. Thank God I quit my job or I'd have to wait until the weekend to do this. I'll start by looking for any motels that are on the beach, first, then check those that are further inland, if necessary. Hopefully I'll see her beat-up, red Camaro in one of the parking lots.

I tried, once again, to contact Twink to see if she'll go with me but got no response. That has me worried, too. Where is she? Has something happened to her? And what will happen to me? I've become dependent on her for help, even if it comes at the price of tolerating her snippiness.

I'm going to bring my faery-phone crystal with me, just in case, and I'm going to wear my new pendant as a protective talisman. I don't know if it'll work for that purpose but it feels right, and I'm making this up as I go along anyway, so I'm going to trust my gut on that one.

Meantime, Onyx is still across the street, hanging around the remains of his home. I fed him last night, again, the poor thing. I don't know if one can of food a day is enough for him. Maybe I'll start bringing some dry food over to hold him until nighttime when I bring his canned food. I'll pick some up at the grocery store later today and hide it in the back of the pantry so Chuck won't see it. I did at least leave the bowl of water.

Okay, there goes Chuck, out the door. I'm heading to Geneva-on-the-Lake now. I'll report back with any news.

###

Wow. A lot to tell. I'll start at the beginning.

It was surprisingly easy to find her. I don't know why she's being so cocky and assuming that the state police won't recognize her easily identifiable car—after all, there is a fresh warrant out for her arrest. Maybe she has an invisibility spell of some sort cloaking her from them, too. Who knows? In my eyes, however, she was "hiding" in plain sight.

I drove straight north to Eastlake and turned east, watching for motels along Lakeshore Boulevard—just in case I was wrong about what town she's in—until I had to take Route 20 the rest of the way to Geneva-on-the-Lake.

I'd forgotten how cute it is along the strip in Geneva-on-the-Lake. I haven't been there since Amanda was little and we stopped going when she got too old to enjoy beach time with the fam. If I hadn't been distracted by Melinda's craziness, I might have stopped to wander through the little shops, but I had no time for fudge-sampling.

I did a local GPS search for motels on the beach and found a few to choose from, so I drove by their parking lots to see if her car was parked in any of them. I found nothing at the first two but, finally, at the third—a rustic row of beat-up rooms called, ironically, the "Row Inn"—I saw her car parked in front of one of the rooms. My heart skipped a beat when I saw the Camaro—a car I barely paid attention to when she lived across the street but, now that I saw it here, I knew I would know it anywhere—especially with its "My other car is a broomstick" bumper sticker.

My first instinct was to call the police because, after all, she's wanted for arson and she needs to be arrested. That's when I remembered that she is a powerful, practicing witch, and it was probably a piece of cake to cloak herself from their notice. After all, look how effectively she was puppeting Chuck and Amanda, with just a couple of sock dolls!

Besides, even if the cops did show up, that wouldn't mean I could take the poppets home with me. In fact, the cops might even take the dolls in with her, for evidence, and I couldn't take the chance of that. First, I needed to get those dolls from her, then I'd call the cops and turn her in.

I parked across the street from the Row Inn at a convenience store, from which I could see the door to her room and her car, to think about what to do next. I went inside the store to get a can of pop and a bag of chips and came back out to sit in my car. I sat there and stuffed myself while I considered my options.

I must have zoned out to the relaxing sounds of the waves and seagulls off the lake, breathing deeply the beach-scented air. After what felt like twenty minutes or so, I saw her come out of her room—dressed in typical beach attire: a bathing suit and a gauzy cover-up—and get into her car. That's when I saw that she had dyed her hair black.

She pulled out of the parking lot and drove right past me, while I ducked down and prayed she wouldn't notice me. After a few seconds, I poked my head up and saw her driving away—she hadn't seen me or my car.

Having no idea how long she'd be gone—she wasn't dressed to go anywhere but the beach, so I had no clue how far she would be going—I had to act fast, which didn't give me much time to come up with a very good plan. I decided that I'd somehow try to get into her room and snatch the dolls before she came back, and I'd figure out how I was going to do that as I went along.

I ran across the street and tried the doorknob to the room she had just exited. It was locked—no surprise there, but I figured I'd try anyway. I looked around to see if any housekeeping staff were nearby, to ask if they would let me in. I could always tell them I was sharing the room with her—I knew enough personal information about Melinda to bullshit my way in, as a "friend" of hers—but I didn't see any motel staff.

So, I went in to the lobby and lied to the clerk, a pudgy young local guy who was reading the back-page classified ads in Scene Magazine. "Excuse me," I asked, "can I have an extra key to my room? My roommate just drove off to the store while I was walking on the beach and she accidentally locked me out."

He scratched himself, bored, and asked "What room?"

I hadn't paid attention to the room number, so I popped my head out the door again and looked. "Room 12," I said, when I came back inside.

"Oh yeah?" he asked, his interest piqued. "You're with her? The chick with the red car? She's hot!"

"Yes," I said, getting anxious now. He was too intrigued by Melinda for me to be able to easily fly under the radar. Melinda was too often able to feel when she was the subject of my focus and now there was a second person in the mix, who was apparently keen on her, so I was afraid that she would feel my presence. I began nervously fingering my topaz pendant and wondered how to stall for enough time to figure out how to handle this kid.

In a flash, I recalled that scene from Star Wars where Obi Wan Kenobi does the Jedi mind trick and says, "These aren't the droids you're looking for." I held the topaz firmly in one hand and waved my other hand dismissively, and said, "I'm in a hurry and need to get into my room."

I gotta tell ya, I was stunned to see that it worked! I could feel the air sort of … bend … as I spoke and waved my hand like that. His eyes glazed over as he reached behind him to grab the room key off a hook on the wall, and handed it to me. The fact is, I don't know if I could have pulled it off without holding the pendant, but that detail doesn't matter right now.

I decided to push it one step further and said, "You don't need to tell my friend you let me in. She'll feel bad that she locked me out."

With that same glazed look, he replied, "I don't need to tell her. She'll feel bad."

It was awesome! I let that buoyant energy carry me out the door and into her room, where I needed confidence to propel me further.

I unlocked the door and went inside, immediately recognizing the dank smell of the room and the scuzzy green bedspread from my vision last night. I saw the dolls right away, no longer on the bed, but instead on the dresser on the back wall the room, with the drawer still open.

I didn't think about it beforehand, but I should have brought a bag with me so I could take them out of the room without anyone seeing me carrying a bunch of creepy voodoo dolls around with me. I checked the bathroom to see if the housekeeper had left any extra plastic bags under the current bag lining the trash can, as they sometimes do.

Just then, as I was about to pick up the little plastic trash can to look for a bag, I heard Melinda's key in the door. I ducked into the tub, thankful for the opaque, plain white shower curtain, and hid.

She opened the outside door and came into the motel room, muttering, "Can't believe there's not a single store in this fucking beach town that isn't sold out of sunscreen! Can you believe that?" I didn't know who she was asking, but whoever it was didn't answer. I wanted to poke my head around the shower curtain to see who was with her, but didn't dare. I couldn't tell where she was standing in the room, from the sounds I was hearing, and I didn't have the time or composure to psychically tune in to find out.

"Are you ready to go to the beach, my darlings?" she asked someone who, again, didn't respond. From the sound of her voice, she was standing toward the front of the room, near the door, so I decided to peek around the curtain. All I could see was the dresser, with the dolls on it.

Just then, I felt something tickling my arm and instinctively brushed it off. I turned to see what it was and saw the biggest goddamned spider I've ever seen in my life—outside of a zoo—scuttling across the bottom of the tub where it had landed, and it was heading right toward me.

I hate spiders—*haaaaaaaaaaaaaate* spiders—and yet, I managed to stay completely quiet, even though I was screaming internally. I've never been so proud of myself. I managed to not panic as I silently climbed up to stand on the edge of the tub, to get as much distance as I could from the freakishly-large arachnid. Apparently, Melinda didn't hear a thing, because all she said was, "Come along, my pretties," and left the room, slamming the door behind her.

Despite my creepy companion in the bathtub, I waited a few seconds to make sure she wasn't coming back. Then I jumped the hell out of the tub and allowed myself a moment for a full-bodied gross-out shudder before I went back to looking for a plastic bag, to package up the voodoo dolls and get outta Dodge. There was a spare bag underneath the trash can liner, so I grabbed it and went to get the sock poppets.

They were gone. They were Melinda's "pretties" and she took them with her to the beach. Why she would do that, I do not know. I pray she doesn't have some further spell to work on them, by drowning them in the lake or burying them in the sand. God only knows what would happen to us if she did!

I darted over to the window and peered through the slit between the curtains, and saw her following a paved path around the side of the building down to the beach, carrying a tote bag full of the sock dolls. Once she was out of sight, I left the room and hurried back to my car. I sat in the driver's seat for a while, trying to decide if there was anything I could or should do at this point.

I wondered, should I follow her to the beach and see what she was up to? It was probably not a good idea because there was no place to hide on the beach and she was bound to see me. I was already thanking my lucky stars that she hadn't sensed my presence, as it was. I'd be taking a big risk, to go any further than I previously had.

However, I couldn't just leave, not without knowing what she had planned for the dolls. Maybe I could snatch them away while she wasn't looking.

I skulked my way through the motel parking lot, watching carefully for her return, and followed the same path she took to get to the beach. I didn't have to go far. She was right there on a stretch of shoreline that was separated from the lakeside-view motel rooms by a scraggly row of rose bushes and marked with signs saying *For use by guests of the Row Inn only.* She was lying on a lounge chair, facing the sun, working on her tan. The dolls were still in the tote bag, which she had stuffed under her chair. So much for darting over and grabbing the bag without her noticing. But at least she wasn't doing anything nefarious with them. Maybe she just liked to keep them close by. Let's hope that's all it is.

I couldn't come up with any good ideas as to what to do next, so I came home and here I sit, still wondering the same thing. What should I do next? I have no clue. But at least I know where she is and I have the key to her room! Fat lot of good it'll do me, if I don't come up with a plan, but at least I'm further along than I was this morning.

My head is so full of thoughts that I need to stop typing for a while and just stew on it all. Meantime, I guess I'll go feed Onyx.

Journal Entry 37

I don't know why, but I feel the need to log this. I woke up this morning feeling bleh, so I decided to call in sick. When Luis, the HR director, answered the phone he was surprised to hear from me, and said, "It's so good to hear your voice, Lola! I was going to call you today, anyway, to ask how long you wanted to extend your insurance."

Puzzled by the odd question, I brushed it off and joked, "For as long as I can, I guess, especially since I'm too sick to work today. Better make sure I'm covered, eh?"

I don't know why, but I feel the need to log this. I woke up this morning feeling bleh, so I decided to call in sick. When Luis, the HR director, answered the phone he was surprised to hear from me, and said, "It's so good to hear your voice, Lola! I was going to call you today, anyway, to ask how long you wanted to extend your insurance."

Puzzled by the odd question, I brushed it off and joked, "For as long as I can, I guess, especially since I'm too sick to work today. Better make sure I'm covered, eh?"

Then he said, "I'm sorry you're not feeling well. And please know that you're welcome back any time you want. We haven't filled your position yet. I'll go ahead and get the paperwork started for your insurance. Meantime, don't be a stranger!" And then he hung up.

It was a bizarre conversation, but Luis is sort of a scatterbrain when he tries to multitask, so I must have caught him when he was in the middle of something. It was a weird start to a weird day. I mostly just laid around and slept. I have a searing headache and my skull feels like it's full of wet cement. My eyes feel like they're being pushed, from behind, out of their sockets. Bleh.

Chuck was so sweet, though. He made sure, before he left for the day, that I had something easy to make for lunch. Then, he brought me tea and toast in bed. He kissed me on the forehead and told me take it easy, saying he'd bring home some takeout for dinner so I wouldn't have to cook.

It was nice to just lie around and watch TV all day, without any guilt about having to go anywhere or do anything. Plus, it was a relief to not have to cook, because I just wasn't up for it. He brought me my favorites: pineapple fried rice and crab Rangoon, with that yummy red dipping sauce, and it was worth the MSG headache I'm sure to wake up with tomorrow, especially since I already had a splitting headache.

It did my heart good to have him take care of me like that. I've been feeling distant from him lately, so it was a relief to see him being so kind and considerate. Maybe I just needed a day off, because I'm a little better now. Thank God, the blistering headache has faded a bit, even though my head still feels heavy. In any case, I'm well enough to get up and sit at the computer for a while, long enough to jot down these quick notes, even if they're not very interesting but—like I said—I felt compelled to type this out for some unknown reason.

###

Holy cow! You're not going to believe this! Chuck just came rushing in, as I was typing that last sentence, and called me to the window. He pointed across the street and asked, "When did that happen?" I looked where he was pointing and saw that somehow, without my even noticing, the house across the street has burned down! I can't believe I slept so hard today that I didn't hear the firetrucks!

I called Amanda into the room to ask her about it, because she must have seen something. She was obviously feeling sorry for her old, sick mom because she didn't give me any lip when I yelled for her. Chuck beckoned her over to the window, to stand between us, and pointed to the charred rubble across the street, asking the same thing, "When did that happen?"

She reacted the same as me, surprised and flabbergasted. Somehow she, too, had missed the biggest event this block has seen in the entire time we've lived here. How can something as massive as a neighbor's house engulfed in flames and, I'm assuming, a full squad of firefighters

—complete with sirens and flashing light—escape everyone's notice???

But then it got even weirder. While the three of us stood by the window, several feet away from my desk, the coffee cup I keep filled with pens fell over and every pen in it went flying across the room. It just … fell right over … for no reason at all. It's not like I had put it down half-on-top of something that made it off balance. It's a sturdy, solid cup with a wide base, which was flat on the desktop, so there's no way it could fall over like that. Except, it did.

And, you'd think that the pens inside it would maybe spill out onto the desk and perhaps scatter a bit, but no. They shot across the room, one even leaving an ink mark on the wall as it hit and fell onto the two-drawer file cabinet beneath it. I've never seen anything like it.

Journal Entry 38

I got up this morning to the strangest sight! The house across the street from mine must have burned down overnight! I didn't see anything until the sun came up and, even then, I was groggy so it took a minute or so to sink in what I was seeing.

I don't usually get up before dawn on Saturdays, but I couldn't sleep. I woke up at about 4:00 AM and just lay there in bed, staring at the ceiling in the dark, until I made myself get up, from sheer boredom.

I made a pot of coffee and sat at my desk surfing the net, feeling the urge to open this journal doc I forgot I had on my computer's desktop (I have so many shortcut icons on there that I lose track of what's what, and why). I thought it might be a

I got up this morning to the strangest sight! The house across the street from mine must have burned down overnight! I didn't see anything until the sun came up and, even then, I was groggy so it took a minute or so to sink in what I was seeing.

I don't usually get up before dawn on Saturdays, but I couldn't sleep. I woke up at about 4:00 AM and just lay there in bed, staring at the ceiling in the dark, until I made myself get up, from sheer boredom.

I made a pot of coffee and sat at my desk surfing the net, feeling the urge to open this journal doc I forgot I had on my computer's desktop (I have so many shortcut icons on there that I lose track of what's what, and why). I thought it might be a hoot to reread some of the things I've written. Isn't that the fun of having a journal, going back to see who you used to be? But before I could do that the sun rose and, in the growing light of day, I saw the charred rubble across the street.

The strange thing is that I've been awake for hours and, even before that, I wasn't sleeping very soundly. I can't believe that I slept through a house fire right across the street! Wouldn't there have been tons of noise? Wouldn't I have heard something? It's safe to assume that Chuck and Amanda slept through it, too, because both of them would have woke me up to watch the show.

I'll have to ask them about it when they get up. Meantime, I see a streak of ink on the wall that needs to be cleaned off. God only knows how it got there. Amanda hasn't colored on the walls since she was little, and there's a file cabinet right underneath the smudge so it's not like anyone could have accidentally brushed by with a pen in their hand.

No matter how it got there, it needs to be wiped off. I'll be back.

Journal Entry 39

I love Sundays so much. I can sleep in as late as I want. I usually have most of my housework and errands done by Saturday afternoon, so I can relax for a couple of hours on Sunday before I have to get back at it. Life is so hectic and time moves so fast that it's almost a blur. Some people whine because they can't remember what they ate for dinner last night, but I can't even remember having dinner last night! I really need some me-time.

So, that's my plan. All I have to do this morning is enjoy a hot cup of Joe while I surf the net and catch up on Facebook.

I love Sundays so much. I can sleep in as late as I want. I usually have most of my housework and errands done by Saturday afternoon, so I can relax for a couple of hours on Sunday before I have to get back at it. Life is so hectic and time moves so fast that it's almost a blur. Some people whine because they can't remember what they ate for dinner last night, but I can't even remember having dinner last night! I really need some me-time.

So, that's my plan. All I have to do this morning is enjoy a hot cup of Joe while I surf the net and catch up on Facebook.

After, that is, I pick up all the pens that I found on the floor this morning. Somehow my pen cup got spilled—Chuck must have come in here after I went to bed and knocked it over. It would be nice if he'd pick up after himself once in a while, but what are you gonna do? You can't teach a sloppy old dog new tricks, right?

Actually, I have to pick up the pens and wipe off a pen mark from the wall. I just noticed it across the room, a streak of red ink on the wall above the filing cabinet. Seriously, what is that man doing? It's almost as if he deliberately drew a downward-pointing arrow on the wall.

And, great. Here comes Amanda, hollering about something. So much for a nice, peaceful Sunday.

###

Holy cow, she actually had something interesting to holler about! I expected she was charging in here to lodge some sort of teen-hormone driven protest about her crisis du jour, but instead she came tearing into my office, yelling, “Mom! Look!” and directed me toward the window.

You’re not going to believe this, but the house across the street burned down overnight! How weird is that? My bedroom window is on the front side of the house and I didn’t hear anything. I can’t imagine that the firefighting team went out of their way to be deliberately quiet, so as not to wake the neighbors. I must have been out cold last night. I guess I really do need some rest.

While we were looking out the window, Amanda pointed at a scraggly looking black cat wandering through the yard over there—the poor thing looked like it’s famished—and said, “Aw, Mom, can I take it some food?”

How could I say no? Only a heartless wretch would allow an animal to starve like that. We went downstairs to look for a can of tuna in the pantry and couldn’t find any, but I was amazed to find a few cans of cat food and an unopened bag of dry cat food.

Isn’t that weird? We’ve never had a cat, and I’ve never bought cat food, but there it was, tucked away in the back behind a lot of big cereal and cracker boxes, almost as if it was hidden. I made a mental note to ask Chuck later if he knew anything about them, and then brought that poor critter some food and water.

When we got across the street, the cat made a beeline for me, almost tripping me while it rubbed up against my ankles, yowling and purring. Amanda, of course, asked if we could take it home. “Please Mom??? Please???” she begged.

I couldn’t say no to feeding it but that I could say no to, because we have no idea where it came from, or whether it had fleas or worse. It had obviously been feral for some time and it was too dirty to bring into the house. I didn’t tell her that, though. What I said instead was, “It may belong to someone. Why don't we make up some flyers and post them around the neighborhood?"

Meantime, the cat finished eating and came back to snake around my ankles, again almost knocking me over with the force of its kitty love. I felt bad for refusing it a home, but something told me that—even beyond the fact that it was filthy—it would be a bad idea to bring it in the house. I'm not normally very intuitive, but I had a very strong "gut feeling" about this that I could not ignore.

After both of us petted it for a while—long enough for it to get bored with us—I took a picture of the cat with my phone and we came back home to make some flyers. I'm printing them now. She and Kirsten can hang them around the neighborhood this afternoon.

Journal Entry 40

I must be losing my mind.
I went to work this morning same as usual and Alexis, the receptionist, made me wait in the lobby while she went to get Luis. She wouldn't let me just go to my desk like I have every weekday for God only knows how long. As I said hello and tried to walk past, she stared at me and asked, "What are you doing here?"
Nonplussed, I said, "The same thing I always do here—spend my day tolerating Ron."

I must be losing my mind.

I went to work this morning same as usual and Alexis, the receptionist, made me wait in the lobby while she went to get Luis. She wouldn't let me just go to my desk like I have every weekday for God only knows how long. As I said hello and tried to walk past, she stared at me and asked, "What are you doing here?"

Nonplussed, I said, "The same thing I always do here—spend my day tolerating Ron."

She turned white and said, "Can you wait here?" and directed me to one of the lobby chairs. Puzzled, I sat down and cooled my jets until she came back with Luis, who took me back to his office.

Imagine my surprise when he told me that I no longer work there! Naturally, I assumed that he meant Ron had fired me but didn't have the guts to tell me to my face and was making Luis do it. But then Luis told me, his twitchy face full of nervous concern, "Lola, you quit, weeks ago!" He even pulled out a folder with my name on it from his file cabinet and showed me a letter of resignation with my signature on it!

While I was reading it, I felt a shiver of déjà vu, like I vaguely remembered writing and signing the letter but that memory was like a wispy dream, so far away I couldn't be sure it was real.

I got scared, wondering if I was losing my marbles. How could I not remember quitting my job? And why would I even do that? The letter offered no clues. It just said that I appreciated my time with the company but it was time to move on.

He offered me a cup of tea and some sympathy, but it was obvious from his fidgeting that he wished I would just leave, so I did. I went straight out the front door and came home, only to find another frightening sign of amnesia, here on my desk. Well, actually, in my printer tray. I saw a stack of ten "Found Cat" flyers, with my phone number on them, which claimed that I had found a lost, black cat across the street from my house and was looking for its owners. I had no recollection of making the flyers, nor of finding a cat across the street!

So, I looked out the window to see if there was a stray cat across the street and saw that the house that used to be there has burned down! I was just out front, mere minutes ago, parking my car in the street, and didn't even see that the house which has always been there is now a burned-out shell of blackened bricks!

Thank God I have this journal. As soon as I finish logging all of today's events, I'll go back and read what I've written in the past. Hopefully I've made better notes and explanations than I did in my resignation letter.

And now, just as I was typing that, my pen holder just fell over by itself, without my touching it. One of the pens went flying across the room and hit the wall over the filing cabinet, leaving a huge streak of ink.

I have to go lie down. My head hurts and it feels like it's filled with sand. I'll reread the journal later. I'm going to call the doctor and make an appointment, after I take a nap. In fact, I'm even going to write a "note to self" reminding me to make that appointment, just in case I forget to do that, just like I've forgotten all of these other important things.

God, I hope I don't have a brain tumor!

Journal Entry 41

I was on the phone with the doctor's office to make an appointment (thanks to the note I left for myself-otherwise I wouldn't have remembered!), when the funniest thing happened. My pen holder toppled over, all by itself! I was just sitting here, on hold, minding my own business, when it fell right over and sent pens flying everywhere. Looking for an Easter Egg? You found it!

After I got off the phone (my appointment is for next week, the soonest opening they had, even though I told them it was urgent), I went to clean the ink off the wall with a rag and obviously wiped down this same wall with a rag and cleanser.

I was on the phone with the doctor's office to make an appointment (thanks to the note I left for myself—otherwise I wouldn't have remembered!), when the funniest thing happened. My pen holder toppled over, all by itself! I was just sitting here, on hold, minding my own business, when it fell right over and sent pens flying everywhere. In fact, one of them went sailing across the entire room and hit the wall, leaving a streak of ink there, right above the filing cabinet.

After I got off the phone (my appointment is next week, the soonest opening they had, even though I said it was urgent), I went to clean the ink off the wall with a rag and some cleanser. But when I got closer to the wall, I saw that this wasn't the only stain. Now that I was standing only a foot or so away, I could see faint remnants of other ink marks in the same location, and streak marks on the paint where someone had obviously wiped down this same wall with a rag and cleanser.

There was no doubt about it. All the ink marks were in the same vicinity and pointing in the same direction. In fact, altogether, they created an almost perfect downward-pointing arrow.

So, I found a flashlight and got down on the floor to peer behind the file cabinet. It was far too heavy to move, so I hoped that whatever the arrow was pointing at would be easy to reach. There was nothing back there, so I looked inside the file drawers.

In the bottom drawer, tucked away far in the back, was a rolled-up plastic grocery bag which held three things: a quartz crystal, a gorgeous silver filigree pendant with a beautifully faceted clear stone, and a key on a fob that said, on one side, "Please return to the Row Inn, Geneva-on-the-Lake Ohio" and the room number, 12, on the other side.

I'm not sure how to describe what happened next. I felt a bunch of mild lightning bolts—for lack of a better way to describe them—inside my head. As if it wasn't scary enough that I may be losing my mind, those zaps and flashes in my brain were terrifying. But with them came a jumble of quick-change scenes: faeries and fires, and a witch's dark spells. I saw Chuck having sex with another woman, an atrocious tart with bright red hair, and Amanda in police handcuffs. It was so horrifying that I screamed and shook my head, hard, to clear it from these scenes of mayhem.

Although I've never seen any of the items from the plastic bag before, there was something about the pendant that made me feel calm, so I put it on and heaved a sigh of relief as it somehow lessened my anxiety. I felt another lightning bolt flash, but this one didn't jolt me as strongly. With that bolt came another memory, this one of me—myself—packing these items in the plastic bag and tucking them away in the back of the drawer.

I swear, I do not remember doing that. Normally, I would trust myself and say that if I didn't remember it, I didn't do it, but since I've had to start leaving notes just to remind myself to call a doctor because I'm losing my ability to remember things, then I'm willing to believe that … perhaps … I did put them in the file cabinet.

But why???

I tucked the crystal into a desk drawer and the key fob into the side pocket of my purse, where I could easily find it again. I made sure to stick it in that side pocket so it wouldn't get lost—my new purse is enormous and I'm always losing things in the main compartment.

I'm not sure what to do next but, for now, I need to lie down again. Maybe when I get up from a nap I'll reread this journal to see if I have left myself any clues. But that can wait. I really do need to shut my eyes for a while. My head is killing me.

Journal Entry 42

I've had to wait a while to write this, because I didn't have access to my laptop until Chuck brought it to me, here at the hospital. I'm a little groggy, so I hope what I type here makes sense. I make no promises. The drugs they've given me make me see trails sometimes, and I tend to nod off to sleep at a moment's notice. Tra la la.
La la.
La la la, la la la la.
Laaaaaaaaaaaaaaaaaaaa!
Oh, look! A faery! How pretty!

I've had to wait a while to write this, because I didn't have access to my laptop until Chuck brought it to me, here at the hospital. I'm a little groggy, so I hope what I type here makes sense. I make no promises. The drugs they've given me make me see trails sometimes, and I tend to nod off to sleep at a moment's notice. Tra la la.

La la.

La la la, la la la la.

Laaaaaaaaaaaaaaaaaaaa!

Oh, look! A faery! How pretty!

###

Okay, sorry, I'm back after a quick nap.

It's hard to type with this IV needle in my arm, but at least it's my left arm, so it's not too in the way. Just a little.

Where to start? Julie Andrews says to start at the very beginning, the very best place to start. So, I think I'll begin with A … B … C. Or perhaps Do Re Mi. Ha! I crack myself up.

Whoops, I feel another nap coming on.

###

God, my mouth hurts. And I'm starving. I haven't had solid food in I don't know how long. I think they've cut back on the pain killers, because I'm awake enough now to realize that those bad dreams I was having weren't dreams, they were memories of what happened when I decided to return that key to the Row Inn.

I didn't remember anything at the time—I was still in an amnesiac fog. All I knew is that I had hidden the crystal, the pendant and the key fob away for some unknown reason—unknown at the time, anyway. Now I know that Melinda had somehow screwed with my head to make me do that, because she also somehow knew that they were powerful tools, in my hands. She used the Lola poppet to direct me to dispose of anything I owned that could be used against her. I'm grateful that, even though she was spellcasting, I had enough inner strength to not throw them away for good.

It turns out she knew I was in her motel room hiding in the shower that day. I don't know how she knew, but she did. She told me so.

I'm getting ahead of myself. I should back up and start from the beginning, the very best place to start, like A-B-C and do-re-mi. But first, I need a nap.

###

Here's what happened. I decided to go to the Row Inn—not to return the key to the front desk but to find out why I had it in the first place. I was more interested in solving the mystery than doing a good deed.

I put the quartz crystal in my pocket, the pendant's chain around my neck and, with the motel key still in my purse, I drove to Geneva-on-the-Lake with an ominous sense of foreboding in my gut. I almost turned around and came home a couple of times, especially as I got closer because the further I drove from home, the stronger my anxiety became.

I pulled in to the parking lot of the junky lakeside motel with vague memories of having been there before. The memories were nothing solid, more like a fleeting déjà vu experience. For all I knew, it could be a memory of another visit to Geneva-on-the-Lake, as a kid, with my parents or even with Chuck, back in the days when we used to come here as a family when Amanda was little.

I saw a red Camaro in the parking lot near Room 12 and it, too, felt familiar and scary, but I didn't know why. It wasn't directly in front of that room, though, because that parking spot was taken up with some minor construction equipment—two-by-fours, a wheelbarrow with a bag of powdered cement in it, and various other items that implied a project. In fact, I saw where the sidewalk between rooms 11 and 12 had been busted out and caution-taped, waiting to be repaired. I parked near Room 14 on the other side of the Camaro.

The lights were on in Room 12, but the curtains were drawn shut. I could only see light along the edges. As I approached the door, I heard the TV blaring.

At that point, I was at a loss about what to do next. Even with the key, I couldn't just enter the room. Who knows how long I'd had the key, and who might be inside? It might be someone completely unrelated to the mystery I was trying to solve and I couldn't break in on them.

I thought about going to the lobby and talking to the desk clerk, but what would I say? Even though this was a skeezy motel, I was sure that they would respect the privacy of their tenants and wouldn't give me the name of Room 12's resident. Or would they? Maybe if I slipped them a finsky or two?

I decided to play it by ear, and went into the lobby anyway. The front desk clerk was a younger guy, maybe in his twenties—wearing a grease-stained, too-tight t-shirt—who was deeply absorbed in playing a game on his smartphone. He barely looked up when I entered, just long enough to register my presence, and said, "Hey, how's it going? She lock you out again?"

"Uh, no …" I stammered, "I have my key." I held up the fob and jingled the key, to show it to him. This was a good sign. He apparently knew me, though God only knew how, so he may be easy to bamboozle. I went for it. "'She' wants me to check to see how long our room is paid for, because she forgot and she's figuring out the budget."

"Lemme check," he said, and put down his phone. "That's room twelve, right?" he asked, tapping away at the motel's computer keyboard.

"Right," I said.

"Got it. You're paid until the end of the month. Do you want me to print you a duplicate receipt?"

I couldn't believe my luck. "Yes, that would be great. Thanks!" I said, as he pressed a few keyboard buttons and the printer shot out a piece of paper that, hopefully, held all the information I would need.

He handed it to me as he winked and said, "Make sure you tell Melinda I said 'your secret is safe with me.'"

"I'll do that. Thanks again," I said, and left the lobby. Something told me that I shouldn't leave my car where it was, so I got in and drove to the end of the motel's parking lot which, granted, wasn't very far away, but at least I wasn't parked so close to Room 12 where I could be more easily seen by "Melinda," whoever that was.

My head is starting to get a little fuzzy, so I'll write more later. I need to call the nurse for some pain meds, too. My mouth hurts so badly that I can barely see.

###

I'm back. Sorry about that. I'm still coming to grips with what happened and why I'm here, and which memories are real and which are chemically induced hallucinations. I'm pretty sure I'm clear headed enough to continue, even though I'm starving from lack of solid food, so I'll keep writing for as long as I'm able.

When I left off, I was sitting in my car, with a receipt for Room 12 in my hand. Before I had a chance to read it, however, the front pocket of my jeans started to get hot. I put down the receipt and reached into my pocket to find out what on earth was going on, and discovered the quartz crystal that I had forgotten I put there. It was unusually warm—I mean, not warmed by my body temperature, it was much warmer than that—and my gut told me to pay attention. This must mean something.

Then, just like the pen holder on my desk kept falling over on its own, the crystal seemed to jump right out of my hand and fell onto the floor mat in front of the passenger seat. I reached down to pick it up and, as I lifted my head, I saw some activity down the row of parking spots. Someone was getting into the red Camaro, a woman with spiky black hair. I felt a fearful thrill of recognition—I knew her, but didn't know why—and sensed that the falling crystal had somehow deliberately caused me to duck down like that so I wouldn't be seen by her. I kept my head down until she pulled out of the parking lot, hoping she hadn't spotted my car.

So now I was faced with a decision. Should I use my key and go into the room, without knowing who she was, where she went or how long she'd be gone? Before deciding, I took a moment to look at the receipt and saw the name, Melinda Underwood, and her address. I was stunned to see that the address was very similar to mine—only the last number was different. This meant she lived on my block, possibly right across the street!

Again, I felt the jarring sense of those mini-lightning bolts in my head, and flashes of memories. This was the woman I had a flash of the day before, the one in bed with Chuck, except her hair was bright red! What the hell!? Had he cheated on me? With that???

I'm going to use the blind fury that I felt then as my excuse for being so stupid. I grabbed my oversized purse and got out of the car, key in hand, and stormed across the parking lot toward Room 12. I jammed the key into the lock and threw the door open.

Good lord, what a pig she was! The room was trashed, with clothes on the floor and empty junk food wrappers all over. And it stunk, not just with the typical cheap motel funk of old, mildewed paneling, but from unwashed laundry and waste baskets full of empty beer cans and wine bottles.

I entered the room, making a path through the dirty laundry with my foot, and looked around. The crystal in my pocket began to grow warm again, which reminded me to not dawdle.

Nothing interesting caught my eye until I got to the dresser against the back wall and lifted the corner of an old newspaper to see what might be underneath. There I saw three homemade dolls, each made from an old gym sock. My first thought was to jam them into my purse and get the hell out of there, but something about the sight of them made me instantly nauseated and I almost puked, right then and there.

I didn't have time to do any of that, however, because I heard a hate-filled voice from the doorway say, "My God, Lola, you are such a fucking idiot."

Journal Entry 43

I need to be more careful telling this story, because just writing that last part made me vomit. Literally. I was typing it out when I got just as sick as I felt then, and had to grab the little tray the nurses keep on my bedside stand for just such occasions.

Fortunately, there wasn't much in my stomach other than Jell-O, so it didn't last long, but … still. Throwing up like that made the stitches in my mouth hurt like mad, and I needed to take some time to recover.

Anyway …

I need to be more careful telling this story, because just writing that last part made me vomit. Literally. I was typing it out when I got just as sick as I felt then, and had to grab the little tray the nurses keep on my bedside stand for just such occasions.

Fortunately, there wasn't much in my stomach other than Jell-O, so it didn't last long, but … still. Throwing up like that made the stitches in my mouth hurt like mad, and I needed to take some time to recover.

Anyway …

Melinda stood in the doorway, calling me a "fucking idiot." I hadn't heard her drive up or even open the door, for that matter, because I had stupidly left it open (although, come to think of it, closing it wouldn't have made any difference anyway—she had a key, too).

I whirled around to face her and instantly knew who she was. It was as if all the amnesia I had been struggling with vaporized and my memories came flooding back. I didn't have time to be frightened, although I felt a rush of adrenaline, fight or flight. I couldn't flee—she was blocking the door—so it looked as if I had to fight.

"Did you really believe," she snarled, "that I didn't know you were here, snooping around? I'm more psychic than you could ever be! I knew you were here the first time when you hid in my shower, and I knew you were here today. I only left, just now, so you'd try it again." She shook her head with disdain, "Yep, quite the idiot."

"I'm the idiot?" I shot back, "I'm not the one who burned my own house down and then stayed in the area with an arrest warrant for arson!"

"Pfft! Please," she scoffed. "I might as well be a whole world away out here in Ashtabula County. The Cuyahoga County boys have better things to do and the locals are easy to manipulate, like puppets on a string." She fluttered her fingers in the air, miming the actions of a marionette puppeteer.

"Speaking of puppets," I said, gesturing toward the sock dolls, "I came for these."

She laughed, long and hard. "You may have come for them, but you ain't leaving with 'em!"

"We'll see about that," I said, marveling at my own bravery. I turned back toward the dresser and flung aside the newspapers that covered the dolls. I snatched up all three of them, stuffed them into my purse and charged toward the door, hoping to duck past her.

I should have known that wouldn't work, but it was worth a try. Melinda was like a linebacker, blocking the exit, and she's bigger than I am. I hoped that my smaller size would help me to dart around her, to slip between the cracks, as it were, but no such luck. She grabbed me by the shoulders and flung me backwards, onto the bed.

She jumped on top of me and straddled my pelvis, pinning me down with my hands over my head, so I couldn't move. It sickened me that she was enjoying this so much, her face in a twisted grin, cheeks red with exertion, a vein in her forehead throbbing. She laughed and said, "Like I said, a fucking idiot." She loomed over me and took a moment to catch her breath. "Now," she asked, "what am I going to do with you?"

I struggled to get free but she was too heavy. I tried to kick her, but most of her weight was on my pelvis and her feet were hooked over my thighs, so I couldn't even do that. "Knock it off," she snapped. "I'm in charge, here."

Her thought-wall kept me from tuning in for the best way to respond so I had to rely on common sense … to fight against her and feed her twisted desire to dominate was exactly the wrong way to go. I calmed down and just lay there, thinking about my next move.

"What's the matter, huh?" she taunted. "Give up, do ya?"

When I didn't reply, she grinned and said, "You know your man wants to fuck me, don't you?" With that, she ground her pelvis into mine and said, "That's right, bitch. He had his hands all over me and I made him rock … fucking … hard." As she said this last, she pumped her pelvis in cadence with her words, humping me.

I was so grossed out that I couldn't hide my reaction from my face.

"Don't like that, do ya?" she leered. "Well, ain't that tough shit?" She brought her face directly over mine and gathered a mouthful of spit, which she then slowly dripped into my eyes.

As much as I knew to not fight her, to not be her victim and feed her frenzy, I couldn't help struggling to get away from her vile spittle. Once again, I had to try to not puke.

I better stop writing for a minute or I'm gonna vomit now.

###

Okay, I've caught my breath again. Man, what a nightmare!

I don't think I should go into so much detail, because it brings the physical feelings back and I'm not up for that yet.

Call me naïve, but I never knew she could be so very awful. No matter how intuitive I may have become, it never occurred to me that anyone I know could act so horribly toward another human being and *mean it*. Maybe it's because I never allowed myself to dive that far into someone else's disturbed psyche. Even with Ron, my ex-boss, I didn't dip into his perversions for this very reason. I didn't want to feel it and I didn't want to believe that real people could act this way.

I know that sounds childlike and ridiculously innocent. I accept that. I also know, academically, that beyond harmless sex play there really are beastly people out there who get off on hurting others. I, personally, have never been face to face with someone like this and it was a rude awakening. A sickening, horrifying, deeply rude awakening.

It became clear that I wasn't dealing with someone who could be reasoned with and this realization chilled me to the bone.

I tried, again, to remain calm and passive while I considered my options which, admittedly, were few. No one knew I was here, and

Chuck and Amanda were still under her forgetfulness spell. I had to get those dolls out of there and figure out how to undo whatever she had done to them—to all of us. But how?

While I lay there, thinking, she also seemed to be pondering her next move. Then, she noticed the chain around my neck, on which was hung the topaz pendant that was under my shirt. She pulled on the chain until the topaz was freed and said, "Well, isn't that a sparkly bauble!" She fingered the silver filigree and ran her thumb across the large stone. "This is mine, now."

She pulled my arms down to my sides and put one knee on each arm. She reached behind my neck for the clasp and pulled it around front, where she worked to undo it. As she struggled with difficult clasp with her beefy, clumsy fingers, I felt the crystal in my pocket heat up again. I knew, now that my memory had come back, that Twink was with me, somehow, somewhere, and she was trying to communicate with me.

I closed my eyes and concentrated, thinking as loudly as I could, *"Twink! Help me!"*

I don't know if she was in the room with me at the time, but I heard her tiny voice shouting in my ear, *"NOW!"*

Now … what??? This was the second time she did that to me, just said "now" without explaining what I was supposed to do. So, I followed my instincts. While Melinda was distracted with the intricate clasp, she wasn't paying much attention to me so I gathered all my strength and bucked my hips upward, sending her airborne.

She kept a strong hold on the chain as she went flying off the bed. I grabbed her wrist, pulled it up toward my mouth, and landed a huge bite on her forearm. She roared and let go of the chain but swung her other arm at my head. I managed to duck away from the coming blow and rolled off the bed, snagging my purse as I went.

I ran out the door and into the parking lot, and headed toward my car with Melinda in close pursuit. The dolls were safely in my purse, but this also meant that they were at the top of everything else, burying my car keys. This was a really bad time to have to dig for them but I knew, from experience, that if I just crammed my arm into my purse and fished around at the bottom the weight of the numerous keys on my keychain would become obvious and I'd find them easily enough.

That's what I was doing when it happened.

Melinda had grabbed one of the two-by-fours from the construction supplies and was coming at me. Even though I'd just had the illuminating realization that she was truly mad with no moral objection to hurting a fellow human being, I still couldn't believe that she meant to hit me with it. Time moved in slow motion and I just stood there, stupidly watching, as she swung the board like a baseball bat aimed right at my face.

Holy Mother of God, I've never felt so much pain in my life. Not even childbirth hurt that bad. And you know how cartoon characters see stars when they get hit in the face with a frying pan? Yep, that's pretty much what happens. I practically saw chirping birdies. But, unlike Wile E. Coyote, I didn't get right back up. The last thing I was conscious of after I went down, hard, onto the parking lot asphalt, was the sight of the front desk clerk running toward us, yelling, "Hey! You stop that! I've called the police!"

I woke up here in the hospital, with a face full of stitches and a mouth full of missing teeth.

I think that's enough for now. I feel another nap coming on, but first, some chocolate pudding with whipped cream. It's the only advantage to having this kind of injury. I get to eat pudding whenever I want.

Journal Entry 44

It's so good to be home! And it's so good to have my family back. The only problem now is that I have no front teeth, up top. It'll take a while yet to recover and learn to talk and eat normally again. My dentist made a partial denture to replace the teeth Melinda bashed out, but it hurts, and feels horrible and clunky in my mouth. I have an annoying lisp now, and I sound like I have a mouth full of rocks. It's going to take some getting used to.

Chuck, of course, thought it would be funny to suggest that my toothlessness will add a new depth (awful pun intended) to our sex life, but one caustically raised eyebrow was all it took to shut him down.

It's so good to be home! And it's so good to have my family back. The only problem now is that I have no front teeth, up top. It'll take a while yet to recover and learn to talk and eat normally again. My dentist made a partial denture to replace the teeth Melinda bashed out, but it hurts, and feels horrible and clunky in my mouth. I have an annoying lisp now, and I sound like I have a mouth full of rocks. It's going to take some getting used to.

Chuck, of course, thought it would be funny to suggest that my toothlessness will add a new depth (awful pun intended) to our sex life, but one caustically raised eyebrow was all it took to shut him down.

By the way, Tammy came by and rescued Onyx after I told Raven that no one had been taking care of him while I was in the hospital. She passed the message on to Tammy and now the poor thing has a home. Thank goodness!

Fortunately, it was easy enough to undo Melinda's spell on Chuck and Amanda's poppets. All I had to do was untie the blindfolds from their heads and remove the hair that she had sewn on. They got most of their memories back right away, although they still didn't recall everything leading up to the fires. But at least they remembered that she burned her house down! I checked with Raven, first, to make sure that I wasn't doing anything to harm them as I removed the blindfolds, but she said it was safe to do that much.

She did, however, suggest that I let her dismantle the dolls. “Just in case,” she said, “because we don’t know what Melinda did while she was creating them. I’ll do some blessings and unbinding rituals over them, to remove any booby traps or other harmful spells.”

I don’t know what I’d do without her. What a good friend.

My doll, on the other hand, wasn’t so easy. Because Melinda didn’t have any of my hair, she had to resort to different methods to affect me so strongly. I asked Twink for her advice one day, shortly after I got home and Chuck went back to work, and she told me, “She filled that poppet’s head with all sorts of spells, so yeh have to take it apart carefully, almost like doing surgery. Remember when yehr head hurt so bad, with that burning headache? That’s when she was working on it, she cut it open and sewed it back up, and yeh felt every cut and stitch!”

“If you knew that,” I demanded, “why didn’t you tell me at the time? Why didn’t you help me? I kept calling for you!”

“I tried,” she insisted, “but yeh couldn’t hear me! I’ve been trying to get through to yeh for ever so long. Only, she somehow managed to block me.”

“Somehow?” I asked, alarmed. “You mean, you don’t know how?”

“Nay, I do not.” Twink admitted. “She’s grown stronger, over time, and she’s a well-armed foe. Yeh’re lucky to come through this.”

This was scary to hear, considering Melinda got away again. When the front desk clerk from the Row Inn came out to stop her from hitting me more than once and told her the police were on their way, she got in her car and sped off. God only knows where she is now. I try not to let myself think about it, too much, otherwise I’d never sleep at night. Twink promises that she’ll do what she can to keep a watchful eye over me, and I’ll have to trust that she can do that. What choice do I have?

Under her direction, I sat at my desk and carefully deconstructed the Lola poppet. She did one of her tricky tricks with her wand and faery dust so I wouldn’t feel it when I clipped through the stitches in the doll’s head. As soon as I opened it, sand began pouring out, and Twink shouted, “Don’t let it spill all over! Save as much of it as yeh can!”

I emptied the pens out of my desktop coffee cup/pen holder and poured the sand in there. Shortly into the process, I heard a soft 'clink' and stopped pouring the sand out of the doll's head to see what it was. It was a small shard of deep purple amethyst, wrapped loosely in a piece of black cloth.

"There, yeh see?" Twink said, "That's how she done it. That's a seer stone. She wrapped it in black to block yehr vision and stuck it into the middle of the poppet's head where yehr third eye is. She bound yeh up, but good!"

"But why the sand?" I asked. "She just used cotton wadding for Chuck and Amanda's dolls."

"Right, like she did with yehrs, at first, but she didn't have any of yehr hair so she couldn't truly block yeh," she explained, fluttering around in the air above the doll's surgical procedure. "And, yehr powers are much stronger than theirs. She had to resort to drastic measures. She bound up yehr intuitive vision and filled yehr head with wet sand from the beach. That's why yehr head felt so heavy and yeh became so forgetful. I'm amazed yeh did so well, even if it did take a thousand tries to get yeh to figure out the message from the pen marks on the wall!" She flew down and landed on the desk next to the empty-headed doll, examining my work.

"What do I do with all of this?" I asked.

"The hard part's done," she said. "Clearing the poppet's head was the main thing."

"My head feels a little better already," I said. "But what do I do with the sand and the amethyst? Should I take it to Raven?"

Twink looked up at me and thought for a moment. "Nah, I think yeh know what yeh ought to do with it."

Flummoxed, I had to admit, "No, I really don't. Please tell me."

"Think about it," she said, "and let me know what yeh come up with." With that, she disappeared in a flash of faery dust, leaving me with a cup full of sand, a little shard of amethyst and a limp, empty-headed poppet.

Journal Entry 45

I keep waking up from the same nightmare. I'm standing in the parking lot of the Row Inn, watching helplessly as Melinda—who, in the dream, is ten feet tall with hair of flames—comes at me with a baseball bat covered in spikes. I stand there, frozen with fear, as she swings the bat and bashes my head in. I float out of my body and hover above, watching as sand pours out of my head. In the middle of the ever-growing pile of sand is a sparkling jewel. I reach down, from way above, to pick it up and admire it but it's snatched away by a tattered black bird.
I usually wake up drenched in sweat, my heart beating like mad.

I keep waking up from the same nightmare. I'm standing in the parking lot of the Row Inn, watching helplessly as Melinda—who, in the dream, is ten feet tall with hair of flames—comes at me with a baseball bat covered in spikes. I stand there, frozen with fear, as she swings the bat and bashes my head in. I float out of my body and hover above, watching as sand pours out of my head. In the middle of the ever-growing pile of sand is a sparkling jewel. I reach down, from way above, to pick it up and admire it but it's snatched away by a tattered black bird.

I usually wake up drenched in sweat, my heart beating like mad.

The first few times I had the dream I shook Chuck awake, demanding to be held. At first, he was more than sympathetic. This whole escapade had terrified him and I was touched by how much he cared. I mean, I knew he loved me and all that, but there's nothing like what we've gone through to make you appreciate one another, ya know?

But as it became obvious that the dream was going to keep recurring, he became less patient with my night terrors and he began to suggest I go to therapy. "Maybe you need to talk this out with a professional," he said. "Maybe you have PTSD."

"That's not a bad idea," I replied, "but I have a feeling there's more to it than that. It feels like maybe Melinda is still behind it, like some sort of psychic attack."

That's where I lost his attention and interest. He wants nothing to do with any of it—Melinda, black magic, psychic abilities (even my harmless ones)—nada. And he wants me to have nothing to do with it, too. As if I can just turn it off and go back to normal! I wish!

The dream has begun to affect my daytime life, too, because every day is tinged with the icky vibe the dream brings with it.

I went to Karma Korner to talk to Raven, and she backed me up. "It's entirely possible that it's a psychic attack, coming from Melinda. As long as she draws breath and holds a grudge against you, you may well be on the receiving end of her wrath, especially if you have any contact objects from her in your home. What did you do with that poppet?"

My heart fluttered with anxiety. It hadn't occurred to me that she could continue to screw with me with that thing still in my home. I thought that, once I had it in my possession, I was safe. "What's a contact object?" I cried.

"It's an item that has been imbued with intention, which can be either good or bad. Blessed objects are good, cursed objects are not so good. The poppets are cursed contact objects and, if they are not discharged properly, they can still affect the person in contact with them."

I explained that Twink helped me to dismantle it, but I still had all the components in my house because I hadn't yet figured out what to do with them. Her eyes grew wide with consternation and she admonished me, "Get them out of your house, lickety split! You don't want anything she used against you in your possession."

"But what do I do with them?" I lisped, my new dental bridge slipping out of place. "You said, yourself, that I have to be careful of what we do with the dolls, because we don't know what she did to them and how any further actions—with or against them—will affect us! What happens if I toss the last one into the trash can? Will I feel it when it gets compacted at the landfill? If I burn it, will I feel the flames?"

"Probably not, literally, but if there is any magic attached to those items, Goddess only knows how the wrong method of disposal could cause destructive ripples in your life." She closed her eyes and said, "Give me a minute. I'll ask my Guides if they have any suggestions."

She was silent for a minute or so and then said, "Bring the sock doll and its stuffing to me, and I'll dispose of it the same way I did with the other two. The sand and the amethyst, however, are for you to take care of. I suggest you connect with one of your own Guides for advice on what to do with them."

I thanked her and went home, both uplifted and discouraged. I was glad that she was willing to take care of the doll carcass, because I was coming up empty with ideas as to what to do with it. But connect with one of my Guides? That was something I had not mastered yet, at least not as easily as she did, by just closing her eyes and asking.

I've tried, believe me, I have tried. I eventually gave up because nothing was happening. But, at her recommendation, I sat at my desk to try again. I pulled out my quartz crystal to call Twink, hoping she'd take pity on me and give me a clue.

"What d'yeh want?" she asked as she popped in, surrounded by a cloud of faery dust.

"Raven says I need to get the sand and the stone out of my house immediately, but I don't know what to do with it," I said.

"Yeh still haven't figured that out?" she demanded.

"No, I have not. And stop trying to make me feel bad. I shouldn't have to even be doing any of this. I never asked for it."

"Like fun, yeh didn't," she muttered.

"Whatever," I muttered back.

"Look, the best thing yeh can do is return it back to where it came from," she said.

That was all I needed to hear. I knew what to do.

The next day, first thing, I dropped the poppet carcass off at Karma Korner and then drove north to Lake Erie with the sand and the amethyst still in the coffee cup. The one-hour drive flew by—it felt like I got there in less than thirty minutes, like I was in a time warp. I took that as a good sign that I was on the right track.

I parked in the motel lot and got out of the car. This was the first time I'd been back since that fateful day and it felt spooky—as if the haunting echoes of the violent scene were still playing out over and over in a timeless loop. Sure enough, when I approached the spot where it all happened, I saw a faint, holographic scene playing out, with the etheric images of the both of us. There was Melinda—huge and looming—swinging her weapon and there was me on the ground—helpless and fragile—blood and teeth spilling onto the asphalt. Over and over the scene kept playing: Melinda, huge and looming …

It occurred to me then that coming here was a stupid idea—I should never have done this alone. What if Melinda psychically lured me here, with the contact objects I brought with me? What if she was lying in wait for me? I called for Twink who, to my immense relief, popped in right away. "Look at yeh, all brave! Well done, you!"

"So, you don't think I might be in danger here?" I asked.

"Oh, aye, but yeh're in danger every day of yehr life, yeah? Yeh still leave yehr house knowing yeh could get hit by a bus."

"Well yeah," I said, "but that only happens if you walk into the street without looking both ways. A scenario like that can be prevented if you use half a brain. The question is, did I 'not look both ways' by coming here alone?"

She was quiet for a moment and put up one finger, as if testing the temperature with a wet digit. "I don't think so," she finally said, "I don't feel her presence here and, besides, yeh asked for guidance from yehr higher sources and that's what led yeh here, yehr gut instinct—that feeling that yeh know yeh're doing the right thing. D'yeh really think yehr own Guides would lead yeh astray?"

I wish she hadn't asked that question because the answer was appalling. "Yes, in fact, they would!" I cried. "They have! It was my gut instinct that led me here in the first place, and look what happened!" I gestured wildly at my still-bruised and swollen face.

"Indeed," she said, fluttering above, "look what happened. It were the only way yeh could end up where yeh are now, innit? By heck, it hurt, but yeh're a changed person and in a good way."

"For crying out loud," I muttered. "I kinda thought my 'Guides' would keep me from harm. Isn't that their purpose?"

"Oh, aye, if it's in yehr overall best interest," she sniffed.

"That doesn't feel very helpful," I said.

"Be that as it may," Twink said, and gestured with a wave of her arm for me to continue with the task at hand. The conversation was over.

I wondered what to do next and my gut told me to walk into the looping scene o' violence and disperse it. I had no idea what that meant, or what it would look like, but I walked forward anyway, breathing deeply—in … and out … in … and out … in … and out—until I stood on the very spot where I was when she hit me. I took a deep breath and held it, as Future Lola to Lola-in-the-past, taking in the pain and transmuting it into love and healing for my younger self who was caught in that loop and in that dream, breathing out a message of "You'll be okay. You'll survive this."

I continued breathing and felt that I should do something with my hands to help disperse the stuck energy so I waved them about as if I was clearing smoke away. I know it probably looked silly to anyone who might be watching, but, whatever. I knew what needed to be done.

Eventually, and surprisingly, I felt as if the recurring nightmare which haunted my dreams left my head. The timeless hologram loop here in the parking lot had been released. I stepped back and watched to see if the scene was still playing out, energetically, and I saw and felt nothing. It was clear.

Impressed with myself, I went back to the car to get the cup of sand and the amethyst.

I didn't know what to do with them, either, but I trusted that the answer would come to me if I just kept moving forward. I felt a subtle nudge to take them to the beach so I followed the path around the motel to the shoreline. It was a weekday, so there weren't many people around. The closest were too far away to be concerned with.

I sat on the warm, dry sand, with the coffee cup beside me, and listened to the waves and the gulls, soaking in the peace and quiet. I've always loved the serenity of having the beach to myself. Then, a waft of rose scent came floating by—not something you usually experience on the shores of Lake Erie where the standard smells were fish and lake water. I looked around and saw the row of neglected rose bushes growing between the motel property line and the beach, so I got up to literally stop and smell the roses.

I saw, on the ground near the base of one of the bushes, an almost-perfect red rose. I picked it up and sat back down near my coffee cup. This rose had to mean something. After all, it was in the Rose Room that I received some exquisite guidance. Maybe I could visit there again, today, using this rose's scent to launch me there.

I couldn't help grinning, because this whole thing felt so right.

I felt nudged to close my eyes before I held the flower to my nose. I was beginning to recognize these nudges. They weren't me, telling me what to do. These weren't my ideas they were expressing. Perhaps this was my "Guide" talking to me, like Raven's talks to her.

I inhaled the rich fragrance of the velvety red rose and felt myself lifted, just as I had when I used the rose oil and was transported to the Rose Room. But this time I didn't ascend all the way up into pink clouds, like the last time I did this.

This time I felt as if I was expanding, larger and larger—not my body, but a sphere of pink light that enveloped and included me—I was the pink light, thick and dense where my body existed, yet emanating outward like incandescence released from the element of a light bulb. I felt All-In-One—excited and calm at the same time, and totally present.

That's when I heard a voice: "It's time to return the sand from whence it came."

I reached over and picked up the coffee cup, removing the amethyst and sticking it into the front pocket of my jeans. Something told me to hold one hand over the opening on top of the cup and the other hand beneath it. As I did that, I felt a ray of light pouring out of my right hand, down through the cup of sand, and into my left hand, below. I felt the sand being purified, all of Melinda's violence and hatred-mojo being zapped away.

I stood and approached the water's edge and poured the sand out in a sweeping motion—as if I was scattering a loved one's ashes—all vestiges of the heaviness in my head going with it. I was released from the illness the cursed sand brought with it. I hadn't realized how lousy I got used to feeling until it was removed. Whew! What a relief.

But what to do with the amethyst? The sand, after all, represented pain and muddled thinking, but the amethyst was supposed to represent my psychic vision that had been bound and buried in the dirt.

Again, acting on pure instinct, I took the amethyst and held it briefly between my hands, bathing it in light as I had with the sand. I then picked up the rose and gently opened it to partially expose the pistil and stamen, inside.

Now that the amethyst had been cleansed of Melinda's ugliness, I placed the sparkling purple stone inside the rose and folded the petals back into place to enclose it. I walked back to the water's edge and bent down to gently place the rose into the water, where the current carried it away.

I took off my shoes and socks, rolled up my jeans into cuffs, and planted my bare feet on the wet sand, allowing the waves to splash up over my ankles. It was icy cold and quite a shock to my system—it jarred me all the way to my shoulders—but it was bracing, as well.

I saw, not too far in the distance, a sparkling reflection of the golden sun on the surface of the water. It shimmered and glistened … so breathtaking. I stared at the exquisite beauty for as long as I could bear, without burning my retinas. It took me a few minutes to realize that this wasn't the sun's reflection, after all. Instead, it was a glowing, growing ball of faery dust and it was coming toward me.

As I watched, the glittering ball of golden light approached me, enveloped me and recolored my formerly pink aura. I was engulfed by an exquisite sphere of unspeakable beauty. I don't remember much beyond this point, because I crossed a threshold, some level of conscious ascension that human beings cannot comprehend and live. I was dying, and it was okay.

When I came to, I was kneeling in the sand, my jeans drenched from the tide, my face wet with joyful tears. I was still on the shore of Lake Erie, on the strip of beach owned by the Row Inn, in Geneva-on-the-Lake, Ohio, but it looked … different. The physical structure of the world was the same, but I saw it as though I was wearing prism glasses—all of the edges of all of the things had little rainbows shooting off of them. Colors were stunningly bright and the sounds of the gulls and waves were transformed into a Song of Love from the Universe.

I whispered, afraid to break the spell. "Twink, are you there?"

"Aye," she responded, as if from far away, "are you?"

"I think so," I replied. "What just happened?"

She popped into the air directly in front of me, only a foot away—the closest and the clearest I've ever seen her. Every detail of her luminescent gown was sharp and crisp, her gorgeous little face was plain as day, no longer too small to truly see. Just like a few minutes ago when I realized how awful I had been feeling once I didn't anymore—I hadn't realized how blind I had been until I could see like this.

"Yeh've crossed the veil, all on yehr own! Again, well done, you!"

"Am I dead?" I asked. I must be, I reckoned, because normally this question would terrify me, but I was okay with the possibility and—in fact—rather hoped I was because this was awesome and the idea of going back to everyday life's drama was less than appealing.

That's when I noticed that my face didn't hurt anymore—the pain and swelling was healed. It was completely, magically gone. I still had stitches and missing teeth, unfortunately, but something told me that—because my memory of the horrific events was still too fresh and vivid—I was unable to, metaphorically, rewrite that part of my hologram's code. Only complete amnesia could accomplish that. But because I was detached enough now from the pain and swelling for it to be instantly cleared, it didn't hurt at all. It reminded me of that frustrating saying about getting what you want as soon as you stop wanting it.

"No, yeh're not dead," Twink said. "That's why I said 'well done'. Yeh've managed to cross the veil and not die. It's an uncommon human can do that! By any chance, are yeh wearing that topaz?"

I pulled on the chain to draw the pendant from inside my shirt.

"If yeh hold that stone in yehr hand, while yeh're here, it'll get an extra boost. Yeh can charge it with yehr current feeling, to help recall it later," she said.

I did as she suggested: I held the filigreed topaz between my hands and sent white light through it from one hand to the other until it felt completely charged, like me. I opened my hands and saw that it was glowing, like a halogen flashlight. I dropped it back inside my shirt and felt it humming against my skin.

I stood up, slowly and mindfully, to test if I could maintain the expanded feeling while walking. That was the tricky part: I knew it was a matter of one right or wrong move to either stay in the groove (I finally understood what the word "groovy" truly means) or to knock myself back to my usual 'reality' … so to speak.

Staying groovy was apparently not affected by large physical movements, as I had feared. It was okay to walk around. Maintaining this good vibe was a thing I did in my head, rather like the time that I steered that psychic vision with my eyes. It felt like I had an inner radar, like a spot in the center of my head where I had to focus.

You know those cheapo plastic maze toys, made of a cardboard disc and a clear plastic cover with a tiny metal ball inside? The object of the game is to roll that little ball into the tiny hole embossed into the cardboard. That's sort of how this felt, like if I moved carefully enough to keep the spot in my head perfectly centered, I could walk around and maintain this fragile, multidimensional awareness.

"What do I do now? Can I stay like this forever?" I asked Twink.

"One question at a time, yeah?" she said, floating alongside me and then landing on my shoulder as I walked carefully along the shoreline, the wet sand squishing between my toes. "Can yeh stay like that forever? It's hard telling. Yeh've already proven able to do things that most humans are still struggling with. So, maybe, but don't be disappointed if it comes and goes."

I could live with that. In fact, the more I thought about how hard it would be to maintain without being obsessively careful, the more I began to come back to normal (whatever that means!). Unfortunately, I didn't realize that was happening until I got too far gone to easily boost myself back up. But at least I knew now what was possible, and I had my charged topaz, which gave me something to look forward to trying again.

"I think I know the answer to my first question, 'what do I do now?'" I said. "What I want is to go home and get back to my real life, which is already in progress."

"Oh, aye," Twink laughed, as we headed back to my car, together. But then she asked "The real question, though, is which is the real life and which is the fantasy?"

I didn't want to even think about it—I had learned to be careful about the questions I asked. The answers would surely come.

Did you enjoy *A Faery on My Shoulder*?
Your review makes a difference.

Visit

lisabonnice.com

The author, wearing a white topaz pendant, in Chagrin Falls, OH.

www.ingramcontent.com/pod-product-compliance
Lightning Source LLC
Chambersburg PA
CBHW051652060726
47593CB00021B/316

* 9 7 8 0 9 7 9 9 9 9 9 7 0 *